Mark inhaled her scent as they danced.

Jess smelled like an exotic combination of flowers and incense, a scent as familiar as it was intoxicating. She'd been burning incense for as long as he'd known her, and he'd never been able to smell it since without thinking of her.

It smelled like sex and fantasies.

His fingers tightened on her waist. She tipped her face up, her brown eyes locking on his. Her red lips were plump and glossy, parted slightly, and he felt his head dipping toward them, drawn to her like a parched man to a desert mirage. His heart beat a frantic rhythm against his ribs.

Jess sucked in a breath, leaning forward. Her breasts pressed against his chest, and he silently cursed the many layers of his tuxedo for muffling the sensation. Still, a hot thrill raced through him, scorching every nerve ending in his body.

Her warm breath teased his lips, and he was absolutely lost.

ACCLAIM FOR RACHEL LACEY

CRAZY FOR YOU

"Lacey's small-town romance is a perfect weekend read."
—*Publishers Weekly*

"4 Stars! Readers will be able to close their eyes and envision themselves looking out over a mountain or standing in a field of poppies. The primary romantic relationship is well-balanced with the strong friendship between the characters."
—*RT Book Reviews*

RUN TO YOU

"4 Stars! Readers will love how the lives of the main characters meld together while still maintaining their individual lives."
—*RT Book Reviews*

"There's much to like in this sweet romance, including the strong hero and heroine, the cast of supporting characters and the beautiful mountain setting."

—Bookpage.com

EVER AFTER

"Lacey's Love to the Rescue contemporary series keeps getting better and better...Olivia's foster dogs, her fluffy kitten, and Pete's dog provide delightful diversions while the humans build their own forever home."

—*Publishers Weekly* (starred review)

CAN'T FORGET YOU

RACHEL LACEY

FOREVER

NEW YORK BOSTON

Copyright © 2017 by Rachel Bates
Excerpt from *Run to You* copyright © 2016 by Rachel Bates
Cover design by Elizabeth Turner. Cover photograph © Jake Olson / Trevillion Images
Cover copyright © 2017 by Hachette Book Group, Inc.

Forever
Hachette Book Group
1290 Avenue of the Americas, New York, NY 10104
forever-romance.com
twitter.com/foreverromance

First Edition: December 2017

Forever is an imprint of Grand Central Publishing. The Forever name and logo are trademarks of Hachette Book Group, Inc.

The publisher is not responsible for websites (or their content) that are not owned by the publisher.

The Hachette Speakers Bureau provides a wide range of authors for speaking events. To find out more, go to www.hachettespeakersbureau.com or call (866) 376-6591.

ISBNs: 978-1-4555-3758-7 (mass market), 978-1-4555-3759-4 (ebook)

Printed in the United States of America

OPM

10 9 8 7 6 5 4 3 2 1

*To my husband, Bill, for showing
me that first love can be the
forever kind*

Acknowledgments

Thank you so much to my amazing agent, Sarah Younger, and my equally wonderful editor, Alex Logan. I'm so incredibly lucky to work with you both. Also, a big thank-you to the whole Forever team—Lexi Smail, Michelle Cashman, Elizabeth Turner, and everyone else who helped bring this book from my laptop to the shelves. You guys are the best!

Thank you to Annie Rains, Anna Shepherd, and Tif Marcelo for reading and critiquing this book for me and to my #girlswritenight ladies, Annie Rains, April Hunt, Sidney Halston, and Tif Marcelo for always being there when I need a nudge.

A special shout-out to the members of my reader group! You guys are the absolute best, and I appreciate your love and support more than you could know. While I was writing *Can't Forget You*, I asked for help choosing and naming a dog for the hero, Mark. You guys had so many great suggestions! Rhonda Ziglar named Bear, and

I also used ideas from Brandy Thornton, Kay Luker, and Kimberly Lucia for other names suggested for various characters. You guys also inspired several of the costumes at Jess's Halloween party—thank you, Josephine Carzo, Amy Bavoso, and Laurie Lemmon.

And the biggest thank-you of all to the readers and bloggers who've bought, read, reviewed, or otherwise supported me along the way. I appreciate you all so much! xoxoxo

CAN'T
FORGET
YOU

CHAPTER ONE

Jessica Flynn picked her way along the grassy roadside. To her right, the forest beckoned, wild and beautiful. The timing wasn't perfect, but after eyeing this undeveloped tract of land next to her spa for years, it had finally been put up for sale. And now it was going to be hers.

She rubbed at the headache squeezing her temples, remembering—belatedly—that she'd meant to take some ibuprofen before she headed out to meet with the realtor. Oh well, too late now. And actually, now that she was away from the hustle and bustle of the spa, she realized her whole body hurt, a deep ache in her joints and a shivery sensitivity on her skin that felt an awful lot like she was coming down with something.

Which was just friggin' great. Half her staff had been out with the flu already this month, and she was booked solid with client appointments for the rest of the week.

But first things first...

About ten yards ahead, a white SUV sat in the gravel driveway beside the For Sale sign. As she approached, the vehicle's front door opened, and a balding, middle-aged man stepped out.

"Ms. Flynn?" he asked.

"Yes."

"I'm Gordon McDermott." He stuck out a hand, and she shook it. "You said on the phone you own the adjacent property?"

"That's right," she said. The Haven Spa was her baby, the culmination of years of sweat, tears, and dreams. And once she'd bought this additional land, she was going to expand the spa into a rustic yet luxurious resort.

"Then he must own the property on the other side because he told me the same thing." Gordon nodded toward a man standing at the end of the gravel driveway, his back to them.

Jessica's spine stiffened as if it had turned to steel. He was tall, lean, and muscular, his black hair close-cropped, hands shoved into the front pockets of his jeans. And she'd know him anywhere.

Mark Dalton, the first man to own—and break—her heart. The man she couldn't get within five feet of without wanting to kick him in the shins for being such a jerk when they were teenagers. And unluckily for her, he was also one of the owners of the property on the other side of this one.

He turned, and their eyes met. His were the color of rich espresso, sizzling in their intensity. His bronzed skin was marred by a vicious scar that slashed his right cheek, the only outwardly visible reminder of the accident that ended his Army career. "Jess," he said, his voice deep and a little scratchy.

"Mark." Her hands clenched into fists. It figured he and his friends would have their eye on this property too. Well, she'd just have to outbid them because she'd been dreaming about expanding the spa for a lot longer than they'd been giving zip-line tours over at Off-the-Grid Adventures.

"I take it you two already know each other?" Gordon said, looking pleased.

She and Mark both nodded, eyeing each other warily.

"Great. Well, as you may have heard, the property owner, Randy Wexler, passed away unexpectedly a few weeks ago, and his family is looking to sell this property as quickly as possible to settle his estate. My impression," he said, raising his eyebrows for emphasis, "is that he left behind quite a few bills that need paying."

"That's sad," Jessica said. "I wonder why he never got around to building anything out here?"

"He'd owned this property for decades, hoped to someday retire and build his dream home here," Gordon said. "Unfortunately, he waited too long to make it happen. Naturally, the family is thrilled that we already have not one, but two, interested buyers for the land."

"I bet." Jessica eyed Mark again. He still stood near the end of the gravel driveway—the driveway that Randy Wexler had envisioned leading to his dream home but instead dead-ended into the forest beyond.

Mark, never one for casual conversation, said nothing.

"As you both know, there's a little over forty acres out there, all undeveloped. The property is zoned residential, but with businesses on both sides, I wouldn't anticipate a problem having it rezoned commercial."

Mark cocked an eyebrow. She'd heard that the guys had had quite a time getting their property rezoned to allow Off-the-Grid to open, but in the end, it had worked out. And the realtor was right—with businesses on both sides, rezoning was a no-brainer.

"You mind if I have a look around?" Mark asked.

"Not at all. Take your time. I imagine you both are familiar with where the property lines lie," Gordon said, gesturing toward the forest before them.

"Thank you," Jessica said. "I'd like to poke around a bit too." She'd already done some snooping on her own, but she couldn't pass up the chance to openly explore. This land wrapped around behind the spa, and since no one used it for anything, she'd occasionally hiked through, daydreaming about little cabins with private hot tubs nestled in the woods.

Mark walked to the end of the driveway then turned and looked back, as if waiting for her to catch up. *Dammit.* She'd been planning to strike out on her own. Well, maybe she could feel him out for how serious he and the guys were about buying. "I didn't know you guys were interested in more land," she said as she fell into step beside him—well, kind of beside him. She'd left a few feet of space between them for good measure. Any closer and she might wind up wanting to strangle him. Because if she looked too deeply into his cocoa eyes, the memories threatened to swamp her. So many stolen kisses and whispered promises. This was the man she'd thought she might spend the rest of her life with, right up until he dropped her like a bad habit when he enlisted in the Army.

Mark kept his eyes on the leaf-strewn ground before them. "We've been talking about adding a mountain bike course. Ethan says there are some hills back here that would be perfect."

A mountain biking course? She wasn't opposed to the idea except for the fact that this property bordered her spa on two sides, and she wasn't sure she wanted adrenaline-seeking men and women racing past her natural spring-fed hot tubs yelling and carrying on while her clients were trying to relax and unwind. "Why can't you build that on the land you already own?"

"Hills on our side are too rocky. Perfect for climbing, not biking."

"So you're pretty serious then? About buying?"

His eyes flicked to hers, just for a moment, and he nodded. "You looking to expand the spa?"

"Yes," she said and left it at that. Her headache was getting worse, and *ugh*, she really felt lousy. She was going to be so pissed if she had to go home from work early today.

She and Mark walked in silence for a few minutes, crunching over the bed of leaves and pine needles that carpeted this part of the woods. Birds twittered overhead, darting through the colorful foliage. Here in Haven, North Carolina, fall had officially arrived, bringing with it a chill on the breeze and a kaleidoscope of color in the trees.

October had always been her favorite month, what with the foliage, cool air, fresh apple cider, and Halloween—which was arguably her favorite holiday—closing things out. Yeah, fall rocked, especially out here in the Smoky Mountains, where Mother Nature really got a chance to put on a show. It was almost enough to take her mind off the stabbing pain behind her eyes and the vicious ache in her bones that intensified with every step she took.

Mark started toward a steep incline to the left, and she

saw her chance to strike out on her own. "I'm headed this way." She gestured to the right, toward the flatter area she'd been scoping out for her spa cabins. "I'll see you back by the road."

He paused, and those dark eyes met hers again, burning right through her. He nodded and turned away, hiking toward the hillside. She turned away too, before she caught herself doing something stupid like watching his very fine ass as he walked away.

* * *

Mark Dalton grabbed the rock and pulled himself up. It didn't compare with the rock face they used over at Off-the-Grid, but he'd never say no to a new rock to climb. His right knee ached as he moved, stiff and tight in a way he'd never fully get used to.

He pulled himself over the top of the rock and stood, finally allowing himself to look in the direction Jess had gone. She was nowhere to be seen.

Just as well.

Since he'd returned to Haven, she'd made it clear she didn't want anything to do with him. Not that he blamed her. It was just his dumb luck that he still wanted her something fierce. In the eleven years since he left Haven—and Jess—behind, no woman had ever come close to what he'd had with Jess. They'd shared something intense, something *real*, that he'd never felt with anyone else.

But that was in the past. These days, he'd gotten so used to the occasional random hook-up that he'd come to prefer it. He enjoyed being on his own. Always been a loner. Probably always would be. No doubt his fantasies about Jess were better off kept as just that...fantasies.

Pausing, he surveyed the hilly area where he and his partners had talked about building a mountain bike course. The terrain out here was ideal, lots of gentle slopes and steep drops. He, Ethan Hunter, and Ryan Blake had opened Off-the-Grid Adventures together last year, offering zip-line tours, rock climbing, survival skills classes, and the like. The whole thing had been Ethan's brainchild, but the timing couldn't have been more perfect for Mark.

After he'd been injured in Iraq two years ago, his Army career had been sidelined. He'd spent a year working on the administrative side of things, but it didn't fucking compare to being out in the field, busting drug deals or securing hostile territory with his Special Forces team.

Now, for the first time in his adult life, he was a civilian. Finally starting to come to terms with it too. There was something reassuring about the peace and quiet of the woods after spending so much time in a war zone. The creatures here weren't capable of evil. They just did their thing and lived their lives. Not so different from him these days.

Movement snagged his attention out of the corner of his right eye. Instinct had him reaching for the weapon he no longer carried. Exhaling slowly, he glanced over his shoulder. He moved more quietly than most hikers and often surprised wildlife out here in the woods. Sure enough, about two hundred feet away, a black bear and two cubs ambled through the trees. One of the cubs paused, looked back at him, and then kept walking.

No cause for alarm. Bears were pretty common out here and rarely bothered people unless people bothered them first. Mark watched as they made their way through the woods, headed roughly in the same direction Jess had gone. And *that* he didn't like.

Unable to help himself, he doubled back. No doubt Jess knew how to handle herself around bears as well as he did, but the duty to protect was too deeply ingrained in him to ignore.

The bear and her cubs had ventured far enough ahead to be out of sight now, but he could still hear their feet crunching through the bed of fallen leaves and twigs that covered the ground and the mama bear's occasional snorts as she called to her cubs. They weren't exactly stealthy, nor did they need to be. They ruled these woods, and they knew it.

He veered to the right in the direction he'd last seen Jess. It wasn't hard to follow her tracks. The leaf bed here was still damp from yesterday's rain, and the imprint of her shoes showed easily. He found her sitting on a tree stump, staring into the trees as if completely lost in thought.

Yep, that was Jess. He stopped and shoved his hands in his pockets to watch her. So damn pretty. Her brown hair hung just past her shoulders. A shaft of sunlight brought out its gold undertones. Probably daydreaming about her plans for expanding the spa. Not wanting to interrupt, he stood back and waited for her to notice him.

After a few moments, she stood and headed in his direction. About two steps before she walked right into him, she let out a little shriek and clutched her chest. "Oh my God, Mark. You almost gave me a friggin' heart attack."

He bit back a smile. "Sorry."

"If you have to do your whole Army stealth thing out here, at least give a girl a heads-up, huh?" She frowned at him, her brown eyes flashing as she brushed past him and kept on walking.

"Didn't mean to sneak up on you."

"Why are you over here anyway? I thought you were checking out the hills for your mountain biking course."

"Saw a family of black bears headed your way," he said, falling into step behind her.

"And you thought I was just some helpless female who needed your protection?" She glared over her shoulder at him.

Nope, Jess was definitely not helpless.

"Well, for your information, I've seen plenty of bears out here over the years," she said. "They don't bother me a bit. I'm perfectly capable of taking care of myself."

"Got it." Knew it was true too. And he also knew he'd do the same thing again, for any hiker out here, male or female, but especially for Jess.

Neither of them spoke as they walked back toward the entrance to the property. Silence was his preferred method of communication, but this silence buzzed with a tension that made his scalp prickle with misgivings. Whichever of them ended up buying this land, they were going to be neighbors, and it would make things a hell of a lot easier if they could get along.

Beside him, Jess rubbed at her forehead. All the color—and the anger—seemed to have drained out of her.

"You okay?" he asked.

"Fine," she muttered, but now that he was close to her, she didn't look fine. She was pale, her movements jerky as if she were in pain.

"Jess..." He touched her arm, hoping to get her to slow down, and *Jesus H. Christ*. "You're burning up."

She jerked her arm away from his touch. "Am I?"

"Hold up a minute here." He reached for her again, and this time she stopped, letting out a weary sigh.

"I might be coming down with the flu. Half my employees have had it already this month."

He pressed a palm against her forehead, frowning. "You're running a high fever. Have you taken anything?"

She shook her head. "I will as soon as I get back to the spa."

"Let me take you home."

She started walking again. "No, thanks."

"You can't go back to work like this."

She let out a frustrated groan. "I know that. Much as it kills me to cancel on my afternoon clients, I can't see as I have any choice. Not good for business if I infect them with my germs, is it?"

He walked beside her, still watching her closely. "Are you limping?"

"Will you cut it out? My joints hurt. I'm sick. I'm going home, I promise."

But she didn't complain when he offered his elbow to lean on, and that spoke volumes. They lapsed back into silence, making their way through the woods. A few minutes later, they rounded an outcrop and found themselves face-to-face with the bear and her cubs, not ten feet in front of them.

Jess gasped, her grip on his arm tightening.

The mama bear had been sharpening her claws on a tree trunk while her cubs climbed the tree. She turned her head at the sudden human intrusion and lunged in their direction, slapping her front paw against the leaf-covered ground as she blew loudly through her nostrils.

Mark raised his hands in the air, beginning to back away. "Easy, girl. We didn't mean to sneak up on you."

"Holy shit," Jess whispered, yanking on his arm. "Let's get out of here."

"We are, but carefully," he said, walking backward away from the bears while still facing them, keeping his body between Jess and the agitated mama. "She's just bluffing. We startled her. She's telling us we're too close to her and her babies."

"No friggin' kidding."

"No need to get upset." He lifted his voice to carry to the bears. "Easy does it."

Mama bear slapped the ground again, huffing loudly.

"Why are you talking to her like that?" Jess hissed in his ear. "You're pissing her off!"

"We're making sure she knows we're not prey, but we're also respecting her wishes and getting out of her space." He kept his voice calm, level, and loud enough for the bears to hear.

Mama bear continued to huff and snort, eyeing them warily until they'd backed out of sight into the surrounding trees. Only then did Mark finally turn around, leading Jess briskly through the trees in the direction of the road, keeping his ears tuned for any sound from behind them.

"Holy shit," she said, looking paler than ever.

"She didn't want to fight us. It was just a warning. You should take my survival skills class sometime," he said, glancing at her.

"I'll think about it."

He took that as a no.

They reached the road a few minutes later, and she removed her hand from his arm, tucking it around her waist. "Thanks for waiting while we poked around," she said to Gordon McDermott.

"You two see everything you needed to see?" the realtor asked.

"Yep," she said. "And then some," she added with a small smile in Mark's direction.

He nodded. "We'll be in touch with our offer."

"So will I," Jess said, her expression hardening.

They said their good-byes, and Gordon climbed back inside his SUV.

"I'll walk you to your car," Mark said to Jess because she didn't look entirely steady on her feet.

"No, thanks." She started off in the direction of the spa, walking quickly.

He fell into step beside her anyway.

She frowned up at him. "You know, maybe some women swoon for your macho style, but I'm not one of them."

"I noticed," he said dryly, wishing her words didn't burrow their way under his skin and stick there like some unwelcome parasite.

"So, bye then." She waved a hand in his direction, picking up her pace.

He didn't argue, just kept walking beside her.

She muttered something under her breath, glared at him, and kept walking. She wasn't limping anymore, but he wasn't sure if she was feeling better or just being stubborn and putting on a brave face so that he'd leave her alone.

The latter, apparently, because when the spa finally came into view, her shoulders slumped and her relief was palpable. She ran a hand through her brown hair and gave him another pointed look. "Okay, thanks for walking with me. I can take it from here."

"Jess... let me drive you home."

Now that she'd stopped walking, she looked like she might topple over if a strong breeze gusted against her. "I'm going inside to finish up a few things first. I'm fine."

"You're not fine, and I'm not taking no for an answer."

"Stubborn man," she mumbled. "Well, I'm going inside to finish up. You can wait here if you really want, but knowing you're out here is not going to make me rush."

On the contrary, she'd probably dawdle just to spite him, but he didn't care. She was in no shape to drive herself home. So he stood to the side of the entrance, hands in his pockets, and waited. Eight years in the Special Forces had given him plenty of experience waiting. He could stand here all afternoon if he needed to.

He didn't much like the idea of going up against Jess to buy this property, but there didn't seem to be any way around it. She was certainly going to do her best to snag it for herself, and there was no way the guys would want to back down, so they would too. May the best man—or woman—win.

Thirty minutes later, she came out the spa's front doors, her purse and another larger bag slung over her right shoulder. And it was a good thing he'd waited because she looked even worse than when she'd gone in.

She stopped in her tracks and gawked at him. "Oh my God. Have you seriously been standing here this whole time?"

He nodded.

"Well, I...I figured you'd leave. I forgot how stubborn you are when you get an idea in your head, but for the record, I'm perfectly capable of driving myself home."

"Jess." He stared at her, frowning. "Stop arguing and let me drive you home."

"Fine." She huffed in annoyance and led the way toward a black Kia Sportage parked around back. She was limping again, moving more slowly than she had during their earlier hike. The doors unlocked with a beep, and she walked to the passenger side. "How's this going to work anyway? How are you going to get back?"

"I'll call someone to pick me up at your place."

She pointed a finger in his direction. "I'm not inviting you in, just so you know."

"Fair enough." He slid behind the steering wheel and texted the one person at Off-the-Grid most likely to be goofing around on his phone this afternoon: Ryan's teenage brother Trent. Sure enough, Trent replied right away. "Trent's going to swing by and get me."

Jess leaned back against the seat and closed her eyes. "Okay...207 Riverbend Road."

"I know." He started the engine and pulled out of the lot. Jess was quiet during the drive. He might have thought she was sleeping except for the lines of tension creasing her brow. Ten minutes later, he turned into the driveway of her little brown-sided house, parked, and shut off the engine.

Her eyes opened, bright with fever, and she gave him a pinched smile. "Thanks for the ride, and you know...saving me from bears." Then her usual attitude flared to life, and her eyes narrowed. "But I'm still going to outbid you on that land."

CHAPTER TWO

Jessica spent most of the next day in bed with the covers pulled over her head, determined to sleep until she felt better. Her body ached, she was wracked with chills, and her head felt like it might burst open at any moment. She hadn't had the flu in years and had forgotten how much it sucked.

Unfortunately, her busybody family hadn't gotten the memo as first her sister and then her brother called to check on her. And just when she'd gotten back to sleep, her mom stopped by with homemade chicken noodle soup. Even though she had no appetite and would rather be sleeping, her mom had insisted on heating up a bowl and staying while she ate it.

"You have to stay hydrated, and the protein will help you heal faster," she'd said.

The truth was that Jessica *did* feel a tiny bit better after the soup. Good enough that she'd propped herself up on the couch and watched this week's episode of *Game of Thrones* on her DVR. By the end, she'd been barely able to keep her eyes open so she'd crawled back in bed and fallen into a fitful, feverish sleep.

A knock at the front door roused her from her stupor sometime later. She squinted through bleary eyes at the clock on her bedside table to see that it was just past six in the evening. And dammit, who the hell was waking her up *this* time? She burrowed her face into her pillow, hoping whoever it was would just leave.

Another quiet knock.

Wishing her bedroom was on the front side of the house so she could at least see who it was, she crawled out of bed. If it was someone from her family and she didn't come to the door, she wouldn't put it past them to call the police for a wellness check. She shuffled to the front door and peeked through the peephole.

Mark.

Her stomach quivered, and it had nothing to do with the germs currently waging war inside her body. His dark, brooding stare was still her kryptonite, which just sucked as far as she was concerned. He'd shown his true colors when he traded her in after high school for his next adventure: the Army. He was a loner, a nomad, not the kind of guy to settle down and get married. Fine, whatever.

But she was twenty-eight now, and she *did* want to get married. Not that she was in any huge rush, but her choice in men these days definitely had more of an emphasis on long-term potential than casual fun.

Groaning inwardly, she pulled open the door. "What are you doing here, Mark?"

He held up a shopping bag. "Just came to see how you were feeling and brought you some sustenance."

Curious, she took the bag and peeked inside. She saw a package of Popsicles and several bottles of Gatorade. And actually...a Popsicle sounded heavenly. "Thanks. That was really nice of you."

"Figured your mom would have already brought over plenty of homemade soup." He cracked a smile. Mark didn't smile all that often, not for her anyway, which was a good thing because his smiles were absolutely dazzling, and she did not want to be dazzled by this man. Not this time.

Still, she felt herself smiling back at him. "She dropped off a big pot this morning."

"That's good. You feelin' any better?"

"No." Maybe even a little worse than yesterday. "I'd invite you in, but...I don't want to infect you with my germs." And truthfully, she was glad for the excuse. It was better that she and Mark see each other as little as possible. He stirred up all kinds of things in her, memories of a time when she'd been young and naïve and foolish.

He nodded. "Don't want to keep you up anyway. I hope you feel better."

"Thanks, Mark." This was probably the most polite conversation they'd had with each other in eleven years.

"'Kay then." With a wave, he headed for his SUV.

She closed the door and walked to the kitchen, pulling out a raspberry Popsicle as she went. *I know*, he'd said yesterday when she told him her address. How and why had he already known where she lived? It probably should have pissed her off, but for some ridiculous reason, it made her smile. She put the box of Popsicles in the freezer and was halfway back to bed when she remembered. Mark...land...she hadn't called to put in her offer.

Crap.

Hoping it wasn't too late, she reached for her cell phone and called the realtor. The asking price for the land was at the very top of her budget, and she'd been hoping to get it for less, but with Mark and the guys at Off-the-Grid also interested and probably having put in their offer yesterday, she decided she'd better offer the full asking price and hope for the best.

With that taken care of, she ate her raspberry Popsicle and crawled back into bed, hoping she felt more human the next time she woke.

* * *

"How come you get to have all the fun on the backhoe?" Ryan asked, watching as Ethan lowered the scoop on their rented machine and scraped up a bucketful of earth.

Ethan gave him a cocky grin. "Because I'm getting married this weekend."

"And your wedding gives you dibs on the backhoe, how?" Mark asked, stepping closer to survey the hole they were digging. Soon this hole would become a mud pit, one of many obstacles that teams would have to cross during the upcoming Adrenaline Rush, their annual team-based obstacle course race.

"It just does," Ethan said.

"I call bullshit," Ryan bellowed, a wide grin on his face.

Mark found himself fighting a grin of his own. Hell, he was so thankful for these guys. Closest thing to a family he'd ever had. Growing up in foster care, bouncing from home to home, about the only sure thing had been that things would change, and usually for the worse. But not with these guys.

They'd landed in a group home together the summer Mark was eleven. Best summer of his whole damn life. They'd been split up soon after, but it was a small town. They'd attended the same middle and high school and so they'd remained friends, thick as thieves through their teens.

After graduation, they'd drifted in different directions, but last year when Ethan had called with his idea for Off-the-Grid Adventures, Mark had jumped at the chance. It had come at just the right time, after his career with the Special Forces had ended. Instead of reenlisting and hoping the Army could find a new post for him, he'd gotten out and come home to Haven. This place, and these guys, had been exactly what he needed.

"Actually, since you're ditching us to run the haunted zip-line without you while you're on your honeymoon, I'd say you owe us one," Ryan said.

Ethan grumbled good-naturedly. "Fine, fine. Let me finish this side, then you can take over."

"That's more like it," Ryan said with a grin, watching as Ethan lifted another load of dirt out of the hole. "Speaking of your wedding, I've got everything set for your bachelor party tomorrow."

"Still not going to tell me where we're going?" Ethan asked.

"Nope," Ryan answered.

Wednesday might be an unconventional day for a bachelor party, but they were the sole owners of Off-the-Grid and it made much more sense financially to shut the place down on a Wednesday than a Saturday so that they could whoop it up with Ethan before he tied the knot.

Ryan had booked them for a skydive outside Boone tomorrow afternoon—that's how adrenaline junkies did bachelor parties—and then a night of bar-hopping. None of them had appointments scheduled back here until Thursday afternoon so they'd have plenty of time to sleep off any resulting hangovers.

"As long as it involves beer, I'm down," Ethan said, but Mark knew it was killing him not to know where they were going.

Ignoring him, Ryan turned to Mark. "Any word on the land?"

Mark shook his head. "Haven't heard anything yet."

"Piss-poor luck that Jessica wants it too," Ryan said.

"Tell me about it."

Ethan flipped the scoop backward, spilling dirt everywhere. "Oops. Listen, I like Jessica as much as the next guy, but this land would be a really sweet addition to our property. I've been thinking about that mountain bike track since we opened this place so I won't be sorry if her offer falls short."

Ryan shot a cautious look in Mark's direction. "I guess we'll wait to hear from the realtor and then see what our next step will be."

Mark nodded. He knew that they couldn't pussyfoot around because of his history with Jess.

"I know my next step," Ethan said with a grin. "I vote we fill this baby with water and give it a go."

"We agreed not to fill the pit with water until a few days before the event," Ryan said.

"But what if, for argument's sake, we add water and find out it's not deep enough? Or too deep? And how much loose dirt do we need to leave in here to create enough mud? All questions that could be answered this afternoon if we just pumped in some water and gave it a test run." Ethan looked positively gleeful at the thought.

There was a reason the three of them ran an outdoor adventure facility. They lived for this kind of shit. And Ethan had a point.

"I'm game," Mark said.

"Two outta three, bro," Ethan said, stepping out of the machine to let Ryan take over.

"Fair enough," Ryan agreed.

They'd chosen this spot for the mud pit because of its proximity to the course but also to the stream, from which they'd be able to pump water to fill it. Two hours later, the hole had been transformed into a mud pit and Ethan was staring at it with a wicked gleam in his eye.

"I'm going in," he announced.

"Figured you would," Mark said. "Let us know how it is."

"Oh, like you pussies aren't coming in too?" Ethan stripped to his boxer shorts and splashed into the mud pit. "Holy balls, this is cold."

"News flash: It's October, and you just filled that shit up with water from the stream that feeds down from the mountains." But Ryan was already stripping down too.

Mark followed suit. Why the hell not? He jumped, landing with a splash in a waist-deep combination of ice cold water and mud. It oozed between his toes and sucked at his body as he walked away from the edge.

Beside him, Ryan was laughing like a crazed hyena, sloshing his way through the muck. "Yo, this may be my favorite obstacle on the course this year."

"No shit." Ethan was laughing too. "Whose idea was this? It's genius."

"I think it was yours, genius," Mark said. The muddy water reached his chest at the center of the pit. Racers were going to love this.

"Oh yeah." Ethan grinned like the cocky bastard he

was. "Hey, why are you two losers just standing there? Get your asses over here so I can race you to the other side."

"You're on, man," Ryan said, hustling toward Ethan.

"Loser treats at Rowdy's tonight," Mark said, sloshing past Ryan.

"Can't," Ethan said. "Promised Gabby I'd help her finalize the seating plan for the wedding."

"Me neither," Ryan said. "Em and I are going to a movie."

Mark hauled himself out on the muddy bank beside Ethan. Things were changing now that Ryan was married and Ethan was only a few days from joining him. They were both properly domesticated now. Which left Mark pretty much where he'd always been in life, on his own. "Well, I'm going to beat your asses anyway. Whichever one of y'all loses can treat at Rowdy's another night."

"Those are fighting words," Ethan said with his trademark grin in place. "You're on."

"You do remember what he does for a living, right?" Ryan asked Mark, one eyebrow cocked. He was referring to the fact that Ethan coached the Pearcy County High swim team and had a couple of Olympic gold medals tucked away in his closet.

"Special Forces trumps Olympics when it comes to mud," Mark said simply.

"Shit, man. He's got some kind of Special Ops stuff up his sleeve," Ryan said to Ethan in mock alarm.

"I'm not worried." Ethan crouched down beside the mud hole, ready to jump.

Ryan took his place beside him. "All right then. Three. Two. One. Go!"

Out of the corner of his eye, Mark saw Ryan jump in

feet first. Yep. He'd be buying at Rowdy's. Mark went in slow, keeping near the edge of the pit where it was shallower. He treaded lightly against the bottom, pulling himself forward with big scoops of his hands through the muddy water. To his right, Ethan was attempting to swim through the muck and going nowhere fast.

He and Ethan were neck and neck until about halfway out when the firmer ground around the edge of the pit came into play as Ethan floundered in the mud. From somewhere behind them, Ryan called out, "Godammit, I'm stuck!"

Mark plowed ahead, not slowing until he'd pulled himself out on the other side. "Hooah!" he hollered, raising his fists in victory.

Ethan climbed out after him. "Sonofabitch."

Ryan hadn't even made it halfway across. "Oh yeah. Go ahead and laugh," he called, grimacing as he sloshed deeper into the mud.

Obligingly, Ethan did just that.

"You're right," Mark told him. "This is a kick-ass new obstacle."

They stood there and watched—and laughed—as Ryan finally made his way to shore. He hauled himself up beside Ethan and Mark with a groan. "That shit is *cold*. My balls have gone so far up inside my body I may never find them again."

Ethan doubled over in laughter.

"Good thing you've already knocked up your wife," Mark commented.

"Funny. Real funny," Ryan said, but he was laughing too.

Mark walked over to the pump and rinsed the worst of the mud from his body and then reached for his clothes where he'd dropped them. His cell phone showed a voice mail from Gordon McDermott. Mark pressed the phone to his ear and listened and then turned to his friends. "Our offer topped Jess's."

Ryan whooped while Ethan did some weird, hip-thrusting victory dance. Mark didn't feel much like celebrating though because his gut told him Jess wanted—needed—that land more than they did. But he couldn't be sorry about winning either.

"The realtor's waiting to hear whether she'll up her offer," he told Ethan and Ryan. "He's given her until five p.m. tomorrow."

* * *

Jessica opened her eyes, blinking to bring the room into focus. Her mouth was dry, and her brain was foggy, but she felt…better. Slowly, she sat up in bed and stretched, relieved to find that, for the first time in three days, her headache had subsided and her fever seemed to have broken. "Hallelujah," she muttered as she climbed out of bed.

Her limbs protested the movement, stiff and creaky as if she hadn't moved in months. Grimacing, she checked her phone to make sure she hadn't somehow been unconscious for days, but no, it was just past ten on Wednesday morning, and she couldn't believe how much better she felt. Honestly, she hadn't expected to bounce back from the flu this quickly.

After a nice, long shower, she was feeling even better. She heated a big bowl of her mom's homemade soup—yes, for breakfast because, why not?—and chased it with one of Mark's Popsicles for good measure.

Mark.

She closed her eyes, remembering his handsome face

in her doorway on Monday, the intensity of his gaze, the heat of his smile. No, the spark between them had never completely faded, not for her anyway. It seemed her body was just chemically programmed to respond to his. And now that he'd come back into her life, a tiny part of her wanted to know more about his time in the Army. The things he'd seen and done. How had it changed him? Were there other scars?

But that was ridiculous. She was overly curious, that's all. This week was the first time she and Mark had really spoken since they broke up all those years ago. She supposed it was natural to be curious about what his life had been like since.

But it didn't matter. What mattered was that he and his business partners wanted her land, and speaking of the land...

She checked her phone and found a voice mail message from the realtor. According to Gordon's message, the guys had come in ahead of her with their initial bid, but just barely. She stared at the phone in her hands. She'd offered the full asking price, and that had already maxed out her budget.

But... maybe they had maxed out their budget as well. Surely she could squeeze out a few more dollars to counteroffer. This had been her dream for so long, and it would needle her every damn day if she had to look outside and see people mountain biking behind the spa instead of her resort cabins.

She dialed the realtor.

"Gordon McDermott," he answered on the first ring.

"Hi, Gordon. It's Jessica Flynn."

"Jessica! I was hoping to hear from you today. Would you like to counteroffer?"

"I can go up ten thousand," she said. That would put her five grand ahead of the guys, and hopefully that would be enough because she couldn't keep playing this game. It wasn't worth it to put herself hopelessly into debt chasing a dream when she already had a profitable business she loved.

She and Gordon talked over the particulars, and he promised to send the documents for her to e-sign shortly. In the meantime, she walked to the living room to boot up her laptop. Her left knee was really painful when she walked on it. Had she twisted it while she was sick? She must have, maybe while she was running away from bears with Mark, and she had been feeling too lousy to notice at the time.

Her phone dinged with a new text message. Tomorrow at 6 at the Oak Branch Trail.

It was her friend Mandy. Jessica, Mandy, Gabby, and Carly would be competing in the upcoming Adrenaline Rush obstacle course race as Team Flower Power, and they'd been getting together a couple of times a week to jog and train together.

I'm going to miss this one, Jessica replied. Getting over the flu. Catch you ladies next time!

Yuck. Feel better soon! Mandy answered.

Someone knocked on Jessica's front door.

She walked to answer it, wincing at the pain in her knee. Seriously, only she could manage to sprain her knee while she had the flu. Her mom stood on the other side of the door, smiling brightly as Jessica pulled it open.

"Hey there, sweetie. Just came to check in and see how you were feeling." Paula Flynn wore her brown hair in a loose ponytail. Her pink scrubs meant she had stopped by on her way to work.

"Much better today, thanks." Jessica walked back toward the couch with her mom beside her. "My fever's gone. I'm still pretty tired and achy, but I think I'm officially on the mend."

"Have you been keeping up on your fluids?" her mom asked, going into full nurse mode.

She nodded. "I just finished a bowl of your soup and one of the Popsicles Mark brought."

"Mark?" Paula's eyes narrowed. "Why was he here?"

Jessica shook her head, wishing she could take the words back. It was insignificant that Mark had been here, and she wouldn't have blurted it out if her mind wasn't still a little sluggish. "I saw him on Sunday so he knew I was sick. He was just being friendly."

"Well, be careful around that man. I'd hate to see you get hurt again."

"We barely know each other anymore, Mom. Our relationship is ancient history." Her parents had never approved of her dating Mark. Everyone in town knew he'd gotten arrested at fifteen for stealing cigarettes from the mini-mart. The owner hadn't pressed charges, but in such a small town, his reputation as a delinquent had been set. By high school, he'd cut so many classes he almost flunked out. He smoked a lot of weed. But he'd always been a perfect gentleman with Jessica while they were dating. "The bigger problem is that he and his business partners just outbid me on that land between our properties."

"Oh no." Her mom's face fell. "So you didn't get it? Oh, sweetie, I know how long you've been saving and planning for this."

"Well, it's not a done deal yet. I'm making a second offer, but this is as high as I can go so cross your fingers for me." While she talked, she clicked through the documents the realtor had sent, adding her electronic signature where it was needed.

"Maybe your father and I could come up with something to help if you—"

"No. Thank you, Mom, but I know you guys are tapped out after Nicole's wedding. It's not worth any of us going outside our means to buy this land."

"But you're so close. Just let me know if there's anything we could do..."

"Thanks, Mom." But there was no way she was taking money from her parents. They'd finally managed to pay off their credit card debt last year, and she wasn't going to let them jeopardize their hard-won financial stability for her. "So if my fever stays gone, how soon can I consider myself germ-free to go back to work?"

"Twenty-four hours without fever is the rule of thumb," her mom said, "but I'd wait until at least Friday to be safe."

"Okay." Friday was doable. She'd been worried she wouldn't be back in time to oversee the spa treatments for her friend Gabby and her bridal party before her wedding on Saturday so this was good news.

Her mom left shortly after to get to work. Jessica called the spa to check in with Dana, her assistant manager. Everything seemed to be running smoothly without her, but Jessica was relieved to put herself back on the appointment calendar for Friday. She was more than ready to get back to work.

Her energy depleted, she leaned back on the couch and closed her eyes. Next thing she knew, her phone was ringing, dragging her from a deep, dreamless sleep. She opened her eyes to see that it was four o'clock, and she'd just slept away most of the day.

And Gordon McDermott was calling.

She cleared her throat and connected the call. "Hello."

"Hi, Jessica. Gordon McDermott here. Calling to let you know Off-the-Grid Adventures has increased their offer by twenty thousand."

Twenty thousand. *Shit.* "Oh."

"If you need some time to think about a counteroffer, I don't need your answer until end of day tomorrow."

"I...um, I don't need any time. I can't compete with that."

"I'm sorry to hear that," he said.

Not nearly as sorry as she was. She slumped on the couch, defeat sitting like a boulder on her chest.

"I'll keep things open until tomorrow anyway, in case you have a change of heart."

"I appreciate that, but unfortunately I'm out. Thanks again." She ended the call before her voice cracked and gave her away. Because she'd been dreaming about this resort almost since she'd opened the spa, and once these guys bought it and put their mountain bike course on it, that land probably wouldn't go back on the market again in her lifetime. Worse, she'd have to watch them out there on their bikes, living it up on the land that should have been hers. Tears pressed against the back of her eyes.

No way around it. Her dream was over.

CHAPTER THREE

$\mathcal{M}$ark plummeted toward the earth, buffeted by the wind rushing past him so that he felt like he was flying, like he was weightless. It was a fucking rush. Unlike Ethan and Ryan, who'd jumped ahead of him—flying tandem with an instructor—Mark got to jump unaccompanied, thanks to his Special Forces training.

Flying solo, the way he did best.

He focused on the landscape below, the green carpet of trees, interwoven with twisting mountain roads and splashed here and there with patches of fall color. For these sixty seconds, he was free as a bird, his mind blissfully empty...just free.

All too soon, it was time to pull the pin and release the chute. The resulting yank of the harness was like reality slamming back into him. It brought with it all the usual chaos in his brain, but today the knowledge that they'd likely crushed Jess's dreams with their last offer weighed heavily on his mind.

High off the adrenaline rush of his first skydive of the morning, Ethan had insisted they go all out with their counteroffer. With Ryan in full agreement, there was no way for Mark to head them off without sounding like a lovesick idiot because they were right. This was just a business transaction.

Jess wasn't his girlfriend, not even his friend.

So he needed to put the whole thing out of his mind because the deed was done, the offer had been made. She might hate him a little bit more now, but she hadn't liked him much to start with so this shouldn't really change anything between them.

And the fact that he still cared about her, still wanted her, the fact that he felt like an absolute tool for snatching this land out from underneath her? Well, it didn't matter. He couldn't let it. He was one-third owner of Off-the-Grid so his ultimate responsibility was to his partners and his business. Not Jess.

Below him, the trees were getting bigger as he drifted toward them. The landing field stood out as a bright rectangle of green grass amid the darker trees with the stray stripe of the runway down one side. He pulled the left toggle, steering for the middle of the field, where he could see Ethan and Ryan engaged in some kind of mock fight.

Fuckers. He felt himself grinning.

He swooped in near them, pulled down on both toggles to slow his descent, and landed at a jog.

"You don't have to make that look so easy," Ethan said as he walked over. "I landed flat on my ass both times."

Mark shrugged, hiding his smile.

"It's good for you to land on your ass every now and then," Ryan told him. "Keeps you humble, bro."

"Fuck you," Ethan shot back. He rammed into Ryan with his shoulder, and they both went down, still laughing.

"Easy," Mark said as he began unclipping himself from his harness and chute. "I promised your wife"—he pointed at Ryan—"and your future wife"—he pointed at Ethan—"that I'd bring you home from this gig in one piece."

Two hours later, they'd just finished devouring three large plates of ribs and were ready to move on to the next stop on their brewery tour of Boone. There were three in town, and they planned to hit them all. Ryan and Ethan hoped to be totally shit-faced by the time they called it a night.

Mark would stay sober enough to drive their sorry asses home at the end of the night. He didn't mind. He hadn't been drunk since high school. Back then, he'd gotten hammered any chance he had and done a lot of stupid shit as a result. Since joining the Army, he preferred to stay in control of his body and his senses.

So he'd have a couple of beers, but that was it.

"You know, I keep waiting for those cold feet everyone talks about," Ethan said. He drained his beer, looking thoughtful. "But the truth is, I can't wait to marry Gabby on Saturday."

"That's because she's The One for you, man," Ryan said. "When it's right, you've got nothing to lose. I never got cold feet with Emma either."

"Might be because you had a shotgun wedding," Mark commented, taking another drink of his beer.

Ryan grinned. "Yo, I make no excuses for that. It all

worked out how it was supposed to. We'd have gotten married sooner or later anyway, but I'm glad it happened sooner. Hey, did you guys know we find out the sex in a few weeks?"

"You're going to find out about sex?" Ethan said with a shit-eating grin on his face. "That ship has already sailed, hasn't it?"

Ryan elbowed him in the ribs. "The sex of the *baby*, dimwit."

"That's great, man," Ethan said, sobering.

"Emma thinks it's a girl. I'm kind of hoping for a boy, but it doesn't really matter to me one way or the other. Our kid's going to be outside climbing rocks and shit regardless."

Mark felt a strange pang as he thought about Ryan and Emma becoming parents. Ethan and Gabby tying the knot this weekend. He felt empty somehow. Hollow. Like the part of him that needed to create a family had shriveled up and died all those years he'd been bounced around foster care with no family of his own.

What would it feel like to come home to a wife, a couple of kids? The idea was so foreign that he couldn't even imagine it. A brief image of Jess flitted through his head. Jess in his arms, holding him tight. Jess beneath him in bed while he lost himself inside her the way he never had with any woman but her.

"You guys ready?" Ethan said, standing from the table.

"Brewery number two, here we come," Ryan said, also standing.

"Hang on a sec." Mark reached for his phone, which was buzzing in his pocket. "Hello?"

"Mark, so glad I caught you. Gordon McDermott here, and I'm afraid I have some bad news."

Jess had outbid them after all. Mark didn't feel nearly as disappointed about that as he ought to. "That so?"

"A third party has come into play," Gordon said.

Mark snapped to attention. "A third party?"

"A developer out of Asheville toured the property this morning. They're looking to build vacation condos, and their offer was more than competitive." He rattled off a number so high that Mark knew he and the guys had no hope of matching it.

And to think he'd worried about crushing Jess's dreams. Now he, Ryan, and Ethan had lost the land too.

* * *

Jessica massaged the muscles in Emma's neck, trying to ignore the shooting pain snaking down her right arm all the way into her fingers. If it had been her left, she might have thought she was having a heart attack, but no…this felt more like a pinched nerve or something. And it was annoying as hell.

After getting the all clear from her doctor that she was no longer contagious, she'd returned to work yesterday, but truly, she still felt like crap. She was so exhausted she could barely make it through the whole day on her feet. Her left knee was still sore and a little bit swollen. And now she had this nerve pain in her arm.

It was all she could do not to scream in frustration.

Because she did *not* have time for this. It was eleven thirty Saturday morning, and she was midway through the wedding party's spa treatment. Stifling a groan, she focused on Emma's massage, making sure her friend achieved complete relaxation here on Jessica's table.

When she'd finished, Emma let out a happy sigh. "It's

a bummer I can't soak in the hot tubs with everyone else because I'm pregnant, but I think this was just as great. Thanks, Jess."

"Absolutely," Jessica said with a smile. "I'll leave you to get dressed, and then we'll get you guys all set up for your manis and pedis."

"Sounds good."

Jessica left the room while Emma got dressed, forcing herself not to limp. She walked to the larger of their treatment rooms, where they often hosted bridal parties and other groups to make sure everything was in place for Gabby and her guests. Four pedicure chairs were ready for the bride-to-be, her mother, and her two bridesmaids, each adorned with a pink satin goodie bag containing essential oils, lotion, and other gifts for the women to take with them, compliments of the spa.

After making sure everything was ready, Jessica went down the hall to the staff room. She grabbed a bottle of ibuprofen from the cabinet and shook two pills onto her palm. Usually, she preferred holistic remedies to medicinal, but right now, her whole body ached, and she had work to do, dammit. *Screw you, flu. I don't have time for this shit.*

Dana poked her head in the room. "You all right?"

"Fine," Jessica answered automatically.

"I just wanted to let you know we had a cancellation at two. Tourists decided to head home a day early. So you could totally clear out of here after we finish with the bridal party."

Oh, thank goodness. "Thanks, Dana. I think I'll do that. That way I won't be cutting it so close to get ready for the wedding myself."

"We got your back, Jess."

"You're the best."

With a wave, her assistant manager left her alone in the break room. Jessica washed the ibuprofen down with a glass of mineral water, bolstered by the knowledge that she got to go home soon. Hopefully a quick nap would revitalize her enough to have fun at Gabby and Ethan's wedding.

Since slowing down for a few minutes seemed to have only made her more aware of her aches and pains, she put down her glass and headed out to greet the bridal party as they made their way into the treatment room for their manis and pedis.

"Is it selfish of me to claim you for myself, Jessica?" Gabby asked with a wide smile. "But I have to assume you're the best, and I *am* the bride after all."

"She's all yours," Emma told her. "You're the only one having close-up photos of your hands taken today." In her yellow knit dress, only the slightest hint of a baby bump showed.

"Besides, you called dibs on me on your own wedding day, if I remember correctly." Jessica gave Emma a friendly nudge, and her friend beamed.

"I sure did, and my hands have never looked prettier."

Jessica ushered Emma, Gabby, Gabby's mom, and her friend Chloe into the treatment room and got them all seated. Three of Jessica's employees followed them in to do the other women's treatments.

The bridal party spent a few minutes picking out polishes. Gabby was the first to make her selection. She took her seat and handed Jessica a glittery silver polish. "That's for my toes," she said. "They'll match my shoes. I want a French manicure for my hands."

"You got it."

An hour later, Jessica was finishing Gabby's French manicure while the girls chatted excitedly about the wedding. Gabby's hands, she noticed, were shaking. "Nervous?" she asked.

"Terrified," Gabby admitted. "Not about marrying Ethan...but the ceremony, the wedding itself. It's all so nerve-wracking."

"You'll be fine," Emma said. "The worst part is walking down the aisle because everyone's looking at you, and you just know you're going to trip or puke or something."

"I'm not sure you're helping," Gabby said, her eyes going wide.

"But really, who cares if you trip?" Emma said with a giggle. "We'll laugh *with* you, not *at* you. And I was two months' pregnant at my wedding so the puking thing was probably just me."

"She's got a good point," Jessica said as she applied the clear, sealing coat of polish to Gabby's left hand. Despite the intermittent shooting pains in her right hand, she'd managed to apply the polish perfectly.

Gabby looked down at her polished fingers with a dreamy smile. "I can't believe it's really happening today."

"I still remember having my nails done the morning I married your father," Gabby's mother said. "I'm so happy for you, sweetie."

"Thanks, Mom." Gabby's eyes had gotten glossy.

Jessica finished up and stood. "You ladies take all the time you need in here and feel free to help yourself to more drinks and snacks in the lounge before you leave. There's no one booked in this room until later this afternoon."

"Thanks so much, Jessica," Gabby said.

"My pleasure. Good luck with the rest of your preparations, Gabby. I can't wait to watch you walk down that aisle in a few hours." Jessica gave her shoulder a squeeze, as both of Gabby's hands were currently resting under the dryer.

Jessica headed for the front desk, where Maritza was on the phone booking an appointment. Dana came up behind them. "Go. We've got everything covered for the rest of the day. Go on. Rest up and get ready for the wedding."

Ordinarily, she'd never bail on them like this, but she'd looked at the schedule, and it was true. They were covered. And she was dead on her feet. "Okay. Thanks, Dana. Just call if anything comes up, okay?"

"Will do, but we're fine. Go on. I can't wait to hear all about the wedding tomorrow." Dana grinned. "Never thought I'd see the day Ethan Hunter got hitched."

Jessica smiled too. Yes, Ethan had been one of Haven's most notorious bachelors. "I'll take pictures."

She said good-bye to Dana and headed to the break room to get her things. Then she was finally, blissfully, on her way home. The exhaustion she'd been fighting all morning rose up and swallowed her the moment she stepped inside. She limped to her bedroom, flopped onto her bed, and was asleep almost before her head hit the pillow.

When she woke up, the clock read two thirty-three, and she felt like a whole new woman. Maybe she'd jumped back into work too quickly after kicking the flu, but she hadn't exactly had a choice. And she hated sitting home doing nothing.

After a long, hot shower, she stepped into the blue satin dress she was wearing to the wedding. She'd originally picked out a pair of strappy heels to go with it, but her knee was still bothering her so she went with simple black flats instead. She added a few chunky necklaces and a pair of matching earrings, and she was ready to go.

The wedding was at a beautiful estate on the outskirts of Haven. Jessica parked in the gravel lot behind the estate house with the other party guests and made her way to the area on the back lawn that had been set up with rows of white chairs facing a flower-draped arbor. The Smoky Mountains smudged the horizon beyond, and a vineyard to the east added to the beautiful scenery with its rolling hills lined with grapevines.

Here and there, couples walked around, laughing and talking before taking their seats. Jessica clutched her bag and looked around for someone she knew. Attending weddings by herself was such a drag. She needed a boyfriend, like yesterday.

Dammit, she was so tired of being serially single, but where were all the eligible bachelors? Because she'd done the online dating thing all summer, and it had yielded nothing but a series of duds and a few seriously cringe-worthy moments.

With some relief, she spotted her friend Carly Taylor and her boyfriend, Sam Weiss, seated about halfway back on the aisle and made her way toward them.

"Hey, you guys," she said, sliding into the empty seat beside Carly.

"Hi." Carly turned to her with a wide smile. "Isn't this place absolutely breathtaking?"

"It really is," Jessica agreed.

"Hey, Jessica," Sam said in his smooth drawl. Despite the fact that he happened to be one of the hottest rock stars in America, Sam had managed to keep a fairly low profile here in Haven. Jessica had been skeptical of her friend's whirlwind romance at first, but Sam seemed like an honest-to-God great guy, and he and Carly were obviously completely smitten with each other.

In fact...

Carly was waggling a blindingly gorgeous diamond solitaire ring in Jessica's direction, her smile almost as dazzling as the ring. "Look what happened last weekend while we were in LA."

"Oh my God!" Jessica whisper-squealed. "That's so exciting. Congrats, you guys."

"Thank you," Carly and Sam said in unison.

"That's some ring. Way to go, Sam." Jessica grinned at him. "So I guess we'll be attending another wedding soon."

It was practically a wedding epidemic at this point, and Jessica was thrilled for her friends, but... *ugh*, she was twenty-eight years old. Almost twenty-nine. And so single she hadn't had sex in almost a year. It was pathetic, really.

"Would it be tacky if we had our wedding here too?" Carly said. "Because this place is so amazing. Oh, look, there are the guys!"

Ethan, Ryan, and Mark had taken their places in front of the crowd, and damn, but they were a good-looking trio. Ethan with his tousled blond hair, blue eyes, and that charming grin that just wouldn't quit. Ryan with his brown hair, plentiful tattoos (which were hidden today beneath his charcoal gray tux), and bad boy attitude in place.

And Mark. Mark with his military-style close-cropped black hair, his dark eyes always so full of mystery, and the deep scar that creased his right cheek. His skin was a beautiful shade of bronze thanks to his father, who was

African-American. Back in high school, Mark had shown her the faded, wrinkled photo in his wallet, the only photo he had of his parents. His mom, petite and blond, his father tall and handsome, much like Mark himself. Just teenagers when they had him. They'd died in a car crash when Mark was six, leaving him adrift in the foster care system.

No doubt it was the reason he was so closed off now. Her heart broke for that little boy, orphaned and all alone. She'd loved that boy when he was on the cusp of becoming a man, loved him with all her heart. And rather than loving her back, he'd walked away. And so, no matter how much she hated the things he'd had to go through, she couldn't make the mistake of falling for him again.

But *damn*, he was something to look at. So handsome in his tux. Somehow, the scar only added to his sexy intrigue. She wanted to trace her fingers over it, kiss it, kiss *him*. And seriously, what was the matter with her right now? She did *not* still want Mark. She didn't even like him. She hated him for walking out on her the way he had.

So what if he looked delicious enough to eat? She shifted in her seat and stared out at the vineyard to her left until the ceremony started. The bridal party came first, radiant in their lavender dresses. Then the music shifted, and beside her, Carly gasped.

Gabby was the vision of beauty and happiness as she walked down the aisle with her father at her side. Her dress was simple but flowing, with lace edging the bodice and a full, lacy train. It was stunning, only slightly less stunning than her smile. She wore tiny white roses in her hair, and . . . yeah, Jessica felt herself getting teary-eyed.

She dabbed at her eyes as Gabby and Ethan exchanged

their vows. The love stamped all over both of their faces was just... wow. That's what Jessica wanted. She wanted a man who looked at her the way Ethan looked at Gabby. She pressed a hand to her heart when they were pronounced husband and wife.

Ethan pulled Gabby into his arms and gave her a kiss that made everyone in attendance whoop and cheer. Yep, Gabby was a lucky lady; that was for sure. After the ceremony, guests drifted to the patio for drinks and hors d'oeuvres while the bridal party had photos taken. Jessica walked around, making casual conversation while trying not to stare at a certain tall, handsome groomsman who was smiling—yes, smiling—for the camera on the other side of the lawn.

Finally, the reception got under way, and Jessica was relieved to find herself at the table with Carly, Sam, and a few other people she'd gone to high school with. She made small talk while she ate (and shared a few giggles with Carly as several female guests came over to their table to fawn all over Sam).

When they opened up the dance floor, she figured why not? She was feeling much better, and a couple of glasses of wine from the open bar had only improved her mood. She moved to the beat of a popular dance song with Carly, Emma, Gabby, and several other women. Their friend Mandy spun around in the center of the group, her red dress twirling. Jessica wished she could be that uninhibited, but no, she was content grooving quietly on the sidelines.

After a couple of dance tunes, the music changed, and a ballad began to play. Dancers coupled up, and Jessica headed for the bar. Halfway there, she almost walked right into Mark. He blocked her path, those dark eyes as serious as ever and locked on hers. "Good to see you back on your feet."

Something warm and tingly grew in her chest. "Yeah...um, thanks again for the Popsicles."

He nodded. "Want to dance?"

Dance? Was he serious? "Actually, I was just headed to the bar..."

"One dance. I have a business proposition for you."

"A what?" And what did that have to do with dancing? "If it's about the Adrenaline Rush, I already agreed to offer discount coupons to the race participants and a spa package to the winners like I did last year."

"And we appreciate that, but this is about something else."

What in the world? "One song. And this better be good." She narrowed her eyes at him before leading the way to the dance floor. She stopped at a quiet corner in back where they might be able to hear each other talk.

"You look beautiful tonight," Mark said, and the way he said it made her cheeks heat and her heart flutter.

"Thanks. You look pretty dashing yourself." Which was true, but this felt a little too much like flirting. She put her hands on his shoulders, keeping an arm's length between them like one of those awkward middle school dances. And still it felt too close.

His hands settled on her waist, warm and strong, and she could smell the fresh scent of his aftershave. Her heart was already beating too fast, and this was so ridiculous. She had to get this silly attraction under control, and pronto. This was *Mark*. Been there, done that.

"We lost the land," he said as they began to sway to the music.

She stopped cold and stared at him. "What? The realtor said you guys had outbid me."

"We did." He looked her straight in the eyes. "But then a developer out of Asheville outbid us to build condos on the property."

Jessica gasped, her hands tightening involuntarily on his shoulders. "Oh my God...but...*condos?*" Oh no. No no no. She didn't want condos next door, crammed in between her and Mark's properties.

"Our thoughts exactly." Mark's expression didn't change, but she knew him well enough to see the frustration in his eyes. "Frankly, we can't believe the Town Council is allowing it, but apparently they've already got preapproval. They'd be luxury vacation rentals, bring some new tourism money into the town."

"Well, this is a disaster," she said, still swaying in his arms. "I wasn't thrilled about a mountain biking course running behind the spa, but you guys respect the land, and I respect what you do. Condos next door?" She scrunched up her face.

"That's where the business proposition I mentioned comes into play."

"I'm listening." Although she couldn't for the life of her figure out what he had in mind, but if it somehow stopped the condos from being built...

"We team up," he said. "Together we outbid the contractor, own the land fifty-fifty. You were interested in the flatter areas on the west side to expand the spa. We wanted the hillier area on the east. We both get what we want, and more importantly, we keep the land."

"Whoa." Okay, she definitely hadn't seen that coming. She'd never fully come to terms with losing so this was awfully damn tempting. But...co-owning land with Mark and the other guys at Off-the-Grid?

"We'd be out a lot more money per acre than we would

have been initially, but still less total cost than either of our original offers on the full property."

"But co-owning?" She could feel herself frowning.

His espresso eyes were as closed off as ever so why did she think she saw a flicker of disappointment in their depths? "We could do a separate sale at a later date, split the acreage, buy each other out."

Dammit, that was an awfully hard offer to refuse. And he was right: The land should be big enough to share. Best of all, no condos. *And she could still build her resort.* "Okay," she murmured over the music. "I'll do it."

Mark's expression lit up, and she almost kissed him for it. "That's great. We can meet tomorrow and work out all the details?"

She nodded and then dropped her hands from his shoulders and turned to leave.

He didn't let go of her but instead smiled. "Song's not over yet."

Was Mark Dalton *flirting* with her? Stunned, she just stared at him for a long second. And then, because she'd clearly lost her mind, she settled into his arms for the rest of the song.

CHAPTER FOUR

*M*ark resisted the urge to bury his face in Jess's soft hair and inhale her scent as they danced. She smelled like an exotic combination of flowers and incense, a scent as familiar as it was intoxicating. She'd been burning incense for as long as he'd known her, and he'd never been able to smell it since without thinking of her.

It smelled like sex and fantasies.

His fingers tightened on her waist. She tipped her face up, her brown eyes locking on his. Her red lips were plump and glossy, parted slightly, and he felt his head dipping toward them, drawn to her like a parched man to a desert mirage. His heart beat a frantic rhythm against his ribs.

Jess sucked in a breath, leaning forward. Her breasts pressed against his chest, and he silently cursed the many layers of his tuxedo for muffling the sensation. Still, a hot thrill raced through him, scorching every nerve ending in his body.

Her warm breath teased his lips, and he was absolutely fucking lost.

Someone bumped into Jess, knocking her sideways. She cleared her throat, stepping backward out of his arms. "The, ah, the song's over."

And just like that, the moment was over too. Mark rocked back on his heels.

"Thanks for the dance," she said, her voice slightly husky.

He nodded. "I'll call tomorrow about the land."

She turned and walked away, weaving through the crowd. He watched the way that blue dress hugged her slender waist and flared around her hips. So beautiful.

He drew several slow, deep breaths and then made his way off the dance floor. Weddings weren't exactly his gig, and that encounter with Jess had left him feeling raw and restless. Too many people. Too much noise. It was time for him to melt into the background until he could leave without being impolite.

He strode toward the exit, intent on the vacant darkness beyond.

"Hey there, Good Lookin'. You want to dance?"

He looked down to see a petite blonde standing in front of him in a low-cut silver dress that revealed ample cleavage. With a grunt, he shook his head and dodged around her.

"Let me know if you change your mind!" she called out from behind him.

Not a chance.

"Yo, what did Jessica say?" Ryan stepped into his path, a beer in each hand. He handed one to Mark.

So much for making a quick escape. He took the beer and drank. "She's on board."

"Great, man. That's great."

Mark nodded. "It is."

He and Ryan walked over to the bridal party's table to tell Ethan the good news. From there, he got sucked into a conversation with Trent, Ryan's younger brother. Trent had a friend who was thinking about enlisting and looking for some advice.

Then Ethan and Gabby went out onto the dance floor to cut the cake.

"I hope Gabby knows what she's in for," Ryan muttered.

Mark smiled in spite of himself. Surely Ethan's new wife knew exactly what she'd married into. The man was an incurable jokester. No way he wasn't going to smear that cake all over her face. As they watched, Ethan and Gabby each took a bite of cake to feed each other, intertwining their arms as they went. Ryan leaned forward in his chair, grinning like a fool. Beside him, Emma looked similarly engaged.

Gabby and Ethan lined up their hands in front of each other's mouths, but at the last moment, Gabby ducked down, simultaneously smashing her handful of cake into Ethan's face. The tent erupted with raucous laughter and whoops.

Smiling victoriously, Gabby gave a little bow before handing her husband a napkin. Ethan was laughing hysterically as he wiped bits of cake and frosting from his face.

"That's my girl!" Emma announced proudly, pointing in Gabby's direction.

"He totally had that coming," Ryan said, looking impressed.

Indeed, it was about time someone put Ethan in his

place, and it seemed Gabby was just the woman for the job. Soon after, plates of cake were being served at their table. Mark dug into his with gusto. He'd always had a sweet tooth, but he'd gone years without anything nearly this good while he was overseas. Fucking delicious.

"Mmm," Emma said from across the table. "Carly really outdid herself on this one."

Carly owned A Piece of Cake bakery downtown. Mark had never been inside the bakery, but being part of the same circle of friends meant he'd gotten to enjoy her baking a few times anyway, and he hadn't had anything yet he didn't like. After cake and coffee, the music slowed again and the dance floor filled with couples. Even Trent had found a girl to dance with.

Mark seized the chance to make his exit. He wove between tables and out into the cool, crisp night. Overhead, the sky twinkled with stars. Looking up at them, he could almost think he was back in the desert. But instead of gunfire, the night around him was peppered with music, voices, and the tinkling of dishes. Right then, he missed the sound of gunfire, the adrenaline rush that came with it, the sense of calm that descended over him right before he jumped headfirst into the enemy's lair.

He followed the path toward a fountain splashing at the other end. When he saw someone else sitting there, he started to turn away. He needed to be alone right now, had used up his capacity for casual conversation for the night, but her profile stopped him in his tracks. "Jess."

She turned, silhouetted by the sliver of moon overhead. "Mark? What are you doing out here?"

"Same as you, I reckon." He pushed his hands into his pockets and watched the spray of water as it splashed into the pool behind her.

She was silent for a moment, which suited him fine. "Just needed some air," she said finally.

"Me too."

"Beautiful wedding."

"Yeah." He watched her, captivated by the sheen of her lips in the moonlight.

"Think it's too early to make an escape?" she asked suddenly.

He cocked his head. "I was just wondering the same."

"I need to be out of here before they toss the bouquet."

"Why's that?"

She made a sound of frustration. "It's just...a stupid, embarrassing tradition."

Well, he'd never thought about it that way, but there was no way in hell he'd get out on that dance floor with all the other single guys here and try to catch flowers or anything else. "I can see that."

"I don't want to hurt Gabby's feelings though."

"I'm sure she'd understand. Just tell her you're still feeling ill from the flu."

Jess sighed. "That's not even a lie. I think I'll do that. Thanks, Mark." She stood and started walking back toward the brightly lit tent behind them.

He stayed by the fountain, allowing the shadows to swallow him up. No matter how badly he wanted to see her to her car, for any number of reasons it was best to let her make her early exit alone.

* * *

Jessica woke up late the next morning, intensely grateful that the spa didn't open until noon on Sundays. Her eyes fluttered shut, and she remembered the wedding. That dance with Mark. The crazy moment when she'd been sure they were about to kiss... *holy crap*. A burst of heat spread through her at the memory. Okay, she needed to step up her dating game ASAP because this attraction to Mark was getting out of control.

What was that about anyway?

Maybe it had to do with the thoughtful, honorable, *sexy* man he'd become. But he'd been all those things in high school too and look how that had turned out. Deep down, he was still the same man who'd cut her out of his life without a second thought, who'd do it again the next time he got restless. Couldn't fault him for being who he was.

He wasn't the man for her, and it was past time for her to suck up her pride and get back in the online dating game. Problem was, she was pretty sure she'd already gone out with every available guy in the area that she had anything in common with. Pitfalls of small town living.

Ugh.

She got up, lit some Nag Champa in her incense burner, and spent the next half hour cleansing her energy through meditation. By the time she'd finished, she felt much better—and more optimistic. The right man would come along. Of course he would.

In the meantime, she showered and got ready for work and then fixed herself a grilled cheese sandwich since it was closer to lunchtime than breakfast and she was starved. She washed it down with a much-overdue cup of tea. Her phone showed a text from Mark.

Okay if I stop by around 6?

She typed back: I'm working until 6. Make it 7?

See you then, he replied.

Another thrill shot through her, and this one had

nothing to do with Mark, or nothing to do with her attraction to him anyway. But the land! If this business partnership worked out, she would get to build her resort after all. And soon. Since she still had a few minutes before she needed to leave for work, she went to her laptop and pulled up her business plan as the bubble of excitement inside her grew.

There would be eight spa cabins to start, each of them equipped with their own personal hot tub fed by the natural hot springs. She envisioned an open area at the center of each cabin so that her guests could soak beneath the stars. Maybe with retractable screens overhead so that the area could be closed during bad weather.

It was going to stretch her budget to its limits to pull this off, but her credit would support a small business loan to help get her up and running. A little hard work had never scared her. She was going to do this, and it was going to be fabulous.

Smiling, she gathered her things and headed for the spa. She worked a solid six hours with a spring in her step and visions of spa cabins dancing through her head. She made it home just in time to change out of her spa uniform before Mark was knocking at her door.

As she walked to answer it, she realized with a start that the pain in her knee was gone. Like, totally gone. Huh. Well, that was good news, especially since she had another training run planned with the girls of Team Flower Power tomorrow. Then she pulled open the door and forgot all about it because Mark stood there in a worn blue T-shirt and khaki cargo shorts, and *oh my*, he was a sight to see.

"Hey," he said, a smile softening the corners of his mouth.

"Come in." She pulled the door open, inviting him inside. "Can I get you anything? Coffee? Tea?"

"No thanks." He held out the papers in his hand. "I've got some numbers for us to look over. Ryan wanted to be here too, but he's holding down the fort at Off-the-Grid right now since Ethan's on his honeymoon."

"Okay." She motioned for him to sit next to her on the couch.

"Once we agree on all our terms, Ethan knows a lawyer who can write up the agreement for us, free of charge. It should be fairly straightforward. We just need to agree on a competitive offer to top the builder. We'll be equal owners in all respects, with the option to separate the land and buy each other out at a later date."

"Sounds good to me." She'd known all three of these guys since they were teenagers and trusted them not to try to screw her over. "How will we divide up who gets what?"

"I've got a topographical map here if you want to try to hash it out now or we can just wing it after we buy the land. From our meeting with Gordon McDermott last week, it seemed like you were interested in a different part of the property than we are. We don't need that much space for our mountain bike course. Should work out."

Jessica reached for the map he'd indicated. He was right. They'd probably be fine, but the businesswoman in her felt like she needed to have some clear boundaries defined in their contract. "Show me where you're planning to put the mountain bike course?"

He leaned in, pointing toward the elevated area on the left-hand side of the map, part of which wrapped around awfully close to the space she wanted for her cabins.

"And I want to build from here to here." She swiped

her finger across the map, landing next to Mark's. "But I don't want a mountain bike course running right behind my cabins."

Mark's brow furrowed. "We'll work it out."

"Yes, but a spa is, by definition, where people go to relax and unwind so I need to make sure there's enough space between us that they aren't listening to your clients being rowdy on the mountain bike course."

"Okay." Mark looked over and met her eyes, waiting for her to offer a solution.

She rubbed her brow, where a migraine seemed to be brewing. The headaches and fatigue had persisted for a week now after getting over the flu, and she was really friggin' sick of it. If she didn't feel better soon, she might have to go back to the doctor. "What if I move my cabins over this way a bit, closer to the stream?"

"And we could do the course like this." He traced again with his long, calloused finger, indicating a route that kept the mountain bike trail farther from her cabins.

"So, if we divide the land right through here, we should be good." She traced an imaginary line and then looked up at Mark for his approval. He nodded. She reached into the drawer of her coffee table and came up with a yellow highlighter, which she used to draw the line separating her half of the land from Off-the-Grid's.

Next, she and Mark talked about money, and once they'd gotten their joint offer all worked out, they sat back and looked at each other.

"So. Business partners." She forced herself to smile.

"Business partners." Mark nodded as he gathered the papers from her table. His hand brushed hers, and her whole body lit up from that simple contact.

Business partners. Nothing more.

* * *

By Monday morning, their business partnership was a done deal. The condo developer dropped out as soon as they presented their joint bid for the land to Gordon McDermott, opting instead to build on the other side of town. And so Off-the-Grid Adventures and the Haven Spa became joint owners of the undeveloped land between their properties.

And Mark was feeling pretty damn good about it. Even Jess had looked triumphant as they signed all the paperwork. Because of the nature of the sale, they'd been able to negotiate a closing date the following Wednesday. None of the parties involved wanted to wait any longer than necessary to seal the deal.

Mark welcomed the new project to keep him busy. With Ethan on his honeymoon and Ryan rushing home to Emma at every available chance, initial work on the mountain bike course had fallen to Mark by default. As soon as the closing papers were signed on Wednesday morning, he headed straight out to the new property to start mapping.

Jess planned to come over after she got off work that evening so that they could begin "marking their territory" on the land itself. He was looking forward to seeing her more than he wanted to admit. Since the land negotiations started, he and Jess had spent more time together than they had since high school, and he enjoyed the fact that she was speaking to him again.

A lot.

He struck out into the woods, allowing the forest to swallow him up. The untouched beauty of this land really resonated with him, and he was reassured to know it wouldn't be clear-cut to accommodate vacation condos but rather subtly altered to accommodate his and Jess's plans. It didn't take him long to reach the hilly area they'd been eyeing for the start of the mountain bike course.

They would need to add a small access road or path that connected to Off-the-Grid's existing network of trails. A wide grin covered his face as he climbed the hill closest to Off-the-Grid's existing property. Wide and flat at the top, with a sloping front, it was the perfect launching point for the mountain bike course.

Movement caught his eye, and he glanced automatically toward it. He glimpsed a patch of brown fur as the creature moved off into the woods. Hopefully it wasn't the mama bear and cubs he and Jess had disturbed the last time they were out here. It wasn't common for bears to hang around one place for this long and might lead to territorial disputes later on. He didn't want that. Especially since, no matter whose name was on the deed, this land belonged to the bears and other wildlife.

He backed up and pulled out one of the orange markers he'd put in his pack, sticking it into the soft earth at the hill's summit. He hoped to mark a rough outline for their course before Jess arrived so that he could get her blessing on it.

He made his way down the hill, marking the trail as he went. This hill led to another and then over a small ravine where they would build a raised wooden bridge for the mountain bikes. Again, there was a rustling in the bushes nearby, and again he glimpsed a furry shape in the trees.

The bear was following him.

A frisson of alarm buzzed through his system. This was not normal bear behavior. If the animal was sick or injured, it might become aggressive. Or if it had been fed by humans in the past, it might be hoping for a tasty treat. Neither option boded well, for Mark or the bear. The last thing he wanted was an encounter that might lead to a black bear being put down, which was almost always the result when a bear became a nuisance or aggressive.

Keeping eyes and ears tuned toward the creature lurking nearby, Mark abandoned the path he'd been marking and headed toward the road. He wasn't armed, had nothing to defend himself with, and though an attack was still unlikely, the bear tracking him was displaying unusual and somewhat alarming behavior.

Better safe than sorry.

The animal darted between two bushes, and Mark's scalp prickled with misgivings. It was small, most likely one of the cubs he'd seen last week with Jess. Was its mother nearby or had something happened to her?

He stopped, listening. A cub was unlikely to attack, but its mother was another story, especially if she decided Mark was too close to her baby.

Silence in the woods around him.

He started walking again, and immediately the sounds of the bear cub scampering through the undergrowth reached his ears. It was definitely following him and appeared to be alone. Was it injured? How had it become separated from its mother and the other cub?

He might need to put in a call to the Park Service and see how they handled orphaned bear cubs. He'd feel better if he could get a good look at the animal, but so far it had remained concealed in the dense undergrowth.

Mark started walking again, leading the cub toward a more open area of the forest, hoping to get a better look at what he was dealing with. It followed, rustling along about twenty feet away, until it reached the clearing.

Mark walked on, continuing a safe distance into the clearing so that the animal could show itself without getting too close.

A brown face peered out at him from a low-lying bush, but it wasn't a bear cub.

It was a dog.

CHAPTER FIVE

$\mathcal{M}$ark stopped in his tracks and stared. The animal staring back at him from within the bush was definitely a dog. Not a bear. No wonder it had followed him through the woods. But what the hell was a dog doing way out here?

He crouched and held out a hand. "Come here, boy."

The dog's ears pricked. Mark couldn't tell what breed it was. Something brown and fuzzy. Maybe a mutt.

"Hungry?" He sat on a fallen log and unzipped his pack, pulling out a stick of beef jerky.

The dog sniffed at the air hungrily and came out of the bushes, walking toward him. It stopped every few feet, eyeing him warily. Mark broke off a big piece of the jerky and held it out.

Apparently deciding beef trumped caution, the dog trotted the rest of the way over and stood before him, brown eyes fixed on the jerky. He was about the size of a German shepherd, but his coloring was all wrong. This dog was a more uniform brown, maybe some kind of Lab mix, but his ears...he had the most ridiculous ears Mark had ever seen. They were big and floppy, and the hair there was significantly longer than the rest of his body, shaggy with some curl to it.

Mark kept holding out the jerky until finally the dog came forward and took it gingerly from his fingers, still watching him warily.

"You lost?" he asked, bending to check for a collar. None.

And "he" was actually a "she." There were burs matted in her fur, and her ribs protruded slightly, but she didn't look to be in terrible shape.

"Thought you were a bear," Mark told the dog as she swallowed the jerky and gazed longingly at the rest of the stick in his hand. "Guessing you're hungrier than I am."

He handed it to her, and she swallowed it in a single gulp, licking her lips and staring at him expectantly. With a sigh, he reached into his pack and pulled out more jerky. "This is the last one I've got though."

He broke it into pieces, and the dog gobbled them down as fast as he held them out to her. Mark considered himself well prepared for just about any situation he might encounter out here, but he wasn't actually sure what to do with a lost dog. Take her to the shelter maybe. They could look for her owners there or find her a new home if she didn't have one.

He didn't have a leash so he'd just have to hope she stuck around. Given the way she'd followed him earlier, he figured there was a good chance she would. He pulled out his water bottle and took a long drink and then drizzled some water onto the ground while she lapped at it.

"Mind hanging out while I finish marking this trail?" He stood, and she darted back a few feet but stayed nearby. Testing his theory, he hiked back to the spot where he'd first heard her in the bushes, near the head of the trail.

The dog followed a few steps behind.

So he got back to work, scouting and marking the mountain bike trail to show Jess when she stopped by later. He had a lot of work to do before he saw her.

* * *

It was just past five when Jessica finally left the spa. She was so excited to explore her new land she could hardly wait. She had her phone ready to take pictures and a copy of the map she and Mark had looked at last week to start scouting cabin locations. She'd already gotten approved for a small business loan so, as soon as she'd gotten the lay of the land, it would be time to hire a contractor and start building.

The sun was starting to dip behind the treetops as she walked out the back of the spa, cutting directly onto her new land. Her land! She was grinning like an idiot. So what if she was going to be stretched as thin as cellophane for the next few years paying for it all? The reward at the other end was going to be *so* worth it.

Leaves crunched beneath her feet as she walked. Around her, the trees blazed with color. The distant babble of the stream filtered through them, steady and soothing. This place was absolute perfection for her spa cabins. She pulled out her phone and started taking pictures, marking dots on the map in her favorite spots.

Eventually, she wound up in the middle of the property,

near the area the guys wanted to use for their mountain bike course. In fact, there was a series of orange flags leading over a nearby hill that she suspected Mark had left for just that purpose.

Curious, she walked to them, following the path he'd marked. It led over the next hill and down the other side, headed for a flat patch of land that bordered Off-the-Grid's original property.

"You approve?"

Stifling a yelp, she whirled to find Mark behind her, a brown dog at his side. It really was unfair that he could move so quietly. "Yes, but... did you get a dog?"

He glanced down at the mutt standing at attention beside him. "Nah. Found her."

"Really? Out here?" Jessica stepped closer, holding out a hand toward the dog, who eyed her warily, never budging from Mark's side.

"Yeah. I'll drop her by the shelter when I leave."

"Hi, girl." Jessica crouched down, talking to the dog. "How'd you wind up out here?"

The dog flicked her ears forward and took a step in Jessica's direction. She was fairly large, with brown fur that was matted in places and adorable, fluffy ears. After a little coaxing, she walked over and licked Jessica's hand.

"Maybe you should keep her," she said to Mark. "At least while you look for her family. She's too sweet to go to the shelter."

He grunted, gazing down at the dog.

Jessica stroked behind the dog's ears. "You know what happens to strays at the shelter who don't find a home, right?"

Mark said nothing.

For some reason, she wanted him to keep this dog.

Maybe it would be good for him to have someone at home to greet him. "You don't want her to be euthanized, do you? She seems so quiet and well behaved."

"Which means she probably has a family out there looking for her."

"And you should definitely let the shelter know you've found her. I think they can even scan her for a microchip. Up to you whether you leave her there." She winked at him.

He said nothing.

The dog really was a sweet thing. She licked Jessica's fingers, her tail wagging shyly, and then returned to Mark's side, looking for all the world like she was waiting for her next command. When he started walking, she followed right at his heels.

So did Jessica. They walked together in easy silence, following the string of orange flags he had placed on the ground. He'd been busy today and also true to his word. His flags were well away from the area she wanted for her cabins.

She couldn't help smiling every time she glanced at the dog by his side. The pooch clearly already viewed Mark as her master. It was easy to see why. He moved with a quiet confidence that obviously set her at ease. Not sure which way to go? Just follow Mark.

Jessica was so busy doing just that that she didn't even see the hole in front of her until she'd stepped in it. Thrown off balance, she groped blindly for something to hang on to, her fingers latching on to Mark's arm. He turned in surprise and grabbed her before she went down in a heap.

His hands gripped her arms, warm and strong, his eyes locked on hers. "You okay?"

She nodded because her heart was pounding so hard she didn't trust herself to speak. There was so much electricity in the air between them that her whole body sizzled with it. Her stumble had landed her close in his arms, so close that, each time she drew breath, the space between them seemed to shrink.

His gaze dropped from her eyes to her lips.

He's going to kiss me!

Her blood heated, and her lips parted, and...what the hell was she thinking? Grabbing on to the last glimmer of reason in her brain, she stepped backward out of his arms. Pain knifed up her left leg, and it folded beneath her, dropping her in a heap onto the forest floor.

The air left her lungs so fast she felt dazed, sitting there, staring at Mark's boots. Then the dog was there, nuzzling her cheek, tail wagging.

Mark crouched in front of her. "What's wrong? Are you hurt?"

Not wanting to get lost in his eyes again, she looked down at her left knee, which, now that she was no longer drunk with lust, hurt like a son of a bitch. "I think I twisted my knee."

"Let me have a look." He straightened her leg out against the bed of pine needles and gently felt her knee through her jeans.

She winced. "It's been bothering me off and on for a few weeks. I don't know what I did to it."

"You have it checked out?"

"No." She sighed. Dammit, she hated going to the doctor. Maybe because, having a nurse for a mother, she'd spent way too much time around hospitals as a kid. "I guess I should though. I thought it was finally better."

She accepted the hand he held out and pushed to her

feet, putting all her weight on her right foot. Her left knee throbbed. She could feel the heat radiating out of it. *Son of a bitch.*

"You able to walk on it?"

"Of course." She took a halting step, biting her tongue to hold back a groan. Well, better to get this over with. She hobbled away from Mark in the direction of the spa.

"In the interest of getting home before dark..." His arms came around her, and he swept her off her feet, lifting her into his arms as if she weighed nothing at all (and thank goodness for that because it took a little of the sting off her pride).

"I can walk," she said, her voice gone all low and husky because now she was closer than ever to him, wrapped up in his warm, masculine scent. She felt his heart thumping against her, and as she met his eyes, it quickened.

So did hers.

Her hands tightened behind his neck, causing his head to dip toward hers. Helpless to fight the pull, she leaned in, and her lips brushed his. Her entire body lit with awareness from her scalp to her toes, like she'd just turned on the light after a very long time in the dark. *Whoa.*

Yeah. Sparks. She and Mark still had them.

She sucked in a ragged breath, her eyes locking on to his, and then he kissed her back. This time his lips crashed into hers with an urgency that matched the need flaring inside her. Her eyes fluttered shut, and her lips parted.

"Woof!"

Jessica's forehead bumped into Mark's. He was looking down at the dog, his expression a mixture of amusement and frustration. At his feet, the dog was staring right back in rapt attention.

Way to ruin the moment, Fluffball.

Mark's gaze flicked back to Jessica's, and almost without thinking, she tipped her face, bringing her lips back to his. Everything inside her went all hot and tingly as his tongue swept into her mouth.

"Woof!"

"Seriously, now you discover your voice?" She glared down at the dog in mock exasperation.

Mark let out a rough laugh. "She hasn't made a peep all day."

"I don't think she likes us kissing." As she spoke, her gaze dropped to his lips. The damn dog was probably the only one here that had any sense. But right now, Jessica. Did. Not. Care.

The only thing she could think about was kissing him again. And again.

Mark shifted her in his arms, reaching behind him. He pulled something out of the pack he wore and tossed it to the dog. She immediately crouched on the ground to eat the treat.

Then he was kissing Jessica again. She leaned forward in his arms, clinging to him as their tongues tangled together, tasting, devouring. It was hot and messy and perfect. His arms tightened around her, holding her close as he kissed all the logic right out of her. Because right then, right there, who cared about being wrong if wrong felt so amazingly *right?*

"Mark," she murmured, pressing a hand over his heart. It pounded against her palm, hard and fast, and already he was kissing her again. It was too much, and not enough, and oh, she had no idea what to do with this man!

She wanted his hands all over her, wanted to explore every inch of his body, so much bigger and stronger than he'd been in high school. She wanted to know if it would be as good between them now as it had been then. *Better.* Could it possibly be better?

Each stroke of his tongue against hers promised a resounding *hell yes*.

There was only one small problem with their current position. While it was quite romantic to be held in his arms while he kissed her bones to jelly, it kept him from being able to do anything fun with his hands...like touch her in any of the places that were screaming to be touched. To fit her good parts against his and see if they still lined up just right.

She squirmed in his arms, restless, aching for more. "Mark..."

He lifted his head, his dark eyes blazing with the reflection of the sunset behind them. God, he was absolutely the most beautiful thing she'd ever seen. She traced a finger over the scar on his cheek. It was smooth, almost slick, puckered against his skin.

He flinched.

"Does it hurt?" she whispered.

He shook his head.

"I'm sorry."

"For what?" His voice rumbled through her.

"For whatever happened to you overseas." Because she had a feeling there were other scars, less visible ones, physical and emotional.

He opted to kiss her again instead of answering, and she couldn't argue with that. Not when kissing him was the most fun she'd had in weeks, months, years...who the hell knew? God, he tasted good, he felt good. *She* felt good in his arms.

And whoa. This was getting out of hand. "Put me down," she murmured against his lips.

He lowered her gently, still supporting her with one arm, and holy shit, she'd forgotten why he was carrying her in the first place because, *ouch*, her left knee screamed in protest when she tried to stand on it.

She shifted her weight to her right leg, holding on to Mark for balance, which refocused her attention to the fact that now their bodies *were* matched up. His hard length pressed against her belly like a sinful invitation.

"You okay?" he asked, his voice a bit more gruff than usual.

"Mm-hmm." Instinctively, she pressed closer.

His hands slid down to her waist, anchoring her against him. "Can you walk?"

"Maybe." But that would mean stepping backward out of his arms, when all she really wanted to do was climb up his body until that bulge in his jeans pressed into her right where she needed it...

"Jess." His voice rumbled through her, making every inch of her tingle with anticipation.

"Mark." Her voice was a whisper as she tipped her face up to his, and dammit, why did he have to be so tall? She went up on her right tiptoe (forget her stupid left knee and its inconvenient issues), and then they were kissing again, and this kiss included all the things she'd been missing the first time.

His hands were on her butt, keeping her hips flush against his, and *God*, he was so hard, and she wanted him so much that she didn't even care about what a bad idea it was. She slid her hands beneath his shirt, exploring the taut muscles beneath. Every inch of him was hard. There probably wasn't an ounce of fat anywhere on his body.

She trailed her fingers over the hard slope of his back and around to the drool-worthy six-pack of his abs. He'd been lean and muscular in high school, but now the guy was seriously built. Honestly, she wasn't sure she'd ever felt muscles as prominently defined as Mark's. As she shamelessly explored his abs, her fingers encountered another scar.

His body tensed against hers. She skimmed his scar with her fingers, and Jesus, it ran all the way from his navel to his hip, smooth and straight like a surgical scar. But there were others, raised and puckered in his flesh, tangible souvenirs of his time at war. Tears burned at the back of her eyes for whatever he'd been through. And since this was definitely not the time or place to ask, she slid her hands up, rewarded by a harsh groan from Mark as she pinched his nipples, causing them to constrict into tight buds.

Yeah, he'd always liked that.

He rocked his hips into her, deepening their kiss. His tongue thrust against hers, and her whole brain just went *poof*, leaving nothing behind but lust and want and need. Next thing she knew, he'd popped the clasp of her bra. His hands slid around to cup her breasts, and her nipples tightened into aching peaks, sending a bolt of fire straight to her core, where she already throbbed for him.

They kissed like that for what might have been minutes, hours, days...she'd lost all track of things like time and place. At some point, his hands slid down to cup her ass, lifting her off the ground so that his cock pressed between her legs. Their hips rocked together as they touched, kissing each other like their lives depended on it. And she was so turned on she might—

"Woof!"

Dammit. Jessica had almost forgotten the mutt was there, but when she looked down, she saw the dog sitting at Mark's feet, staring up at them with a comical expression on her face.

Mark put Jessica down, and she stepped backward out of his arms, relieved to find that her knee felt much better. And wow, somehow things between them had gotten totally out of hand. She just stood there for a moment, gasping for breath, staring at Mark.

He was breathing pretty hard himself, and the heat in his gaze almost knocked her knees right out from under her all over again. Okay, she really, really liked this new and improved, more mature version of Mark. Maybe she'd been wrong to think he couldn't change. And the chemistry between them? *Holy shit.* It had bugged the hell out of her throughout her adult life that sex had never been quite as good as she remembered it being with Mark. She'd been pretty sure she was just overexaggerating in her mind, but now? Maybe not.

"Wow," she said, running a hand through her hair. "That was, um…"

Mark said nothing, his expression as frustratingly hard to read as ever.

She refastened her bra and then bent to pet the dog, for lack of anything better to do. What should she say? What did she even want? She had no idea anymore. Was it so terrible if they had sex? Maybe. Probably. If it got rid of all this sexual tension between them, then it might be a good thing. But if it was as good as it promised to be? It was better for her not to go there. No need to remind herself what she was missing because this was a man who'd never trust her with his heart, and she'd be smart to remember that fact.

She straightened to face him. "So, this kiss...maybe we should—"

"It's forgotten," he said, and turned away.

She blinked. *What?* Had she misread him? Had the attraction been one-sided? No. No way. He'd wanted her every bit as much as she wanted him. And yet it still cost him nothing to walk away.

Same old Mark.

Hurt and anger warred inside her. "Right. Forgotten."

She spun and took off in the direction of the spa, walking as fast as her sore knee would allow. She wouldn't give him the satisfaction of looking back so she kept her gaze straight ahead until she'd reached the back lot of the spa, chest heaving and knee throbbing.

Only then did she glance back into the woods behind her. But he wasn't there.

* * *

Mark stood there for a long time, just staring in the direction Jess had gone. His pulse raced, and his heart...his heart felt full and empty at the same time. Jess had the power to light him up like no one else. She turned him on, sure. His need for her was greater than it had ever been for a woman. But he could control his sexual needs.

The problem was that Jess made him *feel*.

And he hadn't felt anything like this in a long time. Feelings were raw and messy and scary as fuck, and they usually ended with someone getting hurt. So when he'd seen the uncertainty in her eyes after they kissed, he'd seized the chance to put an end to this thing before it got any more out of hand than it already was.

He glanced down at the dog still sitting patiently beside him. Time to get her to the shelter. Pushing Jess from his mind, he hiked back through the woods toward Off-the-Grid. His SUV was the only car left in the lot, which suited him fine.

He and Ryan had to be back here later tonight anyway to man the haunted zip-line. Good thing Ethan would be back from his honeymoon in a few days. They'd been stretched awfully thin here without him. Mark enjoyed the extra work, although he'd never understood why people went out of their way to get scared on purpose. What the hell was the point? There were enough truly terrifying things in the world that you ought to enjoy a little peace and quiet when you could find it, as far as he was concerned.

He opened the back door of the SUV and looked down at the dog. She hopped in obediently. Which meant she was definitely someone's pet. He was doing the right thing taking her to the shelter so that her family could find her.

He started the engine and headed out of town toward the Pearcy County Animal Shelter. The dog settled down on the backseat, head on her front paws, watching him. Quiet thing, except for when he was kissing Jess. What was that about anyway?

The road unfurled ahead of him as he drove, twisting and curling through the mountainside. It was a rush, hugging the curves. It sometimes tempted him to drive too fast. Not today though. Not with a dog on the backseat watching him out of big, trusting brown eyes.

He realized his mistake as soon as he pulled up in front of the animal shelter. The lot was empty. The sign on the front door said they closed at five. It was six thirty. He glanced over his shoulder. "Looks like you're spending the night with me."

The dog watched him out of those soulful eyes, her tail thumping against the leather upholstery.

Right then. He was going to need some food for her. Then he'd have to figure out what to do with her while he worked tonight. Maybe she could come along and hang out in the office. At least there would be people in and out. Who knew what trouble she might get into if he left her all alone in his condo?

He debated stopping in the supermart for some proper dog food, but he needed to be back at Off-the-Grid in half an hour and he still had to change so he pulled through the McDonald's drive-through and ordered three Big Macs—two for him, one for her—because he was starving, dammit, and she probably was too.

Indeed, she sat up once the perky drive-through operator handed him his bag and the car filled with the greasy scent of meat and French fries. The dog leaned forward so that her chin rested on the seat behind his shoulder and stayed that way all the way home.

A few minutes later, he pulled up in front of his building. It was a three-story brick building that had once housed the town's newspaper offices. Recently, it had been converted into three spacious condos, which he, Ethan, and Ryan had bought, intending to turn the place into their bachelor pad. Ethan had since moved in with Gabby, renting his space out to Ryan's younger brother, Trent. Emma had moved in downstairs with Ryan after their wedding. So instead of a bachelor pad, the building now housed Mark on the top floor, a teenager below him, and an expectant married couple on the ground floor.

Awfully fucking domesticated.

"Whose dog?" Trent asked, poking his head out as Mark walked up the steps with the dog at his heels.

He shrugged. "Found her in the woods today. Shelter was already closed."

"Cool." Trent bent to pet her, swiping a shock of black hair out of his eyes. The teen couldn't be any more different than his brother. Where Ryan was boisterous and adventurous, Trent was more shy and reserved. Ryan got his kicks rock climbing while Trent DJ'ed at the local club one night a week. He also helped them out at Off-the-Grid.

"You working tonight?" Mark asked him.

Trent nodded. "Mind if I hitch a ride? My car's acting funny."

"Sure thing. And I'll take a look at your car tomorrow." Mark knew his way around under the hood. He'd worked part time in a repair shop back in high school and again last year before Off-the-Grid started paying his bills.

"Thanks, man. I appreciate it." Trent gave the dog another rub and went back inside.

Mark continued up the steps and let himself into his condo. The dog followed at his heel, bubbles of drool forming at the corners of her mouth as she eyed the McDonald's bag in his hands.

He pulled out a Big Mac, unwrapped it, and set it on the linoleum in front of her. She dove in with unbridled enthusiasm, scarfing down the burger without hardly pausing to chew. Mark ripped open another and began to eat in similar fashion. He'd missed lunch today and given most of his jerky to the dog earlier.

After they'd both stuffed their bellies, he filled a bowl with water, set it down for her, and then popped open a Coke for himself. He sat at the kitchen table and closed his eyes to rest for a moment before he headed back to work. Immediately, his mind filled with memories of kissing Jess. The feel of her in his arms. The taste of her in his mouth. The desperate need to lose himself inside her right before he'd pushed her away.

Fuck. He was so screwed.

CHAPTER SIX

Jessica zipped up her black leather jacket just as the doorbell rang. It was eight thirty on Thursday night, and her sister—as usual—was right on time. "It's open," she called.

The door swung open, and Nicole stepped inside. "I'm so stoked for tonight. If it's as much fun as I've heard, we may have to make this a new annual tradition."

Jessica smiled at her sister's enthusiasm. When they were growing up, their parents had gone overboard on every holiday, but somehow Halloween had taken on special significance for the Flynns. Maybe it was their slightly warped sense of humor, but they'd always enjoyed scaring each other, and the annual Halloween party was a big friggin' deal.

So when Off-the-Grid Adventures announced their new haunted zip-line tour this year? Yeah, they pretty much had to come. Even if it meant seeing Mark again so soon after "the kiss they'd never speak of again."

"Why didn't Brennan and Patrick come?" Jessica asked.

"Bren has some live thing on YouTube tonight, and Patrick's working," Nicole said, walking over to the mirror in the hallway to check her lipstick.

Jessica's older brother was a YouTuber, which meant he earned a living—and a whopping good one at that—making videos to post on YouTube. His husband, Patrick, owned the art gallery downtown. And yes, both her older brother and her younger sister had gotten married before Jessica.

And no, she wasn't bitter about it at all. Or not much anyway.

"All right then. Let's go get scared shitless." Jessica smiled as she led the way toward the front door.

"Are you limping?" her sister asked.

"I did something to my knee a few weeks ago. It keeps hurting off and on."

"And let me guess, you haven't been to the doctor," Nicole said.

Jessica hung her head guiltily. But seriously, as long as she could still walk on it, surely it would get better sooner or later.

"Your mom is a nurse, and yet you still stubbornly refuse to go to the doctor for anything!" Nicole elbowed her playfully as they headed out to the car.

"That's not true. I went last week after I had the flu to make sure I was germ-free."

"So that you could go back to work sooner than you should have. I'll drive," Nicole said, clicking the lock on her car. "I have better music."

"You have *country* music, which you know I hate." Jessica climbed into the passenger side of Nicole's Acura.

"Not my fault you have horrible taste in music." Her sister cranked the engine with a grin, and as Keith Urban began to blast from the speakers, she turned the car toward the outskirts of town, where Off-the-Grid was located. As they passed the spa, Nicole asked, "So have you done anything with the new land yet?"

"Not yet. I'm meeting with a few builders this week to get things moving."

"I get to stay at the nicest cabin free of charge, right?" Nicole asked.

"As long as you don't abuse your little-sister privileges," Jessica answered.

"I would never," Nicole answered, with a look that said she planned to do just that.

They pulled up at Off-the-Grid, and Nicole parked in one of the empty spaces beside the house. A swarm of hyper butterflies took flight in Jessica's stomach, partly in anticipation of the haunted zip-line but mostly because of Mark, dammit.

Why, oh why, had she kissed him yesterday?

"This is going to be so awesome," Nicole said as she climbed out of the car.

"Definitely." They walked inside the office, where Trent stood behind the desk, busily texting on his cell phone. And then the brown dog from yesterday walked out from behind the desk, tail wagging, and Jessica felt a big smile cover her face. She crouched down. "Aww, you're still here."

Mark hadn't taken her to the shelter after all.

"No microchip," Trent said. "Mark left her description at the shelter and the vet in case anyone comes looking for her though."

"That's smart," Jessica said, but something told her

this dog didn't have a family out there looking for her. She had that same lost, haunted look in her eyes Mark had had as a teenager. She might be good for him.

"Whose dog?" Nicole asked.

"Mark found her out in the woods yesterday," Jessica told her.

Her sister's eyebrows rose. "And what were you doing in the woods with Mark yesterday?"

"Scouting who gets to use which parts of our new land." *And kissing.* If she was lucky, she wouldn't even run into him here tonight. The property was huge, after all.

"You guys have tickets already?" Trent asked.

"Yeah, nine o'clock," Jessica told him.

"Oh yeah, I see your names." He pulled off two orange wristbands and handed them to Jessica and Nicole. "Have fun, ladies. It's a screamin' good time out there."

"That's what we're counting on," Nicole told him with a smile.

There weren't any spooky sounds on the breeze as they walked across the lawn, following the arrows that guided them toward the first zip-line platform. No cheesy Halloween props in the yard either. The night was cool and clear, the moon bright overhead. In the distance, something flashed deep in the woods, and Jessica jumped in spite of herself.

Then she grinned. Yep, this was going to be fun. She and Nicole climbed the steps to the first platform, and a figure stepped out of the darkness, standing silently before them. The hairs on Jessica's arms rose, and her heart beat faster, but not out of fear. Somehow, even in the pitch dark, her body recognized Mark's.

A thin, green beam of light pierced the night as he

gestured them forward. She hung back, letting Nicole go first. By the flashes of green light, she saw him strapping her sister into the harness for her zip-line ride, and if she hadn't known him so well, she had to admit it would have been a little freaky, this tall, silent man, dressed all in black, fastening their harnesses.

After he had secured Nicole's harness, he turned to Jessica. Even in the darkness, their gazes clashed and held, and her body started to sizzle from the inside out. Then his hands were on her as he slid the harness over her legs and around her waist, and even though he worked completely professionally, she couldn't help remembering the way he'd grabbed her ass yesterday, how he'd pressed her against him until she'd almost gone off like a rocket right there in his arms, fully clothed.

But equally seared into her brain was the way he'd shut down afterward. Shut her out. The heat that swept through her then had a lot more to do with wanting to kick his ass than wanting to kiss him.

He cinched the harness tight around her and then turned back to Nicole, clipping her harness onto the line overhead, "Put your hands here." He indicated a handle above Nicole's head. "And keep them there until you've landed on the next platform. You can kick off whenever you're ready. Try not to scream."

Nicole gave him a funny look before kicking off into the night, screaming as she went. Which left Jessica alone on the platform with Mark. In the dark. Her heart felt like it might pound right out of her chest.

He said nothing, just a shadowy figure in the darkness.

"You kept her," she said finally, unable to help herself.

"The shelter was closed."

"It was open today."

"I brought her in before work. They scanned her for a chip, told me they were already overcrowded, so I offered to keep her until her family shows up to claim her."

"And if they don't?" She spoke so quietly she was almost whispering. Something about being up here in the dark with him felt way too cozy. Somehow, his voice sounded even sexier when she couldn't see the rest of him. And she was furious with herself for still wanting to kiss him.

He didn't answer her question. "You're up," he said instead, gesturing toward the zip-line.

"Right." She stepped forward, watching as he clipped her to the line. Then she kicked off from the platform, soaring into the darkness after her sister.

* * *

Stifling a scream, Jessica whooshed through the night. Something that felt an awful lot like an enormous spider-web smacked her in the face while a pair of eerie red eyes glowed in the darkness nearby. She sped on through the darkened forest. A light strobed, illuminating a ghoulish scene to her left. As she watched, a blood-spattered monster lunged toward her. Shrieking, she recoiled, swinging on the line as it carried her farther into the night. A glowing ghost fluttered by overhead, and then she was approaching the landing platform, lit by a sliver of moonlight. She lifted her feet as the line slowed, bringing her in for her landing.

An arm reached out of the darkness, groping at her, and she yelped, skittering sideways even as she heard Nicole's laughter somewhere nearby. A teenager, dressed all in black as Mark had been, unclipped her from the line and motioned for her to join her sister in the center of the platform.

Behind them, the line whirred again, and then Mark swung onto the platform. On cue, the teenager attached himself to the next line and whizzed off into the darkness.

"That was so great!" Nicole said, her voice hushed. "And we still have four more lines to go."

"Yes." Jessica felt a warm tingle pass over her skin as Mark came to stand beside her, followed by the all-too-familiar desire to kick him in the shins. She was glad for the darkness hiding the tension between them tonight. He seemed as calm and closed off as ever, but she wasn't nearly that unaffected—or as good at hiding her feelings—and she was certain her eyes had to be spitting red sparks in his direction every time she looked at him.

Mark's phone blipped, letting him know his employee had arrived at the next platform so he stepped forward and attached Nicole to the line. She whooped as she soared off into the night. A few seconds later, she screamed.

Jessica laughed.

"How's your knee?" Mark asked.

"Sore." She glared at him in the darkness, annoyed with him for bringing it up and reminding her how he'd swept her off her feet yesterday when she'd twisted it.

"You should have it looked at. You might have torn something."

"If it's still bothering me in a week or so, I will." She paused. "Have you named her yet?"

"Named who?"

It was unsettlingly intimate to be standing up here on this platform in the dark with him. If she didn't strangle him first, she might end up kissing him again. "The dog, of course. She looks like a Penny to me. Maybe Maggie."

Mark made an unintelligible sound.

She decided to take a page from his book and say nothing. Then it was her turn on the zip-line again. As she soared off into the darkness, something huge flapped over her head, and she screamed, just as Nicole had done.

By the time they'd made it to the end of the course, she could officially say that the haunted zip-line was awesome. She got scared out of her wits several times, which was totally her idea of a good Halloween time. The guys had outdone themselves. She wasn't even sure how they'd done some of the stuff that had jumped out at her during the course. There was something extra thrilling about whizzing through the night sky, unable to stop or even slow down, never knowing what lay ahead.

This was her first visit to Off-the-Grid as a customer, and she definitely would have come back for more if not for the tall, brooding man walking beside her as she and Nicole made their way along the trail from the final zip-line platform to the office.

Naturally, they'd installed a few booby traps along the trail too.

By the time they made it back to their car, Jessica and Nicole were clinging to each other, laughing. "That was so much fun!" Nicole said as they got back into her car. "But the thing that surprised me the *most* tonight?"

"What?" Jessica asked, sensing a trap.

"The tension between you and Mark."

Jessica made a face. "So we don't exactly get along anymore."

"That's not what it looked like to me," Nicole said, giving her a sly look. "From where I was standing, it looked more like you wanted to get naked together."

"Well..." Crap. It was no use lying to her sister. "Fine.

We kissed yesterday, which was a really stupid mistake because the chemistry is definitely still there but the relationship potential isn't."

"Whoa!" Nicole was staring at her, wide-eyed. "You and Mark kissed yesterday? And I'm just finding out about it now?"

Jessica lifted one shoulder halfheartedly. "I wasn't eager to rehash it."

"Well, he is," Nicole said, a gleeful glint in her eye. "He was looking at you like he wanted to eat you up. And you looked pretty hot and bothered around him too."

"Not going there."

"But why not?"

"I already told you—there's no future for us so there's no way I'm going to make things even more awkward by sleeping with him, especially now that we co-own this land."

"Why are you so sure there's no future for you guys?"

"Because he's *Mark*. He's a loner. He's so closed off he doesn't know how to be any other way. He's just passing through life, always in search of his next adventure."

"Are you sure?"

Jessica remembered the way his eyes had shuttered yesterday after their kiss. *It's forgotten.* "Yes, I'm sure."

* * *

Mark spent the next week neck-deep in work. Between regular hours at Off-the-Grid, the haunted zip-line, prepping for the Adrenaline Rush, and initial construction on the mountain bike course, he was too busy to do much of anything but work and sleep.

Which suited him just fine. Too busy to think was the way he operated best.

"Your damn dog needs a name."

He looked up to see Ryan in the doorway to his office, the dog at his side. She wagged her tail with delight. "She's got a name. Whenever her owners come to get her, we'll find out what it is."

"No one's coming for this dog," Ryan said. "You've had her over a week, and she looked like she'd been on her own out there for a while before that. So give her a damn name so we can stop calling her 'the dog.'"

Mark shrugged.

"If you don't name her, I'll let Emma do the honors, and you won't like it."

"Oh please, can I name her?" Emma pushed her way past Ryan into Mark's office. She sat cross-legged on the floor, and the dog walked over to lick her face. Emma giggled. "Daisy. Or Poppy. What about Marigold?"

Mark lifted his eyes to Ryan. "She going to name your daughter after a flower too?" Earlier that week, Ryan and Emma had learned they were expecting a baby girl.

Ryan beamed. "Actually, yes. We decided on Lily. Lily Rose."

Aw hell. Emotion punched Mark hard in the stomach as he imagined Ryan and Emma with their daughter. Lily Rose.

Emma was beaming too. "Flowers make beautiful names, Mark. Don't knock it."

"It's a great name," he said, and he meant it. It would suit their baby perfectly. Emma owned her own landscape design company. She'd planted every flower here at Off-the-Grid.

"So back to the dog," Ryan said, "because if I have to call her 'the dog' one more time…"

The dog in question lifted her head, looking from Ryan to Emma to Mark, tail wagging.

"Thought she was a bear when I first saw her lurking in the bushes out there," Mark said.

"Well, she's obviously not a bear," Emma said, still rubbing the dog's head.

"It'd be a funny name for her though," Ryan commented.

"What? Bear?" Emma frowned at him.

Mark glanced down at the dog, with her big fluffy ears and soft brown eyes. Seemed somehow fitting given how they'd met. "Yeah, I like that. Bear."

"You guys can't be serious!" Emma looked outraged. "You realize she's a girl, right?"

"That makes it funnier," Ryan said.

"I could stick with 'the dog,' if you prefer," Mark told Emma.

"Men are infuriating," she said, climbing to her feet. "I have to get to class. See you guys later."

Mark tuned them out while they kissed and said good-bye. He needed to pack up and head out if he was going to have time to grab supper before coming back here for the haunted zip-line. He looked down at the dog. Bear? Maybe. She lay with her head on her front paws, watching the humans in the room. As soon as Mark stood, she bounced to her feet, ready to follow him. Good damn thing too, since he'd never gotten around to buying her a collar or leash. He'd picked up a bag of dog chow at the supermart, but that was the extent of his dog-related purchases so far.

Suppose Ryan was right and no one was looking for her. What then? Did he leave her at the shelter or keep her?

He didn't know the answer to that question yet, and until he did, she didn't need a name. Instead, he led the way out the back door, headed for his SUV. The shelter was already closed for the night so she was still his, at least until tomorrow.

"Hey, do you mind dropping this paperwork off at the spa on your way out?" Ryan asked, poking his head out the door.

"What is it?" Mark asked, doubling back to take the papers.

"A copy of the zoning approval."

"At least they didn't give us any BS this time." Mark took the papers from Ryan.

"True that." With a wave, Ryan went back inside.

Mark unlocked the SUV and opened the back door for the dog. She hopped right in like an old pro. He cranked the engine and drove a half mile down the road to the spa, but Jess's Kia was nowhere to be seen. She must have already left for the day, and he didn't have time to swing by her house before the haunted zip-line opened so he'd catch up with her in the morning.

Instead, he drove into town and parked at the deli because the fridge at his condo—and his stomach—were running on empty. Leaving the dog in the car with the windows down, he walked inside. The place was packed with the dinnertime crowd so he took his place in line, deciding on a grilled chicken panini for himself. And, what the hell, one for the dog too. She loved her sandwiches as much as he did.

He messed around on his phone while he waited, trying to think of an excuse not to go to the Halloween party at the spa next weekend. Ethan and Ryan had insisted they all put in an appearance as a show of good faith since they were joining forces with Jess on the new land.

But parties weren't Mark's scene. At all.

The very thought made his skin crawl. He'd finally made it to the counter so he ordered his sandwiches and grabbed a can of Coke. With the line pressing in behind him, he moved down the counter to wait for his meal. He didn't see why all three of them needed to go to the party. Surely he could just be a no-show, and no one—other than Ryan and Ethan—would even notice. Okay, Jess might notice, but he suspected she'd be glad for his absence.

The teenager behind the counter pushed a white bag in his direction. Muttering his thanks, Mark turned toward the door.

And froze.

The woman clearing tables in the back...for a second he could swear it was...but it couldn't be. She was blond, slim, early forties maybe. As he watched, she turned her head, and the hairs on the back of his neck stood on end, sending a chill prickling across his skin.

His mother.

No. No way. Not here in Haven. He hadn't seen her in over twenty years. Hell, he had no idea what she looked like now or if she was even still alive. No idea why he'd had such a visceral reaction to this woman, who was nothing but a complete stranger.

No idea why he was hustling out of the deli like he had a sniper trained on his head.

He climbed back into his SUV and was halfway home before his brain caught up with his wheels. He'd made a mistake. That's all. His mother was long gone.

Long fucking gone.

He'd been six years old the last time he saw her, and he intended to keep it that way.

I'm sorry, but I can't do this anymore.

That's what she'd written in the note she left behind. Mark could still remember the funny tightness in his stomach as he'd stood in front of the school, watching the other kids leave with their parents and wondering why his mom was so late picking him up that day. Once all the other kids had gone home, he'd sat in the principal's office until a woman named Mrs. Coates from social services came to get him.

She'd been the one who found the note in his backpack.

When she told him she was taking him to a foster family until they found his mom, he'd been so terrified he'd wet his pants. He remembered the hot, prickly embarrassment of walking out to Mrs. Coates's car in wet pants. Of being driven to a house with people he didn't know in wet pants. He remembered waiting, and waiting, and waiting for his mom to come back for him. Being shuffled from house to house as days became weeks and weeks became months. On his seventh birthday, he'd been sure she would finally come. She'd never miss his birthday.

But she hadn't come. Like the foolish child he'd been, he'd waited and waited for a mother who was never coming back. When life got tough, she'd just dropped him off at school with a note in his backpack and skipped town, leaving him behind for somebody else to pick up the pieces.

He'd finally faced reality when he was ten and overheard his foster mother refer to him as an orphan. For all intents and purposes, he was an orphan. So he'd taken control over his situation the only way he knew how: He decided to pretend that both of his parents had died in the car crash that had killed his father and sent both Mark and his mother to the hospital.

Over time, he'd almost started to believe it was true. His hurt and anger toward her faded a little bit more every time he told someone his parents had both died in a car crash. He'd grown up an orphan, and it was too late to change things now.

CHAPTER SEVEN

The next morning, Mark headed for the Pearcy County Animal Shelter before work. It was time to decide once and for all what to do with the dog. She walked obediently inside with him. No collar. No leash.

"Any word?" he asked the young guy, Logan, behind the desk. He'd been in at least five times already, asking if they'd found her family yet.

Logan shook his head. "We've been in contact with every shelter and vet within fifty miles of here, and no one's missing a dog like that."

The dog in question sat beside Mark and stared at Logan, her ears pricked to attention.

"How's that possible?" Mark asked, frustrated.

Logan glanced down at her and shrugged. "It wouldn't be the first time someone drove a dog out into the middle of nowhere to dump them when they didn't want them anymore."

Mark's scalp prickled. "People do that?"

"All too often, I'm afraid. At least this one doesn't look like she got thrown out of a moving vehicle."

Mark looked down at the dog, imagining her sitting by the side of the road waiting for her family to come back and get her. The abandoned six-year-old boy inside him roared with anger. A dog was a responsibility. A life. You didn't just dump them on the side of the road when you got tired of looking after them.

"So are you going to keep her?" Logan asked.

"What?" Mark's head snapped up. "She's not mine."

"She's not anybody's," Logan said. "We're pretty full right now. I hate to say it, but a nice dog like this one sometimes gets overlooked here at the shelter. She's too quiet. People notice the loud ones, the ones who bark and jump and beg for attention. A dog like this one sits in the back of her cage, gets depressed. No one notices her."

Goddammit. "She's staying with me," Mark said before he'd even consciously made the decision.

"Glad to hear it. We're having a vaccination clinic in a couple of weeks. Bring her in, and we'll get her all taken care of." Logan passed him a yellow flyer.

"Thanks." Mark turned and headed for the door with the dog at his heels. He'd never bring her back to this building full of abandoned animals. Her family might have driven her out here and left her, but she wasn't homeless anymore.

She looked up at him with those big brown eyes as if to say thank you.

He had no idea how much she understood about her situation, but in his estimation, animals were pretty perceptive, sometimes more so than their human counterparts.

He loaded her into his SUV and headed for town. Not

until Jess's house came into view did he realize he'd turned onto Riverbend Road, taking the roundabout way back toward Off-the-Grid. He still had that paperwork for her after all, and her black Kia Sportage was in the driveway. He pulled in behind it and parked.

After cracking the windows for the dog, he grabbed the envelope Ryan had given him and headed for her front door. He knocked and then stood back and waited. And waited. He was about to leave when she pulled the door open, wearing black jogging pants and a green hoodie, her hair swept back into a loose ponytail.

"Hi," she said with a small smile, giving him a "what are you doing here?" look.

"Got some paperwork for you," he said, holding up the envelope. "Zoning request came through."

She took it from him. "That's a relief. Should be clear sailing from here then, huh?"

He nodded. They stared at each other for a few beats of silence. He cleared his throat. "Ah, there's one page in there that you need to sign. If you want to sign it now, I can drop it off later today with ours, make everything official."

"Okay." She stepped back, inviting him in. "I was about to have a cup of tea. Would you like some?"

He hated tea, but he wouldn't mind spending a little more time with Jess. "Sure."

Her eyes focused on something behind him. "Oh, your dog's with you? Well, you can't leave her in the car."

"You mind if she comes inside?"

Jess shook her head, holding the door open as he went and fetched the dog from the car. "So have you named her yet?"

He remembered his conversation with Ryan and

Emma yesterday. "Calling her Bear," he said as the dog followed him through Jess's front door.

"Bear?" Her eyebrows lifted. "That's not very feminine."

Who said the damn dog's name had to be feminine? "Thought she was a bear when I first saw her slinking around in the bushes. It was the first thing that came to mind."

"Have you decided to keep her then?" Jess walked toward the kitchen, where a kettle already sat heating on the stove.

He and Bear stood in the open area between the living room and the kitchen. "Yeah."

Jess smiled. "I'm glad."

"No one came looking for her, and the shelter's full." He glanced down at Bear. She sat at his side, her tail swishing against the hardwood floor.

"She knew she was yours since that afternoon you found her in the woods," Jess said.

"How's your knee?" he asked, both to change the subject and because something seemed off with Jess this morning. He couldn't quite put his finger on it, but something about her movements suggested she was in pain.

She shrugged, rubbing at her knee absently. "Still sore, on and off."

"You had it looked at yet?"

"Keep thinking it's better, and then it's not." The kettle started to whistle, and she walked to it. She filled two cups with hot water and handed him one, gesturing to a box of teabags on the counter.

He just stared at it. "You pick."

She dipped a tea bag with a purple tag into his cup, and then chose a yellow one for herself. He decided not to ask why his was purple. Instead, he followed her to the kitchen table. Bear walked beside him and lay down at his feet, resting her head on her front paws.

"Who would have thought you and I would end up business partners?" she asked, a soft smile curving her lips.

"Yeah." It was something, all right. Hell, it was amazing to be able to sit here with her at her kitchen table, almost like friends. That wasn't something he'd ever thought he'd be able to call Jess, but now that it was within his grasp, he wanted to grab hold with both hands.

"The Halloween party at the spa is next weekend. I had to step up my game this year after you guys put on such a great show at the haunted zip-line." Again with the sweet, sexy smile.

"Ethan's idea," he said.

"I figured. Too bad he missed most of it on his honeymoon."

"They got back a few days ago." Mark swirled his teabag in the cup, watching the water turn a golden brown. They talked while they drank their tea—which wasn't as bad as he was expecting. He still didn't care for it, but it wasn't nearly as bad as some of the excuses for drinking water he'd had overseas. At least Jess's tea wasn't likely to give him dysentery.

He stood to take his empty cup to the sink. When he turned around, he bumped right into Jess, who had come into the kitchen behind him. Automatically, his hands went to her shoulders to steady her. She let out a breathless sound that shot straight to his groin.

Their eyes locked, and she leaned closer.

Fuck. His blood heated, and his pulse pounded. He shouldn't do this. It was better if they stayed friends. But his head bent toward hers, drawn by a force too powerful to resist. Just before their lips touched, her eyes rolled back and she fell limp in his arms. Her teacup hit the floor and shattered, and he could have sworn his heart stopped too.

* * *

Jessica fought against the bursts of light blasting behind her eyelids. She'd been battling a migraine all morning and had been feeling much better, but then right before she kissed Mark, the pain had intensified until she felt like the top of her head might blow off.

"Jess," Mark's voice drifted in through the waves of pain.

"I'm okay," she whispered.

But she wasn't. She was starting to think she wasn't okay at all. These headaches, the constant fatigue...and yesterday, the pain in her knee had switched from her left knee to her right. What if she'd inherited the arthritis that had crippled her grandmother? How would she be able to keep up her duties at the spa if her body rebelled against her?

"Not okay," Mark said, echoing her thoughts. "You blacked out for a second. I'm driving you to the hospital."

"What?" She forced her eyes open, looking up into his concerned face. Spots danced around her vision, and her stomach roiled. "I don't need to go to the hospital..."

He swept her into his arms and started toward the front door, apparently not taking no for an answer.

"It's just a migraine," she protested, but okay, she'd never had them like this until a few weeks ago, and she'd definitely never blacked out during one before. "My purse..."

He bent to lift the black bag from the table by the front door. "I'll come back for Bear."

"Mark, you really—"

"We're going to the hospital," he repeated. Supporting her easily with one arm, he opened the passenger door of his SUV and set her inside.

She would have protested this macho display, but she wasn't altogether sure her legs would hold her right now. The pain in her head was so intense that it seemed to radiate through her whole body. She leaned back and closed her eyes as he fastened the seatbelt around her. His fingers brushed her arm, warm and comforting.

Oh, this man . . . why did he have to be so damn good?

By the time they got to the ER, that intense wave of pain had passed, and she insisted on walking inside. Now that she could think clearly again, she felt a little uncomfortable about being at the hospital, especially with Mark. She signed in at the front desk and then settled into an uncomfortable plastic chair near the back of the waiting room with him at her side. "You really don't have to stay. Aren't you supposed to be at work?"

He shook his head. "I'm not on the schedule until noon today."

Still, she was sure he had better places to be than here with her. "I called in sick today. Hate having to do that."

He gave her a sharp look. "Why didn't you say so when I first stopped by?"

She shrugged. "I was feeling better for a little while there." And there'd been something in his face when he'd shown up, something almost . . . vulnerable. She'd wanted to spend some time with him, maybe see if she'd finally encountered a chink in his seemingly impenetrable armor.

Instead she'd swooned in his arms like an idiot and wound up here at the ER.

"Jess..." He shifted in his seat. "Are you sure it's just a migraine?"

"What do you mean?" She drew back, the movement causing her head to throb.

"You just haven't seemed quite well these last few weeks. Maybe you should get checked out, that's all."

"Well, I'm here, aren't I?" she grumbled, closing her eyes.

They sat there for almost an hour together. She was too groggy to come up with small talk and ended up falling asleep with her head on his shoulder instead. As a result, she was already feeling a lot better by the time she was called back.

And what a big waste it all turned out to be. She'd been poked, prodded, and irritated, and all for nothing. The ER doctor gave her a prescription for the pain and told her to follow up with her regular doctor. She was just signing her discharge paperwork when her mother came bursting into the room, wearing scrubs decorated with brightly colored balloons, huffing for breath as if she'd just run all the way from the pediatric wing (which she probably had).

"I just heard you were here! What's going on?" Paula rushed to her side.

With a sigh, Jessica recounted the events of the morning while her mother buzzed around her in concern. Paula read over the paperwork the ER doctor had given her, gasping dramatically when she learned Jessica had lost consciousness.

"For like a second, Mom. I'm fine."

"But you don't usually have migraines like this."

"No," Jessica acknowledged. "I've been having them a lot the last few weeks though."

"Definitely follow up with Dr. Rimmel to be sure that's all it is," her mom said. "Plus, if they keep up like this, there are some really effective medications available that might help."

"I will." Jessica stood, giving her mom a quick hug. "I promise. You'd better get back to work, Mom. I'm ready to get out of here."

"How are you getting home, sweetie?"

"Mark's here. He'll drive me home."

"Mark?" Her mom raised her eyebrows.

Jessica nodded, regretting it as the movement brought a fresh wave of pain radiating through her head. "He stopped by my house this morning with some paperwork for me to sign. He's the one who insisted I come get checked out."

Paula smiled, her expression softening. "Well, tell him thank you for that. You've always been too stubborn where doctors are concerned."

"Stubborn, but not stupid," Jessica said. "I'll follow up with Dr. Rimmel, I promise."

"Okay, keep me posted," her mom said. "And I want to know more about why Mark's name keeps coming up so often lately, but right now, you need to get home and rest. Lunch later this week?"

"Definitely." Jessica said good-bye to her mom, checked out of the ER, and went to find Mark in the waiting room. He was still sitting right where she'd left him, messing around on his phone, and *oh*, he was a welcome sight. She wanted to lose herself in the comfort of his embrace and let him hold her until she felt better, but that was silly.

Instead, she let him lead the way out to his SUV. She could hardly wait to crawl into her bed for a nice, long nap. Mark insisted on stopping at the pharmacy on the way home to fill her prescription, and while she wanted to protest, the promise of pain relief was too tempting in the end.

"Thanks for your help this morning," she told him when they got back to her house.

He nodded. When she opened her front door, his dog came barreling out, tail wagging, looking more excited than Jessica had ever seen her. "Call if you need anything," he said.

"I'll be fine." She stepped closer. "But thanks…really."

It was such a shame she hadn't gotten to kiss him earlier, but maybe she could still fix that. She leaned in. Her blood heated, and her heart started to pound, but *dammit*, the pain in her head intensified until spots danced in front of her eyes. She closed her eyes and drew a shaky breath. If only she could kiss him without her pulse racing… "I'm going to go in and lay down," she said, accepting defeat.

Mark nodded.

"If I don't see you before, you'll be at the party on Saturday, right?" She suspected he'd only be there if Ryan and Ethan dragged him kicking and screaming, but she didn't care, as long as he was there. Her annual Halloween party was one of the highlights of her year, and she could hardly wait.

Mark made a noncommittal sound.

"Come?" She gave him what she hoped was her sweetest smile. "It'll be fun. Promise."

"I'll stop by," he said.

"Don't forget your costume." She stepped inside,

closed the door behind her, and then released a long, shuddering breath. Dammit, her head really hurt. Her knee hurt—the right one now, not the left—and she just felt generally awful. She walked to the kitchen for a glass of water and washed down one of the pills the ER doctor had prescribed for her.

Please let it help.

She walked to her bedroom and curled up in the middle of her bed, blinking back the tears that burned in her eyes because, if she cried, it would only make her head hurt even worse.

Something's not right.

The feeling had been nagging at her for weeks now. Ever since her bout with the flu earlier this month, she just hadn't been herself. She'd been plagued with fatigue, aches, and pains. She'd managed to keep the feeling at bay until this morning, when Mark had voiced his concern. Now that he'd spoken her fear out loud, she couldn't shove it back into its little hiding place in the back of her mind. She drifted into a fitful sleep filled with frantic, unsettling dreams. When she woke up, it was just past three o'clock, and her head did feel better, but that knot of fear was still wedged in the pit of her stomach.

It was time to call her doctor.

CHAPTER EIGHT

Mark stood inside the front door of the shop, reading an e-mail on his phone from the contractor he'd hired to deliver lumber for the raised portion of the mountain bike course.

"If you don't pick your own, we're going to pick one for you," Ethan said.

Mark scowled. Somehow they'd dragged him into the Halloween store to get costumes for the party tonight at the spa. Ryan and Ethan were excited. Mark was not. "I don't need a costume," he said, even as he remembered Jess's parting words to him last Friday.

Don't forget your costume.

"I totally see you in this," Ethan said, deadpan, as he held up a Batman costume in a clear plastic sack.

"Not a chance in hell," Mark answered.

"Got mine." Ryan held up a package containing a white suit like John Travolta wore in *Saturday Night Fever*.

Mark lifted an eyebrow.

"Emma's going to be a disco ball," Ryan said. "You know, with the baby bump…"

"Coordinating costumes?"

Ryan shot a look at Ethan, who'd gone noticeably quiet.

"You too?" Mark asked.

"We're going as the characters from *King of the Desert*," Ethan said, referencing the adventure-style video game that Gabby had helped develop.

And okay, as far as couples' costumes went, that was pretty cool.

"Which just leaves you," Ryan said, pointing at Mark.

"I don't dress up."

"Today you are," Ethan said, turning his attention to the racks of costumes in front of him. "So what's it going to be?"

Mark gestured to the plain black T-shirt on the wall that read, THIS IS MY COSTUME. "That."

"Yo, even for you, that's lame," Ryan said.

"Agreed," Ethan said. "Look, you could be Darth Vader, complete with the helmet. No one would even know who you were, and then you wouldn't have to talk to anyone."

While the thought of being incognito did hold a certain appeal, no way in hell was he dressing up as Darth Vader. He shot Ethan a look that said as much.

"I've got it," Ryan said, holding up a white mask. "You can be the Phantom of the Opera. Just wear black clothes and this mask."

"Bro, that's perfect." Ethan slapped him a high five. "You're wearing it."

And Mark apparently didn't get any say in it because

Ryan was already walking to the cash register with his disco outfit and the Phantom of the Opera mask in hand. Mark didn't even know who the Phantom of the Opera was—some dude from an opera, he was fairly sure—but if he had to wear a mask and his own clothes to put in an appearance at Jess's party, he could live with that.

Since that was settled, he left the store to wait for his friends outside. He'd happily never step foot inside a Halloween store again.

"Here you go, man." Ryan came out of the store and handed him the white mask.

"Thanks." Mark took it and headed in the direction of their condo building. Ryan followed while Ethan waved good-bye, off to get ready for the party at his and Gabby's house.

"You're cool with the mask, right?" Ryan asked, falling into step beside him.

"Yeah. Sure."

"Everything okay with Jessica? I heard you took her to the ER last week."

"Migraine," Mark said.

"Don't usually go to the ER for that."

"She blacked out for a second, had me worried." He was still worried. Jess hadn't seemed like herself this past month, and he didn't like it one fucking bit.

"Shit, that would have me worried too. Is she all right?" Ryan asked.

"Hope so."

"You don't sound too convinced." Ryan shot him a look.

"I'm not."

"Well, let me know if there's anything I can do."

"Thanks. Appreciate that." He nodded, wondering at

the sudden tightness in his chest. He had an inexplicable urge to give Ryan a hug, which was so completely foreign to him that he instead waved good-bye and headed up the steps to his condo as fast as his legs would carry him.

Bear waited inside, her tail swishing enthusiastically. She'd need a walk before the party. A jog maybe. Mark could use one as well. He went into the bedroom to change into jogging shorts and a T-shirt and then sat on the bed to pull on the compression sleeve he wore over his right knee when he exercised. It didn't do a whole lot for the discomfort he felt when he ran, but it kept his knee stable, and since he was a few ligaments short of whole, that was a good thing.

With Bear at his side, he pounded out a solid three miles through the mountains, releasing the stress and tension that had been building up inside him all afternoon. He showered and fixed sandwiches for himself and Bear, and then it was time to get ready for the damn party. He'd rather tango with a grenade than go mingle with the locals at this Halloween party.

But Jess would be there. And he needed to see her, needed to make sure she was okay. Hell, he just needed her. Period.

* * *

Jessica eyed her reflection in the mirror. "This makeup's not right."

"It *is* right. I'm following a tutorial on Pinterest. Have faith." Nicole frowned in concentration as she swept more white makeup across Jessica's face.

"I look like a clown."

Her sister swatted her arm. "Relax, will you? This is not my first time."

No, Jessica and Nicole's Halloween costumes often included elaborate makeup, and they'd both gotten pretty good at painting each other's faces for the occasion. Tonight, Jessica would go as the Corpse Bride from Tim Burton's 2005 cult classic. Nicole was going as one of the title characters on *The Walking Dead*—and Jessica's handiwork was evident all over her sister's garishly "undead" face.

"Almost there." Nicole pursed her lips as she painted Jessica's eyebrows an exaggerated black, with an upward twist like Emily, the Corpse Bride.

When Nicole had finished, Jessica had to admit she was looking rather corpse-like. Careful not to disturb her makeup, she stepped into the simple white wedding gown she had accented with gray lace to imitate Emily's dress, complete with plastic ribs poking through the bodice. Nicole pinned a gray veil in her hair, and then Jessica reached for her gray-painted bouquet of flowers.

"Wow," Jessica said as she spun before the mirror.

"You look stunning...in a creepy, ghoulish way." Nicole beamed from behind her zombie makeup. "Dennis, come and see!"

Her husband poked his head into the bedroom. "Wow, babe. This might be your best work yet."

"Thank you." Nicole's smile grew even wider.

Dennis was also outfitted as a zombie, in dirty, ripped clothing and similarly disgusting makeup. "You ladies ready?"

"Just about." Nicole turned to give herself one more touch-up in front of the mirror. "How's the head, Jess?"

Jessica flinched, reaching for her forehead reflexively

before remembering she'd ruin her makeup if she touched her face. "Much better." The headache came and went, but she'd taken a pill earlier so she was feeling optimistic about tonight.

"Did you make that appointment?" Nicole turned deadly serious, leveling Jessica with a look that would have made their mother proud.

"Yes. I go on Monday." She'd met her mom for lunch a few days ago, and among other things, her mom had written down a list of doctors for Jessica to visit to get to the bottom of her current health problems. So far, she'd seen her general practitioner, who'd ruled out a few basic things like mono and meningitis. Unfortunately, this left her no closer to figuring out what was actually wrong with her.

Was it one of those invisible illnesses that were so difficult to diagnose but could cause unexplainable pain for a lifetime? The very thought made her shudder. On Monday, she would go for an MRI to make sure she didn't have a brain tumor or something similarly horrifying. And as for being put inside that tube for the test? Well, she wasn't letting herself think about it. Not yet.

"Good." Nicole touched her shoulder. "Look, I know this party's a big deal for you, but if you're not feeling well, just tell me, okay? Dana and the other girls from the spa can totally hold down the fort if you need to rest."

"I'm fine, Nic, honest. There's no way I'm missing my own Halloween party." Jessica had spent the whole day at the spa getting things ready, coming home only long enough to get dressed, and now she was itching to get back there and oversee the final details.

"Let me just get my purse," Nicole said as she bent to pick up a bag that looked like a severed arm.

"That's disgusting," Jessica said with a huge grin.

"I know." Nicole pretended to gnaw on the arm as they walked out to the car.

"First time I spent Halloween with your family, I knew Nic and I were meant to be," Dennis said as he slid behind the wheel. "Y'all are seriously disturbed, and I love it."

That Halloween had been the moment when Jessica was sure her sister had found the right man too. Any man who jumped so enthusiastically into the Flynn Halloween festivities was definitely a keeper.

Her mind flitted to Mark and his hesitance—even as a teenager—to join in the fun. Would he show up tonight? She had a feeling Ethan and Ryan might force him to put in an appearance, but would he dress up? She wasn't sure she'd ever seen him in a costume.

They pulled up outside the spa, and Jessica smiled at the sight. From the grounds behind the building, orange and purple lights filtered through the trees and stage smoke billowed.

Perfect.

Dennis parked, and Jessica hustled straight toward the back patio. Her mom was already there—dressed as Professor McGonagall from *Harry Potter*—while her dad wandered through the woods in purple robes and a long white beard as Dumbledore.

"Oh! The Corpse Bride—I love it!" her mom said as she caught sight of Jessica. "And…a zombie? That's rather unimaginative by your standards, Nic."

"Not just any zombie," their dad said as he walked over. "She's obviously Sophia from *The Walking Dead* after she'd been bitten in season two." He gestured at Nicole's tattered blue T-shirt with a rainbow on the front.

"Thank you." Nicole looked vindicated.

Jessica left them to make sure everything else was

in place. They had various scares staged throughout the surrounding woods, for those brave enough to take a "romantic stroll" through the grounds, and the witches' brewing station was bubbling up plenty of green beer with dry ice smoke billowing.

"I'm here!" Carly announced, crossing the patio with a large white bakery box in her arms.

"Perfect timing." Jessica led her to the dessert table.

"I've got ghost truffles, spider cookies, zombie brain cupcake bites, pumpkin cupcakes, candy corn Jell-O shots, and witch's fingers. Sam's bringing the rest of the boxes." As she spoke, Carly was already placing desserts onto platters on the table. A Piece of Cake had provided the desserts every year since Jessica had turned the party into a charity event.

The deli would be providing finger foods. It saved her a lot of time and expense on food prep and helped draw a larger crowd at the same time.

"This looks amazing. What are you dressed as?" Jessica asked.

Carly wore a hot pink halter top that accentuated her cleavage and a black miniskirt with fishnet stockings and leather boots. "I'm a groupie. Sam's a rock star."

"That's not a costume," Jessica protested.

"Oh yeah?" Sam said from behind her. "Would you rather I was incognito?"

Jessica turned, and her breath caught in her throat. In jeans and a black leather jacket with his guitar slung over his shoulder—sunglasses in place despite the evening hour—Sam looked every inch the rock star, and *no*, she didn't want him to change a thing. Having him here dressed like that…well, it was the best publicity her party could ever receive.

Things got busy after that. She checked on all the refreshments and made sure Maritza was in place at the front door to sell raffle tickets. The prizes had been donated from local businesses, and all proceeds went to the children's ward at the hospital.

By seven thirty, the party was hopping. Music was pumping, and people filled the patio, decked out in costumes ranging from a dancing chicken to Emma's disco ball getup. Jessica's headache still pulsed dully behind her eyes, but thankfully it hadn't gotten any worse. With the adrenaline of the party, she could almost forget she didn't feel well.

She poured herself a cup of punch—the alcohol-free version because of her medicine—and took a sip. On the other side of the patio, she spotted a tall man in a mask, dressed all in black. The Phantom of the Opera. But she didn't need to see his face, or even the smooth brown skin of his hands, to know the identity of this Phantom. She felt it in the tingle at the pit of her stomach when they locked eyes. *Mark.*

Unlike the bitter, brooding Phantom of opera fame, this man was kind, warm, and passionate. And just the sight of him made her heart flutter like a hummingbird.

She crossed the patio to him. "You came."

"You recognized me." He sounded faintly surprised, as though hiding his face could disguise his powerful, masculine presence.

"Of course." This close, the warmth from his body offset the chill of the air around her and made her want to burrow even closer against him.

"You look beautiful." He tipped his head to the side. "And...dead."

"I'm the Corpse Bride." She tugged at the bodice of

her ghastly gown, realizing the irony of her costume choice, considering she'd be undergoing an MRI in two days to check for tumors or other awful—and potentially deadly—things in her brain.

Mark reached out and touched her hair. "Well, you're a beautiful corpse."

"Thank you." Her skin tingled beneath his touch.

Mark seemed to feel it too. He didn't move for a long moment, his fingers still tucked into her hair, his eyes blazing into hers from behind the mask. "How are you?"

"Fine," she answered automatically, but she didn't need to see his face to know he wasn't satisfied with that answer. She blew out a breath, which somehow seemed to bring her even closer to him. "I'm having some tests run to see if anything's wrong."

Mark went very still. "That's good."

"It's really not. I hate being poked and prodded."

His hand slipped from her hair to cup her cheek. "Sometimes it's necessary."

"I know." A shiver ran through her. "But the MRI...I'm claustrophobic."

Mark dropped his hand to her arm, drawing her subtly closer against him. "Bring one of those sleep masks to use as a blindfold, and you can listen to music through headphones too. It's loud in there, and the music helps."

Something inside her chest loosened at his words. "That...yeah, that does sound much better. You've had one then?"

He nodded. "Several."

She thought of his scars—the ones she'd felt beneath his shirt—and the way he sometimes limped. She wanted to ask, but now wasn't the time. "Thanks for the tips."

"Yo, the Phantom of the Opera's here!" Ryan

announced loudly, sliding in beside Mark and clapping him on the back.

Jessica stepped back to a more respectable distance.

"And...don't tell me." Ryan eyed her up and down. "That Tim Burton movie, right?"

"The Corpse Bride." She nodded with a smile, suppressing a laugh to realize he was dressed as John Travolta from *Saturday Night Fever* to match Emma's disco ball.

So many couples' costumes tonight...

Jessica wanted that. She wanted to be part of a couple and wear themed Halloween costumes together, and she wished like hell it wasn't the masked man in front of her that she was imagining as the Victor to her Emily, the Phantom to her Christine. Because it would never, ever happen, no matter how much she might wish for it.

Out of the corner of her eye, she saw her brother walking toward her, wearing jeans and a leather bomber jacket, and... "Oh my God, are you Tom Cruise from *Top Gun*?"

Brennan grinned. "I sure am."

"Holy crap, that's fantastic. And *oh!*" She let out a little shriek as she caught sight of Brennan's husband, Patrick, in a flight suit. "Please tell me you're Iceman."

"Of course." Patrick threw his arm around Brennan's shoulder and grinned.

Ryan fist-bumped them both. "Yo, best costumes of the night, right here."

Even Mark was smiling...or at least she was pretty sure he was. It was hard to tell behind the mask, but his eyes were crinkled, and his posture had relaxed.

Brennan held up his cell phone. "Vlogging the party for my viewers too."

"Seriously?" She gave him a mock-annoyed frown. Her brother was constantly videoing stuff for his

YouTube channel, and while she liked to give him a hard time about it, she was also ridiculously proud of him. Bren had recently surpassed one million subscribers, which was a pretty awesome milestone. He mostly made gaming videos, but his vlogs—or video blogs—were gaining in popularity too.

"Why would we bother to dress up and go out if we didn't record it for YouTube?" Patrick raised his eyebrows dramatically, grinning the whole time.

"I'm donating all my earnings from this episode to the children's wing," Bren said.

"And now you have my blessing," Jessica told him with a wink. "Film away."

Brennan handed his cell phone to Patrick, and they walked off toward the smoking cauldron of witches' brew with Patrick recording while Brennan talked to the camera, gesturing to the party around them.

"I've watched some of his videos," Ryan commented. "Your brother's a trip."

"He's something, all right. I'd better go check on things. See you guys around." She gave Mark and Ryan a smile and headed back toward the party.

And she felt the heat of Mark's stare as she walked away.

* * *

"Yo, what's going on between you and Jessica?"

Mark gave Ryan a look, stymied by the stupid mask. "Nothing."

"Please. You two are so hot for each other I could roast a marshmallow in that fire."

Mark choked. "That is the weirdest analogy I've ever heard."

"Never claimed to be a poet, but I know sex when I see it, and you and Jessica are sending up all kinds of smoke signals. For the record, I think it's a great idea. In fact, she's headed into the woods right now. Maybe you'd better go after her and make sure she's okay." Ryan was grinning like a fool.

Mark scowled, his eyes tracking automatically in the direction Ryan had pointed. Jess was indeed headed into the woods by herself, and *fuck it*. He headed after her.

By the time he caught up to her, she was standing in front of a tree near the back of the spa's property, glaring up at a busted light mounted about ten feet up its trunk.

"Need some help?"

She yelped, spinning to face him with a hand clamped to her chest. "Jesus Christ, Mark! You really need to learn how to make some noise when you walk."

He leaned closer, fighting a smile. "But I thought the whole purpose of tonight was to be scary?"

At that, she grinned. "True enough. For tonight, you get a pass. But next time…seriously, don't sneak up on a girl like that, okay?"

This wasn't the first time she'd accused him of sneaking up on her, and honest to God, he didn't do it on purpose. Didn't like feeling like he'd scared her either. "I'll do my best."

She offered him a pinched smile. "And yes, since you offered, I could use some help. This light's not working."

"Let me have a look." He took off his mask and hung it from a nearby tree branch. Then he reached up and grabbed the branch, swinging himself up into the tree to get a closer look at the light in question. "Bulb's blown," he called down to Jess a few seconds later.

"Hmm, I might have another one in the spa. Mind waiting while I check?"

"No." On the contrary, he was much more comfortable up here in a tree in the darkened woods than he'd been in the noise and commotion of the party. He leaned back against the trunk of the tree and watched her walk away.

She looked hauntingly beautiful tonight in that costume, with her face painted white, her eyes exaggerated with heavy makeup, and her lips a kissable pink. It took every ounce of his self-control not to haul her into his arms and kiss her until they'd both forgotten every stupid thing that stood in their way.

She disappeared into the crowd on the patio, and it was like someone had just turned out all the lights. She lit up the whole room, for him anyway. He had eyes only for Jess, and even if he couldn't have her, he didn't mind.

One minute stretched into five before he spotted her heading back into the woods, empty handed. "No luck?" he asked when she'd reached the tree where he sat.

She shook her head. "Looks like this one is out for the night."

"'S okay," he said as he swung out of the tree. "Don't really need it." On the contrary, it made this corner of the woods nice and dark, which suited him just fine as he stepped closer to Jess.

"Kind of goes with the mood of the party, I guess." She stepped closer too.

All he had to do now was reach out and pull her into his arms, and he just couldn't help himself. He wanted her, needed her, and the thought of her going into that MRI machine on Monday morning was driving him ten kinds of crazy. The thought of what they might find...

He slipped his hands around her waist, drawing her up

against him. She felt so warm and vital in his arms. He didn't even know what he was doing until his lips were on hers. With a soft moan, her hands went around his neck, and she was kissing him back.

She tasted sweet, like whatever fruity punch she'd been drinking at the party. She nipped at his lower lip, and his dick surged against his jeans. Then his tongue was in her mouth, stroking hers, and his whole body was burning up for her. He was on fire in a way he hadn't been in years, maybe not since he'd given her up back in high school.

She pressed closer, all the warm, soft parts of her pressed up against all the hard parts of him. *Heaven.* She felt like heaven in his arms. All those long, cold nights in the desert...he'd been so disconnected from the rest of the world. A lot of the guys turned to porn, but for Mark, it had always been Jess.

His fantasy woman. But his fantasies didn't hold a candle to the real thing. Holding Jess in his arms, kissing her, he felt alive in a way he hadn't in a long damn time.

"Mark." Her breath whispered across his neck, driving a bolt of red-hot need straight to his dick.

He tightened his arms around her, wishing like hell he could touch more of her, but in that dress, all her best parts were completely off limits. Didn't stop him from running his palms over her ass, so frustratingly covered in all that fabric and lace, and giving it a firm squeeze.

In response, Jess went up on her tiptoes, pressing her hips against his. They kissed until he'd all but forgotten where they were, until nothing existed but Jess, her hot, eager mouth and her body fitted against his like a second skin.

Finally, she lifted her head and gave him a dazed smile. "That was...wow."

He had a feeling it had a lot to do with the magic they created every time they touched.

She gave him a funny look. "You have a little, um...my makeup is all over your face."

That would make sense because her makeup was a mess. "Shit, Jess...I'm sorry."

But she was laughing. "It's okay. It was totally worth it."

And now he was smiling too. Hell, yeah, it had been worth it. Kissing Jess was like fuel for his body. It filled him up and turned him on, gave him an energy and a vitality he didn't feel any other time.

She reached up and dabbed at his cheeks, presumably cleaning up some of the makeup that had rubbed off on him. "Got most of it."

"Yours is all messed up." He rubbed her cheek, smoothing out the whisker marks in her white makeup. Around her mouth, it was almost completely gone. It added to the ghoulish effect of her outfit but also made it painfully clear what they'd been doing out here in the woods.

"Nicole's makeup kit is in the car. If we can sneak over there without being seen, you can fix it for me."

"Uh." He had no fuckin' clue how to fix her makeup.

"Just wing it. You'll be fine."

He wasn't so sure about her makeup, but if there was one thing he was good at, it was recon work. Keeping to the shadowy back regions of the spa grounds, he ushered Jess into the parking lot through the woods without being seen. She grabbed a black bag out of the backseat of her sister's car and rummaged through it, coming up with a white tube, which she handed to him.

"Something tells me you're going to regret this." He took the tube and squirted a small amount of the stuff onto his fingers. Hesitantly, he rubbed some of the white cream onto her skin. Okay, that didn't look half bad. He smoothed makeup over all the areas he'd messed up while he'd been kissing her, trying not to think about the feel of her warm, soft skin beneath his fingers and how it made him want to kiss her again.

When he'd finished, she pulled out a pocket-sized mirror and inspected her reflection. "Not bad." Then she opened a tube of pink lipstick and applied it to her lips.

When she turned to smile at him, she looked almost the same as she had before he'd kissed the daylights out of her back in the woods. *Well, I'll be damned.*

"Let's go get some food," she said. "I'm starving."

He nodded. Despite the sandwich he'd eaten earlier, he was hungry too. And the thought of spending more time with Jess made even the prospect of going back to the party sound bearable. He followed her across the patio, heading for the tables of food against the back wall.

He'd just zeroed in on a pile of sandwiches when he saw her, the blond woman from the deli. The woman whose presence made the hair on the back of his neck stand on end every time he laid eyes on her because he was more certain than ever that he was looking at the woman who'd given birth to him.

The woman who'd walked away and abandoned him when he was six years old.

But this time, it was his turn to walk away.

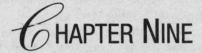 CHAPTER NINE

*W*ho's that?" Mark asked.

Jessica grabbed a ham and cheese slider and glanced over her shoulder at him. He was staring at the woman who'd brought the food. "She's from the deli. I think her name is Sharlene."

Jessica's head was starting to pound, and she hoped food would help. She wanted to find a quiet corner to share with Mark and try to feel him out for where this thing between them was headed. She loaded up a plate and turned around, but Mark was gone, vanished somewhere into the crowd. A particularly vicious pain shot through her temples. He'd done it again. Kissed her and then shut down and bolted.

Goddammit.

"Your makeup looks funny." Nicole stood in front of her, frowning. "You've got all this extra white paint on your left cheek."

Jessica was glad for the heavy coat of makeup that hid the blush she felt creeping over her skin. "I, um, tried to touch it up."

"Why? What happened to it?" Nicole narrowed her eyes. "Were you off kissing Mark again?"

"Why would you think that?" Exasperation laced her tone because how did her sister already know what she'd been up to with Mark?

"Because I saw him follow you into the woods, and you were gone a *long* time, and now your makeup is all messed up." Nicole was grinning now.

"He was helping me fix a lightbulb." Jessica sighed. "And yes, then we kissed, which was so stupid because now he's run off again. Seriously, why am I such an idiot where he's concerned?"

Nicole's grin faded. "What do you mean, he's run off? Where did he go?"

"I don't know. He was just here, and then he was gone. This happened the last time we kissed too, but apparently, I'm a slow learner." Jessica took a big bite of her slider and tried to remember when she could take another pill for her head.

"Well, if I happen to bump into him, we're going to have words," Nicole said, heading off into the crowd.

But Jessica doubted her sister would find him because her suspicion was that he'd left the party altogether. *Coward.* How could such a good guy be so bad at relationships? And why did he have to be the one guy she had such crazy-hot chemistry with? The one guy who could tie her heart up in knots with a single touch?

Over the next few hours, she proved her theory correct because Mark never resurfaced. Not until she was cleaning up sometime after midnight did she find his mask, still hanging in the tree where he'd left it so many hours earlier, like Cinderella's slipper left behind at the ball.

* * *

Sharlene.

With that one word, Mark's whole world had shattered. It was true then. For whatever reason, his mother was here in Haven. Had she come looking for him, after all this time? Or had she forgotten him so completely that her appearance in town was totally unrelated to him?

His first instinct had been to bolt. He'd actually had the duffel bag on his bed and halfway packed before he realized how ludicrous that was. He was one-third owner of Off-the-Grid Adventures. He couldn't just skip town. As solitary as his life still was, there were people in it now. People who depended on him and who he depended on too.

No, it was Sharlene who needed to leave. She might have given birth to him, but she was not his mother. Not anymore.

He slept like shit that night, haunted by dreams he couldn't remember by the time he'd woken up the next morning, but they left him feeling restless. Off.

He couldn't share this town with her. That's all there was to it. With that decided, he drove out to the deli an hour before it opened and sat there, waiting. About thirty minutes later, he got lucky. A gray Honda Accord pulled into the lot, and Sharlene got out. She had on khaki pants and a navy jacket, her blond hair in a messy ponytail.

Mark stepped out of his SUV and intercepted her about halfway across the parking lot, blocking her path. He shoved his hands in the pockets of his jeans and rocked back on his heels. "Sharlene."

She stopped in her tracks and looked up at him. Her brown eyes widened. "Mark?"

"So you do remember."

She swallowed hard. "I do. Of course I do. That's why I'm here." Her voice was low, scratchy, like a smoker's. It stirred nothing inside him. A stranger's voice.

And suddenly, he had no idea what to say. All the air had been sucked out of his lungs. His hands clenched inside the pockets of his jeans. She seemed to have been struck just as silent. She stared at him for several long seconds while a strange feeling of detachment descended over him.

Strangers. That's all they were now.

"I had hoped...I've been trying to find the right time..." She raised her arms as if to give him a hug.

He stepped backward out of her reach. "There is no right time."

She flinched. "You have every right to be angry."

"I'm not angry." Not anymore. In those first weeks after she left, he'd cried himself to sleep every night. His heart had felt like a raw wound in his chest. He hadn't known it was possible for anything to hurt that much. The anger hadn't come until later, and he'd directed it at his various foster families first. He'd yelled, pushed them away because they weren't his real family and he'd so foolishly believed his mom would come back for him.

He'd waited for her for so damn long. By the time he'd finally realized she wasn't coming back, he was an angry kid no one wanted, furious with the world and everyone in it. Eventually, though, even his anger had faded. And then, for a long time, he'd felt nothing at all.

Until Jess.

"You should be angry," Sharlene said, shifting her weight from one foot to the other. "I wish I could say that not a day has gone by when I didn't regret what I did, but that's not true either. For a long time, I thought I'd done the right thing for you, that you were better off without me."

"I was better off without you."

"Yeah." Her face fell. "Maybe you were."

A weighted silence fell between them.

Sharlene fidgeted with the strap of her purse. "Your face." She reached up as if to touch the scar on his cheek.

He gave her a warning look, and she withdrew her hand. "Haven is my home now, but it's not yours. You don't get to just come back after all these years and pretend we're still a family."

"I know it won't be easy, but I'll do whatever it takes."

He shook his head. His heart pumped ice through his veins, leaving him cold. Numb. "There's nothing you can do. It's too late. So do what you do best and leave."

* * *

Jessica kept her eyes closed, despite the sleep mask that she wore at Mark's suggestion. She wore special MRI-approved headphones that filled her ears with a playlist of all her favorite spiritual music. And while she could hardly meditate right now, she could almost forget—almost—that she was lying on a narrow board inside a big metal tube that clanged loudly enough to be heard over the flute music playing through her headphones while a machine took detailed 3-D images of the inside of her brain.

Not freaky at all. Nope.

Not going there. Sunshine. Rainbows. Puppies. Mark kissing every last thought out of her head night before last...Okay, strike that last one because Mark was a jerk and also thinking about kissing him made her horny, which was absolutely inappropriate in her current situation. Still, it kept her mind off her predicament, and really, anything that kept her mind off the fact that she was inside this tube...

Her eyes popped open, and thank God for the mask. All she saw was the faintly pink darkness it provided. Not being able to move was unnerving. Of course, she had an itch on her toe she was dying to scratch. The fingers on her right hand were starting to get tingly from lack of circulation. Her head ached. And now that she was taking stock of her discomfort, she needed to pee too.

She needed to move...couldn't breathe...*oh God, get me out of here!*

She fingered the button they'd given her, the one that would stop the MRI and get her out of this tube right now. But if she pressed it, she'd have to start the MRI all over again another time, and she had to be at least halfway through already. She wasn't a quitter, dammit. Squeezing her eyes shut, she drew in a slow breath and focused on her music, the calming notes of the flute...Mark's lips on hers, his big, strong hands on her body, his iron shaft pressing into her belly. And *phew*, was it getting hot in here?

It was. It definitely was getting hot in here. Sweat beaded on her brow and trickled down into her hair. She wanted to wipe at it. She wanted to *move*, dammit.

And then she was moving. The board she was on was moving, she was almost certain of it. Sure enough, a few seconds later, she felt fresh air blow across her skin and then a hand touched her arm. Someone lifted the mask from her eyes, and she blinked up into the smiling face of the nurse who'd put her into this torture device some thirty minutes earlier.

"Okay?" she asked as she helped Jessica sit up.

"I am now." Even if she was still gulping air like a fish out of water.

"You can get dressed now. Dr. Ledinski will call in the next day or two with the results."

Jessica swallowed over the burst of butterflies in her stomach at what he might find. "Okay." She climbed down off the table and headed for the changing area.

Ten minutes later, she was on her way to the spa. She hadn't put in nearly enough time here this month. Between being sick and everything involved in finalizing the sale of the land, she'd been absent too much and not fully focused when she had been here. Luckily, her staff had been doing an awesome job in her absence, but it was past time for her to pick up her own slack.

"The numbers are in, and we had our biggest year yet," Dana said as Jessica walked through the lobby. "Over five thousand dollars raised for the children's wing."

"That's amazing." Jessica paused, a smile on her face. The fact that her annual Halloween party also helped the pediatric wing of the hospital was just the icing on the cake, and five thousand dollars would buy a lot of new supplies for the kids. She could hardly wait to call her mom and tell her the good news.

"Everything go okay this morning?" Dana asked in a lower voice.

Jessica's smile wilted. "Yeah. I mean, the MRI itself was...not fun, but it's done. I'll know the results in a day or two."

"We're all praying for good news." Dana placed her hand on Jessica's. "Just let us know if there's anything you need."

"Thank you, and really, you've already done way more than I could have asked for."

The phone beside Dana began to ring, and she reached for it with a wave toward Jessica. "Don't mention it."

Jessica continued down the hall to her office to put down her bags and take a look at her schedule for the day. Her cell showed a new text message from Mark.

How did it go?

She fumed so hard her head started to pound. Oh, *now* he wanted to check in? He just vanished in the middle of a conversation two nights ago, right after kissing her, and not a word since, but now he cared? Well, screw him.

She shoved her phone into her desk drawer and went about her day. By lunchtime, though, her manners had gotten the best of her, and she texted back: Fine.

There. She'd answered his question. Let him wonder about the shortness of her response, if he even cared. Quite likely, he wouldn't notice or hadn't expected any more than what she'd sent. After all, it wasn't like he was beating down her door trying to open the lines of communication between them.

Frustrating man.

She powered through the rest of her day, fueled by sheer rage at her stupid body for being so weak these days and at Mark for being...well, for being himself. Whatever was causing the bone-crushing weariness that clung to her like a shroud could just kiss her ass. She didn't have time to lie in bed all day. She had things to do. So. Many. Things.

She worked a full day at the spa and then met with

a contractor for the resort project. She had three more contractors lined up this week, all providing quotes and mock-ups for her spa cabins. She was beyond excited to get this project started, but fear had started to snake its way in through her excitement. What if something serious was wrong with her? What if she had some kind of chronic condition—or worse?

This was not the time for a health crisis, not with the added expense of the mortgage on her new property and the small business loan she'd taken out to pay for the cabins. She dragged herself through her front door and closed it behind her, sucking in deep breaths against the fear suddenly flooding her system. Right at that moment, she hated living alone. She'd have given anything for someone to talk to, and yeah, she had a big, nosy family she could call on. Any one of them would come over at a moment's notice. But the person whose company she was craving was more proof that she was losing her mind. Mark was the absolute last person she needed right now.

Only try convincing her stupid, naïve heart of that.

She pulled out her phone and checked her messages, but of course he hadn't texted back.

CHAPTER TEN

Mark couldn't think of anything but Jess. Had she gotten her test results yet? It was driving him absolutely crazy not knowing, and the waiting had to be even worse for her. Things at Off-the-Grid had slowed down a lot this week now that Halloween was past and the haunted zipline had ended. They were still giving a fair amount of zip-line tours, and Mark had a survival skills class booked later in the week, but right now, this morning, he had nothing to do and too damn much on his mind.

He'd spent the last two days working on the mountain bike course from sunup to sundown, pounding boards into place until Sharlene's face had faded from his mind, until his chest loosened and he no longer felt like he might suffocate from the memories. But now he'd run out of wood, and Jess had consumed his every waking thought. Rather than sit behind his desk, ready to crawl out of his own skin, he headed for his SUV. He'd just drive by her house and see if she was home. He thought he remembered her once telling him that Tuesday was her day off, the quietest day at the spa.

And he needed to see her.

He cranked the engine and turned down Mountain Breeze Road. Ten minutes later, he turned onto Jess's street and could have cheered out loud when he saw her car in the driveway. He was out of his SUV and up her front steps so fast he probably should have been embarrassed, but he was too desperate to see her to care.

He knocked, greeted by silence from within. Was she asleep? She'd been so tired lately, and that, combined with the headaches, had him worried. He didn't want to knock again and risk waking her, but what if she was unconscious inside and needed help?

As he stood there debating his best course of action, the door swung slowly open, and Jess stood there, blinking up at him through damp eyelashes. She'd been crying. *Fuck.*

Emotion detonated inside him, shattering his composure. "Is it...did you..." He sucked in a deep breath. "I just came to see how you were feeling and if you'd gotten your test results yet."

"I just got off the phone with my doctor." She motioned him in, wiping discreetly at her eyes.

And the results had left her in tears. The bottom of his stomach dropped out, leaving him sick and shaky. He reached for her, but she took a step back, folding her arms over her chest.

"The MRI was clean. Everything was normal."

Normal. All the air whooshed from his lungs. "That's...that's good news."

"Yeah." She swiped at another tear. "It is. I was worried."

He had a feeling that was an understatement. He reached out, and this time she let him fold her into his arms. He held her close, savoring the warmth of her body against his, the faint scent of incense in her hair that brought so many memories roaring to life inside him. "I was worried too."

Her breath hitched, and he tightened his arms around her. They stayed like that for several long seconds, and everything that had been restless and raging inside him all morning calmed and went still. He could stay like this with Jess forever.

When she looked up, her eyes were dry, and he recognized the hungry gleam in them a split second before her lips crashed into his. Then they were kissing, and everything that had been calm inside him was on fire.

"I'm so mad at you," she whispered, yanking him closer.

"What?" He lifted his head.

"You kiss me, and then you leave, and here I am, kissing you again." She met his gaze, her eyes sparking.

Fuck. His leaving the party hadn't had anything to do with Jess. "I don't—"

"Just shut up and kiss me."

"Jess—"

She sighed. "It hurt when you pushed me away after we kissed before, okay? Promise me you won't do that this time."

His ribs constricted around his lungs. "I promise. The truth is, I can't stay away from you no matter how hard I try."

"That makes two of us," she said, and kissed him again.

He kissed her back, his tongue stroking hers, mimicking the act of sex as Jess moaned deep in her throat. Her hips moved restlessly against his, and this time, they weren't in the forest or hiding from the crowd during her Halloween party. This time they were alone in Jess's house, and God help him, but he had to touch more of her.

His hands slid beneath her top, finding and releasing the clasp of her bra. Her breasts sprang free, and as he cupped them in his palms, it was his turn to moan. So soft. So full. They filled his hands perfectly, just the way they always had.

"Mark," she whimpered, her head falling back as he scraped the pad of his thumb across her nipple, causing it to harden beneath his touch.

"I'm here." His voice was low and gruff, his blood like liquid fire in his veins. "Tell me what you need."

"More," she whispered, pressing closer against him.

Never let it be said that he didn't give a woman what she wanted. He lifted her top, baring her gorgeous breasts. So pale, with perfect rosebuds in the center. He'd always loved the contrast of his skin against hers, and the sight of her breasts in his hands made him hard as steel.

He bent his head, drawing one of those perfect nipples into his mouth. He nipped, teasing and tasting with his tongue as Jess panted. Her hips rocked rhythmically against his, and maybe because it had been so long since he'd been with a woman, or maybe because this was *Jess*, the urgency pounding inside him was almost overwhelming.

"Touch me," she whispered.

He didn't need to hear that invitation twice. The skirt she wore was knee-length, a soft, stretchy cotton. He reached beneath it, sliding his fingers up her thigh until he reached her panties. He stroked her, drawing another gasp from Jess, and then pushed them to the side.

He swallowed her moan with a deep, drunken kiss as he began to stroke her. He pushed two fingers inside her, plunging in and out as his thumb rubbed against her clit. God, she was beautiful. So beautiful. He kissed her thoroughly, but it was never enough. It could never be enough.

Her movements became frantic as she grew closer to her release, and he increased his tempo, matching her urgency with his own until she moaned, her internal muscles clenching around his fingers in a series of breathtaking spasms. His cock throbbed. Watching Jess come was like nothing else. It was the most beautiful—and arousing—thing in the world.

"Wow," she whispered, her head falling against his shoulder, her body gone limp in his arms.

He looked around for the couch, but as he started to lead her that way, she shook her head, gesturing instead to her bedroom.

"You sure?" he asked.

"Yes." Cheeks still flushed with pleasure, she led him down the hall to her bedroom.

Her bed was covered in a purple quilt, and the aroma of incense was stronger here. That scent alone was enough to turn him on, never mind the woman in his arms, the only woman he'd ever needed this way.

She tugged his shirt over his head and slid her fingers down his chest. "So beautiful," she murmured, her fingernails scraping gently across his skin. Her gaze lingered on the scars on his lower abdomen, and his stomach clenched.

He wasn't ashamed of his battle scars, just intensely aware that Jess was the first woman to see them. He'd thought them to be dead tissue, devoid of feeling, but as she traced her fingers along his surgical scar, he felt the sensation to the tips of his toes.

When she looked up, her eyes swam with questions. But she didn't ask them. Instead she kissed him. She kissed him until his heart was about to pound its way out of his chest, and then she inched her way over his jaw and down his neck. Next thing he knew, her tongue slid across his nipple, sending a burst of fire straight to his groin.

It had been so long since he'd felt a woman's tongue on any part of his body that he'd almost forgotten how much pleasure it could bring. He'd forgotten a lot of things, like how exquisite it was to be with Jess. Everything with her was intense. She made him feel things he hadn't thought he'd ever feel again, things he'd never felt with anyone else.

He lifted her shirt over her head, and her bra—already unclasped—tumbled to the floor with it. She leaned forward, allowing her breasts to brush against his chest, skin to skin.

"Mark," she murmured against his neck, "do you think it will be as good as we remember it?"

How could it not be? "Yeah."

"So do I," she whispered, guiding his hands to the waistband of her skirt.

He hooked his thumbs inside, pushing down her skirt and her panties in one swift movement and allowing his hungry gaze to take her in. "Even more beautiful than I remembered."

"That was my line." She smiled against his lips. Then the button on his jeans sprang free, and she lowered his zipper.

He stepped out of his jeans and pushed down his boxer briefs. And then, they were naked, her body pressed against his. *Finally*. He slid his hands down her back, anchoring her even closer, until not a millimeter of air separated their bodies.

Then he dipped his head and kissed her. Next thing he knew, they were rolling onto the bed together. He was flat on his back with Jess straddling him, his cock pressed into the heat between her legs, and he was so hard that he couldn't think of anything but getting inside her and losing himself there.

"Do you have a condom?" she asked, rocking her hips so that she slid up and down his length.

And *fuck*, how had he allowed himself to go this far without realizing he didn't have protection? He lifted her, settling her next to him in the bed. "No."

Jess looked crestfallen. Then she slid closer, draping her leg over his. "I don't usually, but I'm on the pill..."

"Jess, it's okay. We should wait."

"I'm clean." Her voice had grown husky again as she wrapped her fingers around his dick, stroking him.

"I'm—" He cleared his throat, having lost the ability to speak as she stroked him. "I'm clean, too. They tested us regularly in the Army."

Her brow furrowed, and her hand stilled. He held his breath to keep in the groan that threatened to escape his lips.

"But, Mark...you've been out of the Army for, what, a year and a half?"

"That's right."

"And you haven't..."

"I haven't been with anyone, not since before my last deployment." Two years. Maybe longer. Too fucking long.

"That's a long time." Her fingers tightened around his dick.

Tell me about it. The problem was, he'd gotten so used to taking care of his own needs—and fantasizing about Jess while he was at it—that he'd let himself go too long without a woman's touch. And now, here, with Jess of all women, his control was stretched closer to its limit than he would have ever believed possible.

Her scent, the soft brush of her skin on his, so many sensations combined to light him up like a firecracker about to blow. "It's okay. It's enough to lie here with you."

"Liar." She pressed her palm against his pulsing shaft.

But he wasn't lying. Every moment with Jess was more than he'd thought he would have, and even if they had to stop now, this would still have been worth it.

"Wait." Her eyes lit, and she slid out of bed.

His body mourned the loss of hers with an ache that bordered on pain.

She went into the bathroom and came back a moment later, carrying a little cardboard box. "They're probably expired, but I'm on the pill, and we're both clean so we're basically safe anyway." She slid back into bed beside him. "So, what do you say?"

"I'd say we've got our bases covered." He didn't realize he was smiling until he saw her smiling back at him, and damn, it was a beautiful sight.

"Hurry up then." She ripped open the box and tossed a condom at him.

He ripped open the packet and sheathed himself. He reached down to stroke her, finding her already wet, *so wet*, for him. That same need burned inside him, settling into a throbbing ache in his dick. He lowered his hips, positioning himself against her, and Jess moaned, digging her heels into his ass, urging him on.

He pushed inside her, lost in the feeling of her hot body wrapped so tightly around him. *Fuck.* How had he forgotten how good this was? She gripped him, rocking her hips up to take him even deeper.

"You good?" he gritted out.

"No," she panted.

He froze and then shifted his weight to pull out.

"I need you moving inside me, Mark. Stop holding back."

Stop holding back. He didn't know how. He withdrew until only the swollen head of his cock remained inside her and then plunged back in, burying himself balls deep inside her. Ah, fuck. Pleasure pounded through him. Hot. Fast. *Jess*...

He pistoned his hips, finally allowing himself to give in to the need that had been burning him up pretty much since the moment he'd walked in her front door. But still he held himself in check, drawing out her pleasure, making the moment last as long as he could physically manage.

He reached between them, stroking her where their bodies joined, and she surged beneath him with a wild cry that caused his balls to draw up tight against his body.

"Yes!" she panted, her hands still gripping his ass, plunging him ever deeper inside her. "More."

And that's exactly what he gave her. He thrust inside her again and again as his own need built to an inferno. He held on with what remained of his control, savoring every moment until she tensed beneath him. Her body clamped down on him as she found her release, and it sent him right over the edge. As Jess cried out with pleasure, he came so hard he was lost to everything but the waves of release pounding through him.

When he was spent, he lowered himself to the bed beside her, his muscles limp and trembling, but none so much as his heart. Never again would the fantasy of Jess be enough.

* * *

Jessica lay there in his arms as the last aftershocks of pleasure echoed inside her body. *Wow.* Sex with Mark had been everything. After all these years, she had been sure she'd just built up the memory of him in her mind, but no, if anything, this was better than she remembered.

And if he tried to close himself off and run away like he'd done every time they kissed lately, well, she might just have to hunt him down and...what? Kicking him in the shins felt insufficient. But she was finished letting him hold her at arm's length.

Right now, he was flat on his back, one arm flung over his eyes. His chest heaved as he caught his breath. She allowed her gaze to roam lower. His body was a thing of wonder, all that smooth brown skin and sharply defined muscles. Her eyes landed on the scars on his abdomen. She'd felt them that day in the forest, but seeing them still left her somewhat shaken.

Something major had happened to him; that much was for sure.

She bent her head and kissed the biggest scar, allowing her lips to linger against its puckered surface. He said nothing. She traced each scar with her fingers, kissing her way over every inch of his damaged skin. No, *damaged* wasn't the right word because these scars seemed to make him stronger. He'd survived.

She pressed her lips against the small, round scar

above his hip. "Mark"—she lifted her head to meet his eyes—"will you tell me?"

He looked down at her, his dark eyes blazing. "War injury."

She fought not to roll her eyes. "I worked that much out for myself, thanks."

"I was in the Special Forces. A lot of what we did was classified."

"Then give me the unclassified version." She splayed her hand over his scarred abdomen, noticing that his cock had already begun to harden again from her touch.

"Suicide bomber." He stared up at the ceiling, his expression unreadable.

She was quiet, her hand still resting on his scars as she waited for him to continue.

"We were outside a market, never even saw him until it was too late."

Her breath caught. "Your team?"

"Only minor injuries, apart from me. We were lucky."

She wrapped her arms around him and held him tight. *Lucky.* Maybe, but she had a feeling skill had played a bigger role in his survival. She had nothing but the utmost respect for Mark and all the other men and women who risked their lives serving their country. Her father and uncle had both served in the military.

"There was a shoe," Mark said, his body tensing beneath her, "on the ground beside me. A little girl's shoe. I'll never forget it."

Jessica's stomach lurched. "Just a shoe?"

He nodded, his expression hard. "War is an ugly thing."

It sure as hell was. "And your injuries were too severe to return to duty?"

"I lost a kidney and two ligaments in my right knee, ended my time in the Special Forces."

She looked down at the knee in question, also marred with a long, twisted scar. "I'm sorry."

"So am I, but there's nothing for it now. Off-the-Grid came along at the right time for me."

"I'm glad." She slid up to kiss him.

His arms came around her, drawing her close, and he kissed her back. *This.* This was what she'd wanted from him. Not just sex, but intimacy.

She lowered her head to rest against his chest, listening to the steady thump of his heart. "You want to know something stupid? I almost wanted them to find something on the MRI this morning."

He sucked in a breath. "Why?"

"Because something's not right," she whispered. "I know it, and now I'm no closer to figuring out what it is."

"You'll figure it out, Jess, but I'm so glad they didn't find anything in your brain. Whatever it is, we'll deal with it, okay?" His voice had gone low, gruff.

And it spread a warm, fuzzy sensation inside her. She really liked the sound of "we," even if he didn't mean it in the sense she might have wanted him to. "Okay."

Then they were kissing again. Mark was deliciously hard beneath her, and an answering ache grew between her thighs. She wasn't sure she could ever get enough of this man. They kissed and caressed for a long time, and when he finally sheathed himself in a condom and pushed inside her, she felt him fill her all the way up to her heart.

She was no fool. She knew they still had a long way to go before this thing between them had a chance of becoming something real, but after today, the Mark-sized crack in her heart had grown a little bit bigger. But as he took her over the edge with another soul-shattering orgasm, she really didn't care.

For today, this was enough. So much more than enough.

Afterward, they lay together, arms and legs entwined, and she was feeling all kinds of mushy, romantic things for the man beside her. All. The. Feels.

Then he rolled toward her, his expression turned serious. "I need to go."

CHAPTER ELEVEN

Jessica steeled herself against Mark's words. He'd promised not to shut her out this time, and yet, here he was, running out on her anyway. It was barely lunchtime. She'd hoped they could at least enjoy a meal together before he had to leave.

He gave her an apologetic smile. "I'm supposed to be at work right now."

And...she felt like an idiot for jumping to conclusions. "Really?"

He slid out of bed and started pulling on his clothes. "Didn't have much on the schedule this morning, and I needed to see how you were doing, but Ethan and Ryan may be wondering where I am by now."

She wrapped the sheet around herself and hugged her knees. "What will you tell them?"

He buttoned his jeans and then straightened. "I don't...why would I tell them anything?"

Right. Because he was a man, a man who preferred not to communicate at all whenever possible. But maybe he was right this time. Their relationship felt too delicate to share just yet, especially given their history together. "Maybe it's best if we keep this between us for now."

He nodded, gave her a quick kiss, and headed for the door, still pulling his shirt over his head. After he'd gone, she lay back in bed, waiting for it all to sink in. She and Mark had just had sex. Really, really great sex. And he'd even opened up a little bit afterward.

Wow.

He was still holding back, and that might not ever change. His concern for her was real. She had no doubt of that. And the chemistry between them was scorchingly real. Beyond that, she didn't know, but she couldn't help feeling excited at the possibility of a second chance.

Her head ached. What else was new? But today her fatigue was compounded by the very real fact that she hadn't slept well last night, fretting about receiving her MRI results. And now that she had them, she was no closer to figuring out what was wrong with her, but she couldn't think about it anymore right now without getting frustrated. She'd missed her last training session with the girls because of a migraine so she really needed to sneak in a quick jog this afternoon or they were going to leave her in the dust at the Adrenaline Rush next weekend.

She grabbed her phone to check her messages, but a glance at the calendar on her screen stopped her cold. She had appointments scheduled this afternoon with two more contractors, and she'd nearly forgotten all about it. Groaning, she climbed out of bed, took a shower, and headed to the spa.

The first contractor was someone she knew—he'd done

some work for her at the spa a few years back. He was reliable, and he did good work. The second contractor was the daughter of one of her father's friends, and Jessica was so smitten with the idea of a woman building her spa cabins that she'd nearly hired her on the spot. But in the end, she had to make a responsible decision, and Melissa Gormier's quote might not be competitive. Still, as she climbed back into her car, Jessica found herself looking for an excuse to hire Melissa.

It was just past four, and *oops*, she'd forgotten to grab lunch in her rush to get to the spa after Mark left. That might explain the buzzing in her ears.

Food. Stat.

Her cell phone chimed, and she found a flurry of text messages from Carly, Gabby, Mandy, and Emma. Apparently, an impromptu meet-up was happening at the bakery to look at photos from Gabby's wedding. And while a sandwich would be better, a cup of coffee and a slice of fresh apple pie might just hit the spot too.

Jessica turned her car toward downtown and parked by the town square near the bakery. The memorial gardens Emma had designed this past summer bloomed to her left with red, orange, and purple mums, a beautiful splash of fall color in the town square.

She pulled open the door to the bakery, and the warm, sweet scent inside put an instant smile on her face. She saw Emma and Mandy already seated at a table near the back, looking at something on Mandy's phone. Emma spotted Jessica and waved.

"Be right over," she called. First, she needed sustenance. Her stomach gurgled in agreement.

"What can I get for you?" Carly asked with a smile from behind the counter.

"Coffee, definitely. And I was thinking pie, but those apple turnovers look amazing."

"They are," Carly confirmed with a nod. "I've got apple *everything* this month while they're fresh. Baked those this morning."

"Perfect. Coffee and an apple turnover."

"Coming right up."

Jessica checked her phone again while Carly dished up her coffee and turnover to see if Mark had called or texted. He hadn't, and it would be ridiculous for her to read anything into it. He'd been at work, probably out on the zip-lines all afternoon. But hopefully he'd text her later... Grumbling at herself for being so needy, she paid, gathered her food, and made her way over to the table where Emma and Mandy were sitting.

"Hey," Emma said, scooting over to make room for her. "How are things?"

"Okay." Jessica took a big sip of her coffee, feeling it burn all the way down to her stomach. "And you? How's the baby?" She glanced down at the baby bump rounding out the front of her friend's blouse.

"I think she's having a dance party right now," Emma said with a giggle, rubbing her stomach. "It's like I've been eating sugar or something." An empty plate in front of her at the table confirmed she'd been doing just that. "Want to feel?"

"Um, sure." Jessica held her hand out, and Emma placed it on her stomach. Almost immediately, Jessica felt a little tap from inside, like a tiny hand giving her a fist bump. "Whoa. That's so cool."

"It is, right? Growing a human is the coolest thing ever." Emma was beaming.

Jessica still felt a little bit light-headed so she took a

big bite of her apple turnover, hoping the sugar would do its thing for her too.

"You okay?" Emma asked.

"Yeah, you do look a little pale." Mandy frowned at her.

"Low blood sugar," Jessica said once she'd swallowed. "Missed lunch, but I'm making up for it now."

"Good plan." Mandy took a sip of her own coffee. "Hey, we've been so focused on training for the Adrenaline Rush that we're way overdue for a girls' night, don't you think?"

"We are," Emma agreed. "I've got classes tonight and Thursday. Are you guys free tomorrow?"

"Works for me," Mandy said.

"I should be able to make it." Jessica glanced at her calendar between bites of apple turnover. She should be able to leave the spa by seven, and she could really use a night out.

"Count me in," Carly said, walking up behind them. "We're definitely behind on our gossip. In fact, Jessica, I heard a rumor you kissed Mark at the Halloween party."

Jessica choked on her coffee. It seared its way into her lungs, and if she wasn't mistaken, some went up her nose too. She coughed and spluttered. "What?"

Emma and Mandy stared at her, eyes wide.

Carly was grinning like a fool. "Way to go, girlfriend. He is seriously hot, especially with that whole silent, mysterious vibe he's got going. He's always been my favorite of the Off-the-Grid trio. No offense, Emma."

"None taken." Emma was grinning now too. "You and Mark? When did this happen?"

"I never said . . ." Jessica coughed again. Her eyes were watering, and she definitely had coffee up her nose.

Mandy raised her eyebrows dramatically. "I don't think you have to at this point."

"Aw, man, it looks like I just missed something good!" Gabby hurried up to their table, iPad in hand. "That's what I get for being late."

"Jessica was just about to tell us all about kissing Mark at the Halloween party," Emma said.

"What?" Gabby dropped the iPad. It clattered to the table, sloshing coffee onto Jessica's fingers.

Goddamn coffee. She cleared her throat. "Um."

They were all staring at her with huge smiles on their faces.

"Fine." She wiped her fingers on a napkin. "I kissed Mark at the Halloween party. And...a couple of other times." No need to mention the fact she'd slept with him that morning, not until she and Mark had had more of a chance to talk.

"Yes!" Emma fist-pumped the air.

Gabby looked thoughtful as she picked up her iPad. "When I first met you, I thought you guys hated each other, but it was attraction all along, wasn't it?"

"I did hate him, or I tried really hard to anyway." Jessica swallowed the last bite of her turnover. "He was an idiot in high school. He broke my heart, and he hasn't changed a bit so I don't know why I'm even wasting my time kissing him." *Or sleeping with him.*

"Well, I didn't know him in high school," Gabby said. "But he strikes me as a really honorable guy. Are you sure he hasn't changed?"

Jessica stared into her mostly empty coffee cup. "He *is* honorable. He always has been. He wouldn't hurt me on purpose...but he's just so closed off. I was naïve enough in high school to think we'd be fine anyway, and look where that got me."

Emma frowned. "It's true. He's always been like that."

"Yes, he has. We were inseparable back then. We were soulmates, or at least I thought we were. But while I was planning our future together, he was enlisting in the Army. He didn't even tell me until the day before he shipped out."

"He didn't tell you he'd enlisted?" Carly asked, eyes wide.

Jessica shook her head. "He's just . . . he's all in his own head. He never opens up, not to me, not to anyone."

Emma sighed. "The hopeless romantic in me wants to tell you to keep trying until you crack through that tough shell of his."

"I want to. I do." Jessica polished off her coffee, relieved that the buzzing in her ears had stopped. "I know it was awful for him losing his parents so young and growing up in foster care. He's used to being on his own. I'm not sure he even knows how to be in a real relationship. What if it's too late for him to change?"

"I think you need to be careful," Emma said quietly.

Jessica's back stiffened. "Why?"

"Because it's obvious that you care about him. And you're right. He might be too much of a loner to ever settle down. I don't want to see you get hurt."

* * *

It was past eight before Mark finished up at Off-the-Grid that night. He didn't like the way he'd left Jess that morning. He'd gone over out of concern, not expecting to wind up in her bed, and then he'd had to run off and leave her to get to work. He was far from an expert where women were concerned, but even he knew that wasn't ideal.

And besides that, he wanted to see her again.

He loaded Bear into the car with him and then made a quick stop at the drugstore for condoms...just in case. He wouldn't be caught empty-handed twice. Then he headed for Jess's house. When he saw her car in the driveway, his pulse started to pound. She'd always had this effect on him, but now it was even stronger.

He parked behind her car and walked to the front door. She pulled it open before he'd had a chance to knock, wearing a loose T-shirt and leggings.

"I wasn't sure I'd see you again today," she said.

He hadn't been sure either, until a few minutes ago. "Just left work. Bear's with me."

"Bring her in. Did you eat yet?" She motioned for him to come inside.

He shook his head as he unloaded Bear from the backseat and followed her inside.

"We could order a pizza," Jess suggested. "I don't really feel like going out."

"You okay?" He pulled her into his arms.

She nodded, her body so soft and warm against his. "Just tired."

"I should let you rest."

"I'm not that tired." She smiled against his chest. "I was hoping you'd come."

Good. That was the only thought that broke through his lust-filled brain. When Jess was in his arms, he couldn't think of anything else. Gently, he tipped her face to his, and the moment their lips met, he felt his whole world come into focus. Kissing Jess felt like coming home.

She slid her hands into his back pockets. "Because if you hadn't come over, I couldn't do this." And she bent her head to kiss his neck, applying a gentle suction with her mouth that turned his blood to steam.

"Woof!"

"No one asked your opinion, Bear." But he could hear the laughter in Jess's voice.

"I could put her back in the car."

Jess peeked up at him, a half smile on her face. "Sometimes I can't tell when you're joking."

He was joking. Mostly. But seriously, the damn mutt needed to stop interrupting every time he tried to kiss Jess.

She slipped from his arms and knelt before the dog. "Did you need a few kisses of your own?" She took Bear's head in her hands and placed a kiss right between her eyes.

The dog's tail went nuts, swishing back and forth against the hardwood floors. Such a ridiculous-looking thing with those enormous, fluffy ears. He never would have picked her if he'd gone to the shelter looking for a dog. Couldn't say he minded having her around though. She was good company, cock-blocking aside.

"Okay, so now that we've gotten that out of the way, is it okay if I kiss Mark again?" She was still talking to the dog.

And he was still entertaining ideas of putting Bear in the car if she interfered again.

Jess stood and pressed a quick kiss to his lips before picking up her phone. "So what do you like on your pizza?"

"Anything."

"Okay then." She tapped away on her phone for a few minutes and then set it down. "Done." She stepped back into his arms. "Now where were we?"

"Here." He sank his hands into her back pockets, drawing her up against him as he bent his head to nibble her neck, reversing their earlier position.

"That's right," she whispered. A shiver rippled through her as he traced his tongue over the pulse point in her neck.

He was here. Bear was here. She'd ordered a pizza. And unless she kicked him out later, he was going to do things right this time, make love to her and stick around, spend the whole night if she'd have him. Because tonight, there was no place else he'd rather be.

* * *

Mark woke sometime before dawn, disoriented for a moment in the semi-darkness. A purple glow illuminated the room, and purplish shadows swirled on the wall. The familiar scent of incense reminded him where he was. Jess lay sprawled on her stomach on the other side of the bed.

They'd spent only one full night together before tonight. She'd told her parents she was going to a sleepover, and he'd snuck out of his foster home. They'd driven out of town and camped on a blanket under the stars. The memory of that night had gotten him through a lot of tough times in the years since.

He rose up on one elbow to spot the source of the bizarre purple shadows on the wall. Her lava lamp. Of course. He felt a smile tug at his lips. Not that he'd gotten to spend much time in her bedroom back in high school—her parents had forbidden them from shutting the door, which had been a smart move on their part, in retrospect—but she'd had one back then too. Blue, if he remembered correctly. It was oddly hypnotizing to lie there, watching the blobs of wax in the lamp float to the top and then sink slowly back toward the light.

Jess's bedroom was a peaceful place with the incense and the lava lamp. Or maybe it was just that both of those things reminded him of her, and she'd always been his source of peace.

He rolled over, intending to slip out of bed and go to the bathroom, when he encountered another warm body in the bed on his other side.

Bear.

The damn dog had crawled in bed with them after they'd fallen asleep. He nudged her with his foot, and she lifted her head, fixing him with a wide-eyed, innocent stare, daring him to give her the boot. But her puppy eyes were no match for him. He gave her another nudge, and this time she hopped down, slinking off to the blanket Jess had put down for her in the corner.

He got up, used the bathroom, and then walked to the kitchen for a glass of water. This happened to him a lot in the middle of the night. He'd get these random bouts of wakefulness. No doubt they were the result of his years in the military, too many shifts worked at odd hours. Too many sleepless nights.

He climbed silently back into bed, annoyed to find Bear curled up in a furry ball by Jess's feet. He shooed her off again.

"Let her stay," Jess mumbled, rolling toward him.

"Didn't mean to wake you."

"I'm a light sleeper." She wrapped her arms around him and gave him a kiss. "Couldn't sleep?"

"Happens sometimes."

"I know a cure."

"Oh yeah. What's that?"

She didn't answer. Instead, she wrapped her hand around his dick, which hardened in record time beneath her touch. A warm ache pulsed in his groin, and he pulled her closer, kissing her slow and deep.

They kissed as the lava lamp threw swirling shadows onto the ceiling above them, as the friction between their bodies built to scorching. By the time he rolled on a condom and sank inside her, he was so far gone he couldn't think of anything else. There was nothing but the rhythm of their bodies, the tidal wave of need rising inside him, and Jess.

Beautiful, wonderful Jess.

She cried out beneath him as she found release. He thrust again, his whole body shaking as he exploded inside her. He'd never felt more alive than he did at that moment. And then, as she'd predicted, he closed his eyes and slept.

Deep. Hard. Dreamless.

When he woke the next time, sunlight streamed through the windows. Jess was nowhere to be seen. Instead, Bear lay sprawled across the bed beside him, her head on Jess's pillow. *Jesus.* What time was it? How had he not heard Jess get out of bed?

The answer to the first question, as he squinted at the clock beside the bed, was five past eight. And as for the second, he had no explanation other than that Jess and her wonderfully peaceful bedroom had worked some kind of voodoo on him because he hadn't slept past eight in . . . well, he couldn't remember how many years.

The sound of the shower filtered through the bathroom door so he slid out of bed and went to her. He found her standing beneath the steamy spray, seemingly lost in thought.

"Oh, hey. Good morning." She gave him a shy smile as he stepped into the shower behind her. "I didn't want to wake you, but I had to start getting ready for work."

He pulled her into his arms and kissed her. "Your sleeping charm worked a little too well."

"It was nice, you know." She looked him straight in the eye. "Spending the night together, in a bed, after all these years."

"Yeah." Although *nice* wasn't quite the word he'd use. He felt anchored to Jess in a way he hadn't before, not even in their teens. Things between them then had been passionate but volatile. They'd been so young, and he'd been so lost, just drifting through life trying to keep his head above water.

He sure as hell hadn't been an adult, not even close. But he was an adult now, and he fully appreciated the beautiful, amazing woman in his arms. And he was going to cherish the hell out of every single moment he got to spend with her.

He bent his head and kissed her as the shower's hot spray cascaded over their bodies. But it was nothing compared to the fire raging inside him. Each time he held Jess in his arms, his need for her grew even more intense, more powerful.

"Sometimes I imagined what it would be like," she murmured as she kissed her way down his neck. "You and me together like this."

"You thought about us?" He cupped her breasts, rewarded by a moan of pleasure from Jess. In all the years he'd spent fantasizing about her, he'd never imagined she might have done the same. She'd been so angry, so hurt, when he left that he'd assumed she'd never thought of him again.

"Of course." She took his nipple between her teeth and tugged.

His dick pulsed with increasing intensity. He let that ache fuel him as he touched her, kissing and caressing every inch of her beautiful body. Her breath caught as he slid a hand between her legs, stroking her while he kissed her neck.

He needed to memorize everything, the soft sounds of pleasure she made as he brought her closer to the edge, the sweet scent of her skin, the way the shower pounded on his shoulders, heightening his senses. He held her closer, taking pleasure from the way her hips rocked against his. She was so responsive to his touch, so passionate.

She threw her head back, and it was the most erotic thing he'd ever seen. Her eyes closed, and she whimpered, her hips thrusting erratically against him as she lost control. It was beautiful. So fucking beautiful.

"Oh God, Mark..." Her body tensed as she came, and then she collapsed against his chest. "That was...amazing."

Fuck, yeah. As good as it was between them, and it was fucking spectacular, he'd never lost control like that during sex. Never lost control, period. It was addictive though, watching her lose control. He wanted to do it again. And again.

"Your turn," she whispered, gripping him.

His balls tightened as she stroked his shaft, and he hissed out a breath, thrusting his hips against her.

"How bad do you need me right now?" She stroked her thumb over his head, and his vision grew hazy.

Pretty fuckin' bad. So bad it scared him. He reached down and pushed her hand away. "Not as bad as I need to taste you."

"No time," she said, even as a blush crept across her cheeks. "I have to get ready for work."

"There's time." He reached up to turn off the water and then swept her into his arms and carried her to the bed.

He kissed his way down her stomach and knelt between her legs.

"Mark, really, you don't have to..."

But her whimper when he touched her let him know that she wanted this as much as he did. He put his mouth on her, reveling in her salty taste, the way her hips bucked and her knees parted, inviting him in. He used his tongue to drive her wild, letting her pleasure fuel him. He lost himself to the sensations as he nipped and plunged, driving her higher and higher. She let out a cry that echoed throughout his body. His dick was so hard he felt like he hadn't come in years, when it had only been hours.

This was the effect she had on him.

"Wow," Jess whispered when she'd recovered.

He looked up at her, ridiculously pleased by the ravished look on her face.

She sat up and reached for him. "I can be a few minutes late."

"No, you can't." He gave her a quick kiss, then slid out of bed. He pulled on his boxers and jeans and reached for his shirt.

"Mark..."

"Call me later."

She frowned. "I have a girls' night tonight, I think."

"No problem." He gave her another kiss. "Bye, Jess."

With Bear at his heels, he headed for his SUV and pointed it toward his condo. Jess tested the limits of his control, something no woman had ever done before. Which meant he needed to get ahold of himself.

Back at his condo, he took Bear for a walk and fed her breakfast. For himself, he devoured a few donuts from the box in his pantry while he boiled a couple of eggs to round out the meal. Sweets were his indulgence, but protein was necessary to fuel him through a day at Off-the-Grid.

With that taken care of, he headed for work. Bear rode along with him, as usual. She would hang out in the office with whoever was working the desk today, probably Trent. Mark had a zip-line tour booked at one, but he'd be spending the morning on the new property, working on the mountain bike course with Ethan.

As business slowed for the winter, they had more time to get the course in shape. And since both he and Ethan had some experience with woodworking, they'd volunteered to lay the raised portion of the course themselves. Kept costs down and kept them busy.

"Ready?" Ethan asked, walking out of the office. "I've got Ryan's truck already loaded up."

Mark nodded. Bear took one look at the truck and hopped into the bed with their lumber and tools. "Guess she's hanging with us today."

"Cool with me." Ethan climbed into the driver's seat. "You've been kind of absent lately. Everything okay?"

Absent? "Yeah."

"Okay, bro. I'll take you at your word. Just, you know, check in with us every once in a while, let us know how you're doing."

Mark shot him a look.

Ethan grinned. "Just trying to be a good friend, man. Yesterday, you walked out of here for a few hours in the middle of the day. It's not like you, that's all."

"Had an errand to take care of."

"This errand have a name?" Ethan gave him a questioning smile.

Dammit. "No." Because it was none of his business, and Jess had asked him to keep things private for now.

Ethan guided the truck back into the woods beyond the end of the zip-line course. Already they'd built a platform where the mountain bike course would originate. Today, they would begin constructing the course itself. It would run on a raised wooden track for the first quarter mile or so over the rocky terrain on their original property. Then they'd carve a dirt trail into their new land, twisting and turning down the hillside, ending in another raised portion that branched, offering a moderate finish for those looking to play it safe and a hair-raising drop on the other side for the true adrenaline junkies.

If all went well, the new course would be ready to open for business in the spring. And he couldn't fucking wait. It had been years since he'd been on a mountain bike. This course was going to be a rush.

He and Ethan spent the rest of the morning hammering wood. They made pretty good progress too. It was exciting to see their vision starting to come to fruition. He wondered how Jess was coming with her plans for the cabins.

Just past noon, they loaded up the pickup truck and headed back to the main building for lunch before the one o'clock zip-line tour. He and Ethan would be taking out a group of locals. Mark had been helping out on the zip-line a lot since his survival skills class had been a slow starter, and he didn't mind. He enjoyed the zip-line, but it involved a lot of face-to-face time with the clientele, and he preferred being behind the scenes or one-on-one teaching survival skills in the forest.

He'd just finished his roast beef sandwich when their clients arrived in the lobby, a group of middle-aged men and women who all looked suitably excited about their afternoon adventure. His gaze fell on a woman near the back, a small woman with bleached blond hair and a timid smile that made his sandwich curdle in his stomach.

What was Sharlene doing here?

He thought he'd made himself perfectly clear when he confronted her in the deli parking lot last week. She wasn't welcome, not here or anywhere else in his life.

CHAPTER TWELVE

Jessica stood in front of the bathroom mirror, scowling at herself. She looked tired. She *felt* tired, but surely she could hide it through the magic of makeup. Emma would be picking her up in a few minutes for girls' night out, and she was going to have fun tonight no matter what. She blotted concealer beneath her eyes, smoothed it in, and then gave herself a final once-over. She had on a low-cut purple sweater, skinny jeans, and boots, and with the dark circles under her eyes successfully camouflaged, she looked ready for a night out on the town.

Bring it.

Right on time, she heard Emma knocking at the front door.

"Coming," Jessica called. She grabbed her purse and jacket off the end table and opened the door. "Thanks again for picking me up," she told Emma as they walked to her SUV.

"No problem. You're on my way, and I can't drink anyway so I might as well put my sobriety to good use," Emma said with a grin.

And since she'd been able to manage her headaches holistically for the last few days, Jessica really appreciated the fact that she could drink freely tonight. After the month she'd had, she needed to cut loose with her friends and enjoy a drink or three. "I'll return the favor once the baby's born."

"Definitely taking you up on that." Emma pointed a finger in her direction before climbing into the driver's seat. "My college experience is totally lacking in the beer department so far."

"How's everything going?" Jessica got into the passenger seat and fastened her seatbelt.

Emma had started taking night classes a few months ago to earn her college degree, right around the same time she found out she was pregnant. "Honestly, between college and work, I'm exhausted." Emma brushed back a lock of blond hair as she pulled out onto the road. "Once I've finished the gardens for the Silver Springs Lodge, I'm going to cut back my hours until after the baby's born."

"That sounds smart." Jessica chewed her bottom lip. "Have you seen the inside of the lodge?"

"Checking up on the competition?" Emma asked with a sly smile.

And yep, that's exactly what she'd been doing. Not for nothing, but the Haven Spa had been the only spa in the county for a long time. It was definitely not ideal to have a new luxury lodge with its own spa opening right before she expanded her own spa into a resort. "I'm curious, yeah."

"It's nice...really nice, but it has a totally different vibe than your place, Jess. I don't think you have anything to worry about."

"How so?"

"It just feels like any other hotel spa. Everything's shiny and pretty, but there's nothing unique either. The Haven Spa has so much more character, plus you have the hot springs. And your spa cabins are going to be to-die-for."

Emma pulled into an empty spot along the town commons, and they got out of the car. The evening air was cool and crisp. Jessica slipped into her jacket as they walked toward The Drunken Bear.

"Is Ryan working tonight?" she asked.

Emma nodded. "He's been picking up as many extra shifts as he can get."

"Makes sense while you're taking evening classes."

"Yep. Saving up as much as we can before the baby comes."

They pushed through the front doors of The Drunken Bear and found Gabby and Carly already seated at a table by the window. Mandy joined them soon after.

Carly passed her cell phone around the table, showing them photos of her wedding dress.

"It's gorgeous," Jessica said, and she meant it. The dress was a classic ballgown style, strapless with a full skirt and a heavily beaded bodice. "You're going to look like a princess."

"I can't wait." Carly had a dreamy look in her eyes.

"It's like a wedding epidemic around here," Mandy said, tossing a meaningful look in Jessica's direction.

She nodded in solidarity, as the only other single (or at least semi-single) person at the table.

"More importantly," Mandy added, "does Sam have any single, famous friends? Because I wouldn't mind a rock star of my own."

"Ooh, I hadn't even thought of that," Gabby said. "The town is going to be crawling with celebrities that weekend, I bet."

Carly nodded. "There will be some famous faces around here, no doubt about it. And Sam does have some single friends you and Jessica might swoon for, although I'm not sure yet how many of them will fly out for the wedding."

"And I'm not so sure how single Jess actually is," Emma said with a smile.

Jessica took a long drink from her beer to save herself from having to answer.

"That's right!" Carly's eyes lit. "Because you've been kissing Mark."

"I know you guys have history together," Gabby said. "So is this like a chemistry thing or a feelings thing?"

"It's supposed to be a *private* thing," Jessica said, her cheeks burning.

"No privacy here," Emma said, grinning. "But you can also trust that nothing you say will be repeated outside our group."

"Does that include Ethan and Ryan?" Jessica gave Emma and Gabby questioning looks. "Because we're talking about one of their best friends."

"If you ask us to keep it between us girls, we will," Gabby said.

Emma nodded in agreement.

"This sounds like more than just kissing," Carly said, sipping from her beer with wide eyes.

"It is." Jessica took another drink from her own beer. "He spent the night at my place last night."

Mandy whooped, while a collective murmur of excitement ran around the table.

"That sounds like a *lot* more than kissing," Emma said.

Jessica nodded. "This chemistry between us...well, I guess it was simmering for a while. Maybe we still had some unfinished business we needed to get out of our systems."

"So it's just sex?" Mandy asked.

"For now, it is, and that's why I don't want word of it getting out around town."

"So you won't be inviting him to your parents' house for Thanksgiving?" Emma asked, her expression deadpan.

Jessica set her beer down on the table a little more forcefully than she'd intended to. "No way." Although truthfully, Thanksgiving hadn't even crossed her mind yet. Her family knew him, of course, and she did hate the thought of him spending holidays alone...*crap*.

"Your face right now!" Emma was laughing. "But don't worry, we've already invited him to have Thanksgiving with us so you don't have to worry about him being alone."

"Oh good. I mean...not that I was worried, but I'm glad he'll be with you guys." A ridiculous burst of relief flooded through her.

"Maybe you could stop by for dessert," Emma said, her eyes gleaming mischievously. "I do bake a mean pumpkin cheesecake."

"Um." Jessica sensed that she was in over her head with no way out. She gulped from her beer. "Yeah. Sure. I could stop by for dessert."

"I'm so sorry we're going to miss this," Gabby said, grinning from ear to ear.

"Sam and I are staying in town to spend Thanksgiving with my parents," Carly said.

"Come on over," Emma said. "Ryan and I love any excuse to have extra people around the table at the holidays, and I bet you could bring something really yummy too."

"Oh, I'm sure I could whip something up." Carly winked.

"Your pecan pie tarts are my favorite," Jessica chimed in, for a moment forgetting the potential awkwardness of Thanksgiving with Emma, Ryan, Carly, Sam, and *Mark*.

"Duly noted," Carly said, sipping from her beer.

"So if I might be nosy for a moment," Emma said, raising her eyebrows. "What's he like in bed? I mean, he's so reserved. Does he ever let loose?"

"And is he a dirty talker?" Mandy asked.

They were all leaning in close, grinning like fools.

Jessica felt her cheeks burning again. Reserved... yes, that was a good word for Mark, but she wanted to see him let loose. Ooh, yeah, she might make that her new mission in life. "Not much of a dirty talker, no. And yes, he likes to keep himself in control, but that's kind of a plus because he always takes plenty of time for me first."

Gabby nodded solemnly. "And kudos for that. There are way too many men out there who only think about themselves in bed."

"Sad but true." Jessica nodded. "Mark definitely scores a perfect ten on delivering orgasms, but—" She cut herself off and reached for her beer, semi-embarrassed by what she'd almost said.

"But what?" Carly asked.

"You can't leave us hanging like this," Gabby said.

"If you ever repeat this to anyone, I'll ban you all from the spa." She raised her eyebrows for effect, and they all nodded vigorously. "He's holding back. There's this passion, something really raw and intense. I can see it just beneath the surface, but he reins it in. I'm not sure he's ever really let go, and I really, *really* want to see it. I mean, don't get me wrong, he's already great in bed, but Mark unleashed? That might be like holy shit, off-the-charts amazing."

"Whoa," Mandy said. "I may have underestimated you, Jessica. I always thought you were kind of buttoned-up, but you go, girl. I hope he takes you on the ride of your life."

Jessica chugged the remainder of her beer. "If so much as a word of this makes it to Ethan or Ryan, you guys are dead to me."

"Our lips are sealed." Emma mimed zipping her lips with a grin.

"Absolutely," Gabby agreed. "But you have to let us know how it turns out."

"Girls' night," Carly said, "at one of our houses so that you can spill all the deets in total privacy."

"Do I even want to know?" a masculine voice asked.

Jessica looked up to see Ryan standing beside their table, a wide grin on his face.

"Nope," Emma told him. "This is for girls' ears only."

"Hmm." Ryan surveyed the table. "Interesting. Very interesting. So who's ready for the Adrenaline Rush this weekend?"

"Totally pumped," Mandy said.

Emma pouted. "I'm so sad I can't race this year."

"Team Flower Power won't be the same without you," Carly told her.

"But we're *finishing* this time." Gabby lifted her beer, a determined expression on her face.

"Yo, I have no doubt about it," Ryan said, giving Gabby a fist bump. "All right, ladies. I've got to get back to the bar. Behave yourselves." He winked as he walked away.

A mixture of excitement and trepidation swam in Jessica's stomach. Maybe running in an obstacle course race wasn't the best idea for her right now, but then again, why not? She had several appointments scheduled next week to have more tests done, and in the meantime, there was absolutely no reason she shouldn't go about her life as usual.

Emma had to drop out of the race when she got pregnant, and they needed four members to compete, which meant Team Flower Power was counting on Jessica. If she was lucky, she might even forget about her aches and pains for a few hours while she was at it.

"Here's to Team Flower Power," Mandy said, lifting her beer.

* * *

Saturday morning dawned cold but clear. With a projected high of sixty-five degrees and sunny skies, it was the perfect day for a race. Mark was at Off-the-Grid by five to run final checks on the course.

"Fuckin' freezing out here," Ryan grumbled as he met Mark out front.

Mark nodded. Probably wasn't much more than forty degrees right now, but that would change once the sun was all the way up.

"That mud pit's going to be cold as balls," Ethan said with a grin. "You guys ready?"

Together, they set out into the woods, checking and double-checking every obstacle on the course. This year, teams would start out on the ropes course and then navigate their way into the woods using compasses through a series of team-based obstacles ending in the mud pit. Once the entire team had completed the course, it would be a race to the finish line.

After making sure everything was ready, he, Ryan, and Ethan headed back to the registration area. Already their volunteers were starting to arrive. Emma came out of the office carrying three coffees in a cup carrier from the coffee shop.

"Thought you might need these," she said, setting the tray down on the registration table.

"Do we ever." Ryan leaned in to give her a kiss. "Thanks, babe."

"Lifesaver. I mean it," Ethan said, grabbing one of the cups.

Mark nodded. "Thanks, Emma." He snagged a coffee for himself and took a grateful sip.

"As bummed as I am that I can't race this year," Emma said, "I'm not all that sad about staying warm and dry today."

Ethan grinned. "The Adrenaline Rush is late this year because of mine and Gabby's wedding, but we'll be back to our summer schedule next year."

"I'm so there," Emma said with a smile.

Mark's gaze caught on a familiar figure headed their way. Jess had on black jogging pants and a long-sleeved purple athletic shirt, her hair in a ponytail.

"Hey, Jess!" Emma called out, heading toward her. "I've got flowers inside for everyone's hair. Plus, we can hide out in there for a while where it's warm."

"That sounds perfect." Jess glanced over and caught his gaze. She looked tired. More than that, she looked *ill*, and it raised his protective hackles.

More than anything, he wanted to go to her, pull her into his arms, and hold her tight, but he couldn't do that. She'd been the one to suggest they keep their relationship under wraps. It had suited him fine at the time. But right now, he fucking hated everything about it.

* * *

Jessica sucked in a deep breath and jumped. With a splash, the muddy water swallowed her up, and *holy shit*, it was cold. She kicked against the muck beneath her feet, and her head broke the surface. Spluttering, she scooped mud off her face while her feet scrambled for purchase against the bottom of the pit.

Gabby shrieked as she splashed into the mud beside her. Carly, the tallest of their group, was already walking along the edge of the pit. She hadn't even gotten her head dirty! Jessica scowled as she swiped more mud out of her eyes. Her whole body tingled from the cold.

"Come on, ladies," Mandy—the smallest member of Team Flower Power but also their leader in Emma's absence—called as she swam through the muddy water, headed for the opposite side.

"I'm going to kill Ethan for dreaming this up," Gabby grumbled as she sloshed—half walking, half swimming—after Mandy.

"Oh, come on, this is fun!" Mandy said with a laugh.

"Sorry, but I have to agree with Gabby on this one." Jessica headed for the edge of the pit, where it was shallower, so that she could walk like Carly was doing. The muddy bottom sucked at her shoes and oozed around her ankles.

"Gross. Gross. Gross!" Gabby chanted as she splashed after Mandy.

Jessica slipped and almost went under again. She enjoyed the mud baths she offered at the spa, but this was not at all the same. For one thing, she had mud up her nose, in her ears, and who knew how many other places she'd rather keep clean. For another, it was so friggin' cold, she couldn't think of anything else but getting out as quickly as possible.

She'd had a headache since she got up this morning, and the icy mud didn't seem to be helping matters. Pain stabbed at her temples, matching the throb of her pulse. Her hands cramped, and *ugh*...

"Oh no!" Gabby stopped, staring down into the muddy water swirling around her. "I lost a shoe."

"Uh-oh." Jessica sloshed over to her, feeling around in the mud with her sneakers as best as she could.

"This is so bad." Gabby giggled as she bent lower, searching for her shoe.

Mandy and Carly had already reached the other side. They stood on the bank, dripping with mud and staring back at Jessica and Gabby.

"I don't feel it anywhere," Jessica said.

"Me neither." Gabby's foot bumped into Jessica's as they rooted around in the mud looking for the missing sneaker. "Screw it. I can finish barefoot."

"Um, are you sure?" Jessica was shivering now, and pains were shooting up her arms. "How much of the race is left after we get out of the mud?"

"It's not far. We just have to run past the zip-line to the field behind the house. I can totally do it."

"If you're sure." Jessica hated the thought of Gabby running all that way without a shoe, but they couldn't stand here all day in freezing cold mud looking for it either.

"I'm sure. Last year, I fell and was disqualified. This year, I'm crossing the finish line no matter what." Gabby pulled herself up straight, muddy water dripping from her chin.

"All right then, let's get the hell out of this mud." Jessica had no idea why it was causing her so much pain, but the longer she stayed in here, the worse she felt. She sloshed off toward Mandy and Carly as fast as she could go with Gabby at her heels. A few minutes later, she finally, *finally* pulled herself out onto dry land. Her knees buckled under her, and she landed on her butt at the edge of the muddy trail.

"You all right, Jess?" Mandy asked, extending a hand to help her up.

"My muscles are cramping up from the cold." And she couldn't stop shivering.

"Better keep moving then," Mandy said. "Oh crap, Gabby, you lost a shoe!"

"I know," Gabby said with a smile. "I'm ready to run for it in my sock. Let's go."

They certainly weren't the fastest team as they headed for the finish line. Gabby half limped, half jogged over the rocky terrain in one shoe. Jessica was powering through on sheer adrenaline as her muscles cramped and chills wracked her body. Carly looked similarly miserable. Only Mandy was still in good spirits, jogging energetically and cheering the rest of them on.

"Almost there, ladies!" Mandy called as they rounded a bend on the trail and the finish line came into sight. "Come on. Let's finish strong."

I can do this. Jessica forced her legs to keep moving. Gabby grabbed her hand, and together they sprinted toward the finish line.

"You got this, sweetheart!" Ethan called out from beyond the finish line, and Gabby lurched forward, dragging Jessica along with her.

Then they were through the inflated archway marking the end of the race. A volunteer draped a medal around Jessica's neck. Someone handed her a bottle of water and one of those space blankets that looked like tin foil to warm up with. She wrapped it around her shoulders, but it didn't seem to do much good.

"We did it!" Mandy pulled them all in for a group hug.

Gabby was grinning from ear to ear. "I finished. I really did it. This was so great!"

Emma ran toward them from across the field. She barged into their group hug, flinging her arms around Jessica and Carly, and then she shrieked, "Holy shit, you guys are cold and wet!"

"Um, yeah. We just swam through a mud pit that was slightly warmer than ice," Carly told her, teeth chattering.

"Jess, are you okay?" Emma's eyes crinkled in concern.

"Really c-cold." Jessica couldn't stop shivering, and these awful pains were shooting down her arms and legs.

"You look...blue," Gabby said.

Mandy gave her a discerning look. "Yeah, you really do."

"Sweetie, let me get you some hot chocolate," Emma said.

"I'm f-fine, you guys." Jessica hugged the silver blanket closer around herself. "We should go rinse off." There was a line of outdoor showers along the edge of the field so that they could douse themselves in fresh water to rinse off the worst of the mud. But, oh God, it was going to be cold. And she was already so friggin' cold.

"Hang on a second." Gabby toed out of her remaining sneaker and then ran off toward Ethan in her socks.

Jessica looked down at her hands, which were shaking uncontrollably and still caked in mud. She'd just rinse off quickly here so that she could go straight home and take a long, hot shower.

Gabby walked back over and nudged Jessica in the direction of the house. "Come on. Spouse privileges."

"What?" Jessica started walking in the direction Gabby was guiding her.

"We'll catch up with you guys in a little bit, okay?" Gabby called over her shoulder to Carly and Mandy. They both nodded.

"You get Jessica warmed up," Mandy said. "Beers later to celebrate?"

"Definitely," Gabby said, still marching Jessica toward the house. She led them over to the table where they'd checked bags earlier with clean clothes to change into. "Grab your bag."

Jessica handed her claim tag to the teenager behind the table, and he handed her the black duffel bag she'd brought. "Where's yours?" she asked Gabby.

"Inside. Spouse privileges, like I said." She winked at Jessica over her shoulder.

Right. Because Ethan and the guys owned this building. That was handy. Jessica stumbled as they reached the front door. Seriously, what was the matter with her?

Inside, Gabby led her down the hall behind the reception area. "You know Ethan used to live here, right? There's a full bathroom in back. The guys shower here all the time."

"Really?"

Gabby nodded. She went to a closet and pulled out a blue towel, which she shoved into Jessica's arms. "So go on in and take a long, hot shower."

Too miserably cold to argue, Jessica did just that.

* * *

Mark made his way up to the main building around three o'clock, long overdue for some grub and eager to see how Jess and her team had done. He hadn't seen her since she'd passed by his station on the ropes course hours ago. The yard was filled now with muddy racers wearing finishers' medals and the friends and family who'd come to cheer them on. Here and there, groups posed for selfies, and all around, he heard happy laughter.

Looked like a successful event, and he'd relax and appreciate that fact as soon as he knew Jess was okay.

"Hey, man," Ethan called from his position near the finish line, "everything secure on your end?"

Mark nodded. The last team had completed the ropes course about thirty minutes ago. He and a couple of volunteers had just finished securing all the equipment and closed up the area.

"There are sandwiches at the house," Ethan told him. "Emma brought enough food to feed a small army."

"Great. How did Team Flower Power do?" he asked, careful to keep his tone neutral.

Ethan broke into a wide smile. "They're in tenth so far overall. Gabby lost a shoe in the mud pit, but she still finished strong."

Mark smiled too, relieved to know that the women had finished the race successfully.

"She took Jessica up to the house, said she was really cold or something," Ethan said with a shrug.

Mark was already striding toward the house by the time Ethan had finished speaking. He'd known Jess didn't look well that morning. Dammit, if she'd aggravated whatever was wrong with her by racing today or worse...

By the time he'd reached the house, his heart was pounding against his ribs. He shoved through the front door and then stopped in his tracks as the sound of laughter reached his ears. Jess and Gabby sat on the leather couch in the reception area, coffee mugs in hand. They both had towels wrapped around their hair and looked fresh from the shower. Jess glanced up at him and gave him a small smile.

"Hey, uh, everything okay?" he asked.

"We're great now that we're warm and dry," Gabby told him.

Jess nodded, both hands wrapped around her coffee mug.

"Good," he said.

"I'm just so happy I finished this time." Gabby held up the medal around her neck. "We're going out for beers later to celebrate."

"Okay." His gaze slid back to Jess. She was awfully quiet. "You okay?" he couldn't help asking.

"I'm fine," she said.

"She got really cold in the mud pit," Gabby added, "so I brought her up here for a hot shower and some coffee."

"Good thinking." He hoped that's all it had been, but at least she seemed okay now. As he turned to go into the kitchen and fix himself a sandwich, he could have sworn he saw Gabby give Jess a high five out of the corner of his eye.

What was that about?

CHAPTER THIRTEEN

$\mathcal{M}$ark was deep in the woods, taking down a wooden platform they'd built for one of the obstacles on the Adrenaline Rush, when his cell phone rang in his back pocket. The sound seemed so out of place here among the trees, surrounded by nature. He slid it out of his pocket and checked the screen.

Jess was calling.

His heart picked up its pace as a sizzling jolt of awareness raced through his body at just the sight of her name. After their group went out for beers on Saturday night, she'd begged off early to rest up before work the next day so he hadn't been alone with her—hadn't even kissed her—in days, and he was missing her something fierce. He brought the phone to his ear. "Jess?"

"Hi," she said. "Got plans tonight?"

"No." And if he had, he'd have canceled them at the urgency in her voice.

"The Leonid meteor shower peaks tonight. I thought maybe we could take some blankets and find a nice spot to watch them."

Memories of their one full night together as teenagers on a blanket beneath the stars swept over him. Fuck, yes, he wanted to do that again. "Yes."

"Great. And Mark, I was thinking we should make a night of it, for old times' sake." Her voice had gone all low and throaty.

His dick grew heavy. "Yes."

"You bring the condoms. I'll bring the blankets."

"Done."

"Mark...where are you right now?" Her voice had dropped to a whisper, and the sound was so erotic his whole body tightened with the need to hold her, touch her, taste her.

"In the woods."

"Are you alone?"

"Yes."

"I am too," she breathed. "Alone, not in the woods."

"Where are you?" His voice sounded like gravel. He was rock hard and aching for her. Tonight felt like a million years away. The sweetest form of torture.

"I'm at the spa, in my office. I'm about to close up for the night. Everyone else has already gone home." She paused, and when she spoke again, her voice had gone even lower. "Sometimes, after everyone's left, I take a dip in one of the spring-fed hot tubs. They're amazing, you know."

"I'll take your word for it." He adjusted himself in his jeans, but the mental image of Jess alone at the spa, getting ready to go into the hot tub, only intensified the ache in his groin. "Do you wear a swimsuit?"

"No."

Fuck. He clenched his fist, desperate to touch her.

"Mark..." She made a breathless sound that he felt all the way to his dick. "Are you as turned on as I am right now?"

"Yes." He eased himself onto what remained of the wooden platform, wincing at the pressure in his jeans.

"Are you touching yourself?" she asked.

"No." His fist clenched tighter. "Are you?"

"Yes." She whimpered, and his vision went hazy.

"Fuck, Jess. Don't hang up. Let me hear you come."

"Only if you'll come with me."

He gritted his teeth. Phone sex? Not his style. Certainly not while he was sitting here in the middle of the woods, exposed to the world. "That's a negative. But I'm with you. Keep going. Tell me what you're doing."

"Mark..." She sighed. "Don't be a prude. No one will know. No one but me."

"Public indecency and all that."

"You're on *our* property," she said. "I'm the last one here at the spa. What about your guys?"

"Gone home." To their wives.

"Unzip your pants," she said, sounding so sexy he found himself obeying before he'd even realized what he was doing. His fingers fumbled the button, and then he eased the zipper down, relieved beyond words to be free of its painful constraint.

Jess moaned into the phone. "I almost came from the sound of your zipper."

Her words sent a bolt of lust through him so red-hot that he reached down and freed himself from his boxers, fisting his aching dick. "Your turn. Let me hear you."

She gasped. "I'm so wet. I can't wait to have you inside me later tonight."

"Yes." He stroked himself. Just until she came. He could wait until tonight for his release. To be with Jess. Inside her. Consumed by her.

"Tell me," she whispered, her breath coming in rapid pants.

"I'm going to make you come so hard." He tightened his fist, holding still. Control. Always control.

"I can't hear you, Mark. Tell me what you're doing."

"I'm holding my cock and picturing you naked in your office, touching yourself." He forced himself to stay still as his cock pulsed in his hand.

She moaned. "I'm not naked, but tonight I will be."

"Fuck, yes."

"Stroke yourself. Let me hear how turned on you are."

He gave himself one long, slow stroke, unable to contain the groan that tore from his throat.

"That was really sexy," Jess murmured. "Keep going."

He did, keeping his pace painfully slow so that he could focus on Jess as she moaned and panted into the phone, the sounds more erotic than anything he'd ever experienced.

"I'm so close," she whispered. "Are you?"

"Yes," he gritted.

"You sound so sexy right now. Keep talking..."

"Listening to you come over the phone is going to be the hottest thing I've ever heard. I can't fucking wait."

"Oh," she panted, and her breathing grew even more rapid. "Yes..."

"Keep going, Jess. Take your time. Make it good."

"Mark," she moaned, and her breath caught, "I'm coming..."

"Yes. Fuck, yes." His balls tightened, and he stroked harder, faster, consumed by the sounds of Jess's pleasure.

She cried out, mumbling incoherently in his ear as she found release.

Fuck. She was amazing. So sexy. So perfect. He'd only meant to listen to her come, but while he'd been focused on Jess, his fist kept going, moving at a frenzied pace to match her breathless moans, and now..."Fuck." He lurched forward onto his knees as his own orgasm barreled into him, angling his hips so that he came into the fallen leaves carpeting the forest instead of all over his pants like a horny teenager. His balls burned, his dick pulsed, and relief poured through him.

"Wow," she whispered breathlessly. "You really did this with me."

"Yeah." He sagged back on his heels, boneless and shaky.

"I wasn't sure you'd go through with it," she said.

"Didn't mean to," he admitted. He tucked himself back inside his jeans, zipped them, and then flopped back on the wooden platform behind him, not trusting his knees to hold him up just yet.

"I'm glad you did," she murmured. "This was...it was really sexy and intimate."

"Yeah."

"Mark?"

"Yeah?"

"See you tonight at seven."

CHAPTER FOURTEEN

Jessica heard Mark's SUV pull up outside right at seven. The man was punctual to a fault. She shouldered her backpack and reached for the cooler she'd packed, right next to the roll of blankets and sleeping bag. They would need them. It was going to drop into the forties overnight, but she knew they wouldn't be cold. Not the way they heated each other up...

And not inside her flannel-lined sleeping bag, which was rated for colder weather than this anyway. She pulled open the front door and smiled at Mark. He had on well-worn jeans that hugged him like perfection, a long-sleeved black tee, an insulated black vest, and hiking boots.

"Hi." She felt herself blushing as their eyes locked. The phone sex hadn't been planned, but holy hell, it had been *hot*.

"Hi yourself." He pulled her in for a kiss, taking the

blankets and cooler from her hands in the process. "I brought my sleeping bag too. We can zip them together. What's in the cooler?"

"Cold fried chicken, cornbread, and some of Carly's butterscotch cookies."

"Nice."

"There's a bottle of wine in my backpack."

"Sounds like you've thought of everything." He kissed her again, his hands sliding down to palm her ass.

"Did you remember the condoms?"

He nodded, his dark eyes heated.

"Good," she murmured against his lips. "Because after our phone call earlier, I really need to have you naked."

"That makes two of us." He deepened his kiss, his tongue dancing against hers, an erotic promise of things to come.

"Better get going then," she said when they'd come up for air. "We need to set up before it gets dark. We could go back to that same field we camped in as teenagers. Do you remember the place?"

"That old access road is still there. I've thought about you every time I drove past it."

"Aww." She pressed a quick kiss to his lips even as she wondered if he was serious. Why would he have been thinking about her when he passed their old make-out spot? He'd been the one to run off and leave her without looking back. She'd assumed he'd wiped her from his mind when he enlisted. He sure as hell hadn't gotten in touch.

He led the way to his SUV and loaded her things into the back.

"Where's Bear?" she asked.

"Trent's watching her tonight."

"Oh." She smiled at the thought. "What did you tell him?"

"Said I had business out of town."

"Technically true," she said as they climbed in and Mark turned the car out of Haven toward the wilderness beyond. They rode in silence. Once they'd left Haven town limits, there were only a few cabins tucked here and there in the woods.

About fifteen minutes later, they arrived at the old access road that had been the scene of many stolen afternoons as teenagers. They never knew what the road had been intended for. The pavement was cracked and worn, punctured here and there by hardy weeds that sprouted through the cracks as nature attempted to reclaim the space. It led about a quarter mile into the woods then dead-ended.

And if they walked straight ahead for another quarter mile or so, they'd come into the clearing where they'd often gone as teenagers to cuddle and make out and, once, to camp beneath the stars. She could hardly wait to do it again.

"Think the field is still there?" she asked as they set out through the trees, carrying all their makeshift camping materials.

"Yeah."

Did he sound so certain because he was Mark and never expressed doubt, or had he been here since that night? She pulled her jacket closer around her as they walked. It was already past chilly and headed toward flat-out *cold* here in the woods. Not to mention dark. She stayed close to him as they hiked together toward the field. It wasn't long before it came into view before them, lit in a yellowish glow by the fading sun.

"It looks just like I remember it," Jess said softly.

Mark nodded, leading the way toward the middle of the clearing. The ground here was soft and leaf-strewn. He stomped down a few weeds and saplings so that she could spread out the large, waterproof picnic blanket she'd brought to serve as their bottom layer. Once it was in place, she dropped the rest of the blankets and sleeping bags on top of it, toed out of her boots, and sat down in the middle to zip the two sleeping bags together.

Mark sat beside her, staring up at the sky.

"The meteor shower isn't supposed to really get going until around midnight," she said.

"I'm sure we can keep ourselves busy until then," he said drily.

She laughed. "Hungry?"

He nodded, reaching for the cooler. He unlatched it and flipped it open, tossing her a paper plate. "You make this?" he asked as he opened the container of fried chicken.

"You're kidding, right? This is from the café."

He grinned as he loaded up a plate. "You might have learned to cook in the last ten years. How would I know?"

"Well, I haven't. At least, not like this." She put two pieces of crispy fried chicken and a slice of cornbread onto her plate.

Mark shrugged. "It's what restaurants are for, if you ask me."

She smiled as she bit into her chicken. "Agreed. Oh man, that's good."

"Missed this kind of food when I was overseas," he said.

She looked at him, surprised. It might be the first time he'd ever volunteered information about his time in the

Army. "Nothing beats good Southern cooking. What did you miss most?"

"Dessert," he answered without hesitation.

"You've always had a sweet tooth."

He nodded as he polished off his first piece of chicken and started in on the second. "Chocolate cake. Every time I came home on leave, I'd buy myself a chocolate cake."

"And eat the whole thing by yourself?"

"Yep."

She laughed. "Good thing I remembered to pack cookies for tonight."

Mark had almost finished his second piece of chicken and showed no signs of slowing down.

Jessica finished her first and picked up her cornbread. "Do you keep in touch with any of the men from your unit?"

He chewed and swallowed a bite of chicken. "E-mail sometimes. They're in Syria now."

It must be hard for him being here while they were over there. "I'm sorry. I don't know what it was like for you, Mark. We had never talked about the Army or anything. You completely blindsided me when you enlisted."

He was silent for a moment. "It was something I needed to do."

"I get that. But I would have supported you, you know that, right? I'd have waited for you."

"I couldn't ask you to do that." He had a faraway look in his eyes that was as disconcerting as it was frustrating.

"With all due respect, that was my decision to make."

* * *

"I did what I had to do." Mark had heard the frustration in her voice, but he couldn't apologize for what he'd done. He'd done it for her as much as he'd done it for himself.

"If you could go back and do it over, would you change anything?" She crawled closer to him on the blanket, her brown eyes shining in the near darkness.

"No," he answered truthfully.

She grumbled under her breath, something about a "stubborn, stupid man."

He couldn't argue with her words. "I'm sorry, Jess."

She huffed out a breath. "Well, at least you're honest."

"I've always been honest with you."

"And yet, sometimes I still don't feel like I know you at all."

"I'm sorry for that too." Sometimes he wasn't sure he even knew himself.

"What is it, Mark? What makes you tick?" She crawled closer so that her knees bumped his.

You. He knew it as sure as he knew his own name, but he couldn't tell her that, not after he'd just pushed her away with his words. Maybe he'd already hurt her too badly to deserve a second chance. The truth was that he might be too damaged for a relationship, a real relationship like Jess deserved. He might be better off on his own, the way he'd always been. And since he had no fucking clue how to tell her any of this, he kissed her instead.

She slid into his lap and kissed him back. "That's not an answer," she whispered against his lips.

"I know." He tangled his fingers in her hair, pressing his forehead to hers. "But it's all I've got."

"Do you realize how infuriating that is?"

"Yeah." He kissed her again.

She poured her frustration into her kiss, nipping at his

lip, lashing her tongue against his until he was totally drunk with lust. "I'd hate you if I didn't want you so damn much," she murmured.

He knew it was true too.

She climbed out of his lap and reached into her backpack, coming up with a bottle of red wine. She handed it to him with a corkscrew while she went over to the cooler.

He jammed the corkscrew into the cork and twisted it out. She took it from him, poured wine into two plastic cups, and handed one to him, setting a plate of cookies down on the blanket beside them.

"Hell of a picnic," he said.

"My favorite kind of picnic." She snagged a cookie from the plate and spread a blanket over their legs. Then she leaned back against his chest, looking up at the stars.

He grabbed a cookie for himself and bit in, washing it down with wine. He wasn't much of a wine drinker but this, tonight, was good. The wine was bold and spicy and put a warmth in his belly that chased away the chill of the night around them. Of course, all he really needed to keep warm was the woman in his arms. His blood turned to steam every time he touched her.

"Oh!" Jess exclaimed, lurching upright and elbowing him in the chest in the process. "I just saw one."

"Yeah?" He looked up into the night sky. The heavens twinkled above them, sparkling with what looked like millions of stars. "It's the one thing that's the same everywhere."

"What?" She craned her head to look at him, her brow wrinkled in confusion.

"The sky. Whether you're here, California, Iraq, Germany . . . it always looks the same when you look up."

"I never thought of that." She leaned back against him again.

"Sometimes you just want to see something that reminds you of home. The stars always did it for me."

"I thought about you a lot those first few years," she said quietly. "I'd wonder what you were doing, where you were... if you were safe."

"Thought about you too." He wrapped his free arm around her and pulled her in closer.

"Did you miss me?" she asked, her voice nothing but a whisper.

"Yeah." Like he'd left a piece of himself behind here in Haven. He'd mourned the loss of Jess until... well, pretty much until he'd gotten her back.

"You could have written to me. I'd have written you back."

"No." He couldn't have kept in touch with her. He was a part of her past, and he'd wanted her to have a future free of the uncertainty that came with military life, waiting to see if he'd survive, if he'd come home, and what kind of man he'd be if he did make it back.

"I don't understand you, Mark Dalton."

"Not sure I understand myself half the time."

She laughed, twisting around in his arms to face him. "No matter how angry I still am about our past, you're one of the good guys, you know?"

He drew her in for another kiss. She tasted like a mixture of butterscotch and red wine, a heady combination that lit a slow burn deep in his gut. He lifted her, settling her so that his cock pressed between her legs.

She moaned, rocking her hips against him. "This afternoon... that was my first phone sex."

"Mine too." He slid his hands beneath her jacket, popping the clasp of her bra.

"I liked it." She nipped at his lip. "A lot."

"Yeah." He still couldn't quite believe he'd done it, but yeah...it had been hot. If he lost her again, *when* he lost her again, the memory of that phone call would fuel his fantasies for years to come.

"I think I'll call you again the next time I'm feeling horny." She rocked her hips, moaning as he cupped her breasts.

"Please do."

"Mark," she whispered, reaching down to grip him through his jeans. "I want you to let go tonight."

"What?"

"I want to see you lose control." She ran her palm up and down his length, and his dick surged beneath her touch.

"No can do, baby." He lifted her hand, settling it on his shoulder. "I don't lose control." *Ever.*

"Everybody loses control sometimes." She pushed him back on the blanket, straddling him.

"Not me." Not since he'd turned eighteen and enlisted in the Army. He'd left behind the foolish, impulsive kid he'd been before.

"It's fun to let yourself go," she whispered, tugging at the zipper of his vest. He unzipped it and tossed it aside and then let her tug his shirt off over his head.

"I do love watching *you* lose control though," he said.

"I give it freely." She bent her head to kiss his chest, tracing her tongue around the tight bud of his nipple, igniting that slow burn inside him into an inferno. "And tonight I'm going to take yours. I'm going to make you beg."

"You're welcome to try." He watched in amusement as she unzipped his pants. Never in a million years would he beg, but he was going to enjoy the hell out of whatever torture she had in mind.

"This is going to be so much fun." She tugged at his pants with a wicked grin on her face.

He lifted his hips, allowing her to slide him out of his jeans. "Fair is fair though." He sat up, making short work of her clothes.

Once they were both naked, she sat straddling him, her head thrown back. Moonlight illuminated her, gleaming over the perfect peaks of her breasts and the creamy expanse of her stomach. He sucked in a breath. God, she was beautiful. So fucking beautiful.

She wrapped a blanket around her shoulders, leaning forward so that it covered him too, keeping the cold night air off their overheated bodies. With a wicked smile, she rocked her hips, sliding up and down his cock, and she was so wet. Her heat was burning him up. He gripped her hips, guiding her up and down his length, but she broke free with a laugh.

"You're not in control tonight, remember?" She straddled his left thigh, so close yet so frustratingly far from where he wanted her.

"I remember." He reached down to touch her, needing to feel her arousal. He wanted to taste her something fierce, but she wanted to take the lead tonight so he'd just have to lie there and see what she had planned. In the meantime though...He stroked her, groaning low in his throat when he felt how hot she burned for him.

She rocked her hips, riding his thigh as he teased her with his fingers, living vicariously through her as she grew nearer to her release.

"This is what it looks like," she panted, "when you lose control." Then she threw her head back and surrendered, her hips bucking wildly as she rode her way right over the edge, crying out as she found release.

He plunged a finger inside her, heightening her pleasure—and his—as she convulsed around him. His dick pulsed in rhythm with her release, aching to be inside her, but he could wait however long he needed.

He could always wait.

"Wow." Jess collapsed against him, breathless. "See?" she said, turning her face to meet his gaze.

And hell if he didn't see what she meant. He imagined what it would be like to surrender himself one hundred percent to his desires, to give himself over to the need burning inside him and let go, pound his hips against hers until release crashed into him as strong as it had just taken Jess.

But he couldn't do it. He could never be free of the control binding him. Too many years of practice held him tight as a board.

She slid down his chest, disappearing beneath the blanket, and kissed the head of his dick, just a quick kiss that nonetheless made him jerk against her lips. "How bad do you need me right now?" she asked, her warm breath teasing his aching flesh. "On a scale of one to ten. One being a total limp dick." She kissed him again, proving his dick was anything but limp. "And ten being ready to beg for mercy."

Pretty damn close to an eight. "Five."

"You're such a liar." She traced her tongue over him, and his cock throbbed painfully. "It is going to be so much fun making you beg tonight."

"I'm not going to beg."

"Oh yes, you are." She took him in her mouth, plunging him so deep, his vision went hazy. She sucked hard, once, twice, and then released him from her mouth with a wet pop. "Because I'd say you're already at least at an eight."

Fucking hell. For the first time in his life, he actually considered begging.

CHAPTER FIFTEEN

Maybe it's already a nine." Jessica grinned as Mark lay still as a statue beneath her. His jaw was clenched so tight, he could have crushed stone, and his dick strained against his belly, so impossibly hard. She took him in her fist. His shaft was still wet from her mouth, soft on the surface and like steel inside. "You're so hard, Mark. It's turning me on again just feeling how hard you are."

He said nothing, but one arm snaked around her waist, drawing her down against him.

"Oh, would you like to cuddle for a while?" She was enjoying torturing him, maybe a little too much.

"Sure." His voice sounded like sandpaper.

She snuggled up against him so that her thigh pressed against his cock, and she'd meant what she said before. Feeling him pressing into her like this was turning her on *big time*. "I could cuddle with you like this all night."

"Yep." His voice was casual, but his body was anything but. There was no hiding the way his cock pulsed against her thigh, poking urgently against her.

"Still a five?" she asked.

"Maybe only a four now that we're just cuddling."

He was such a liar! Oh, this was going to be so worth it when he finally broke. She shifted her leg against him, restless in her own desire, and he'd already gotten her off once. She might feel guilty about letting him get her off a second time before she'd done the same for him, but hey, she wasn't too proud to beg. He, on the other hand...

"See any meteors yet?" she asked.

"No."

She rested her cheek against his chest and looked up at the sky, twinkling with millions of stars above them. It was hypnotizing. She'd always loved stargazing, especially during meteor showers. As she watched, another bright streak shot across the sky. "Oh! Did you see that?"

"No."

"Too busy thinking about the fact you're only at a four, huh?"

"Yep. Four."

"Well, I guess I have my work cut out for me then." She swung around to straddle him. His cock pressed between her legs. She rolled her hips, sliding up and down, never quite letting his tip reach her core. Teasing him. She'd never done anything like this before, trying so hard to drive a man mad with need. For her. To make him *snap*.

Mark closed his eyes, still and silent beneath her.

"Have we at least made it back to five yet?" she asked. He nodded.

"Halfway there," she whispered, bending down to kiss his chest. She kissed his nipple, sucking hard. He surged beneath her, his hips arching up into hers. Smiling, she kissed her way over to the other side of his chest, licking and sucking the tight bud of his nipple until he released a harsh groan. He'd always been so sensitive there.

And *dammit*. He had willpower of steel.

She rocked faster as her own need rose up, burning her up from the inside out. "How are you, Mark?"

"Fine," he mumbled. "Still a five."

"You are the world's most frustrating man." She ground herself against him, and *boom*, another orgasm slammed through her. She bucked against him, riding it out, and then collapsed against his chest.

Mark swore, tossing an arm over his eyes.

"I think I'm having a lot more fun than you are." She grinned, panting, still tingling with pleasure. "You know, all you have to do is say please…" She pressed her palm against him, and his cock pulsed so hard she thought he might come right there in her hand.

"I'm tired of this game." He sat up, reaching for his jeans.

"Seriously?" She gawked at him. "You'd quit now rather than risk losing control?"

"I told you." He looked at her, his expression stony. "I don't beg, and I don't lose control."

"No way, mister." She pushed him back down. "No quitting. Here. I'll make it easy for you." She reached into her backpack and pulled out a condom. She pressed the foil packet into his palm. "Because I know you're not much of a talker, you don't even have to say please. When you're ready to beg for mercy, just roll on the condom and go crazy."

He said nothing, but his fist clenched around the condom.

"But when you put on the condom, it is the nonverbal equivalent of begging." She took him in her fist and squeezed. "And no holding back once you get inside me."

"What if you're not ready?"

"Oh, I'll be ready." She was so turned on again just from talking to him she could barely sit still. She had no idea how he was still holding on when she was ready for orgasm number three.

She straddled his thigh, letting his coarse hair rub her just right. Then she pumped her fist up and down his shaft, allowing her thumb to swirl through the dampness at the tip on each stroke, keeping her tempo slow enough to drive him mad, not giving him the speed or the grip he needed to find his own release.

Torturing him.

She rocked against his thigh, feeling her own arousal grow, but she was not, absolutely *not*, coming again until he was inside her. So she slowed down, torturing herself as much as she tortured him, and when she couldn't stand it anymore, she bent forward to suck his nipple into her mouth. She sucked hard, again and again, while her fingers traced the head of his dick, teasing, teasing...

Mark lurched upright so fast she fell to the side, startled. He had the condom in place almost before she'd realized what was happening. Then he'd pinned her against the blanket, his big body covering hers, his cock already pushing against her entrance.

"No holding back," she whispered as she wrapped her legs around his hips.

"Couldn't if I tried." He plunged inside her, filling her up so hard and so fast she gasped.

"Yes," she moaned, digging her heels into his ass.

His hips flew as he plunged into her again and again, each time better than the last. He hooked his right arm beneath her left knee, adjusting their position, bringing him even deeper inside her, so deep her whole body rocked with the power of each thrust. She could feel one of the strongest orgasms of her life building inside her, ready to rock her world.

"Fuck, Jess," he ground out, thrusting harder, faster…

Yes, yes, yes…

His arms began to shake. "I'm too close…"

"Go," she whispered as her own orgasm crested inside her.

He pumped his hips like a man possessed, swearing a blue streak.

"I'm coming," she moaned, and her body clamped down around him.

"Fuck. Me. Holy shit…" Mark kept swearing, his hips slamming into hers, each stroke taking her higher and higher.

She was coming, and coming, and *holy shit* indeed…the pleasure grew so intense, she almost couldn't take it. "Mark!"

"Jess." He stiffened, holding himself still for a long moment. Then he thrust again, and a guttural cry tore from this throat, so wild, so uninhibited that she came even harder.

He pounded into her. "Holy…fucking…shit…"

She could feel him pulsing inside her, and her body gripped him in response, his pleasure fueling hers. Finally, he went still, dropping his forehead against hers, his chest heaving for breath.

"You did it," she whispered, aftershocks of pleasure still ricocheting around inside her. "You lost control."

"I have never come so hard in my life," he gasped.

"I don't think I have either. And yet I never managed to get you past a six." She winked playfully.

Mark thrust inside her again, making her moan. "Baby, I was at an eleven the whole damn time."

"I knew it!"

He withdrew, rolling off the condom and placing it inside their bag of picnic trash. Then he lay back, tucking the blanket around them. "When the Army trained me to withstand torture, they'd obviously never met you."

"But this was a good kind of torture," she said, snuggling in against him, not wanting to think about him undergoing any other kind.

"Yeah."

They lay like that together for a few minutes, neither of them moving. Overhead, a meteor blazed, and she was too awestruck to say a word.

Finally, he sat up, gesturing toward their picnic trash. "I need to get this back to the truck before we attract any bears."

"Um, Mark." She was staring at his dick, which was still semi-hard.

He followed her gaze, hardening even more. "Already at a six."

"That is impressive."

"I may be hard for the rest of my life after everything you put me through tonight."

She grinned, reaching for him. "Let me help you out with that."

"As soon as I take the trash back to the car." He reached for his jeans and pulled them on.

"Stubborn man." She rolled over, wrapping the blanket tighter around herself. "Hurry back."

* * *

Mark woke sometime during the night. Jess had zipped their two sleeping bags together, and it was toasty warm inside them. He was naked. So was she. She slept next to him, curled on her side, her brown hair fanning around her face. So beautiful.

A flash of light caught his eye, and he looked up. The night glistened overhead in a shimmering blanket of stars, and there went another meteor. It shot across the sky, disappearing behind the treetops at the edge of the clearing. Mark had never been that interested in outer space, never dreamed of being an astronaut or any of that. But okay, this was pretty cool.

As he watched, another fireball blazed in the sky, then another. Should he make a wish? Were meteors the same as a shooting star? He wasn't sure. Still, it couldn't hurt.

He closed his eyes and wished for Jess's health. Then he reached out and brushed a lock of hair back from her face.

Her eyes fluttered open, and she smiled, scooting up against him.

"Look up," he said.

She did. He held her close while they stared up at the stars. A meteor shot across the sky, and Jess gasped.

"It's so beautiful," she whispered. "I don't know why, but there's just something so magical about it, especially being out here in the middle of the woods under the stars."

As he held her close, he felt the magic too. He would never have done this, never have even known there was a meteor shower tonight, if not for Jess.

She lay in his arms, a peaceful smile on her face. They lay together like that for a long time, and he saw more meteors than he ever would have imagined possible. After a while, Jess fell back to sleep, and then he finally did too.

When he woke up again, the sky had begun to brighten with dawn, and Jess was still asleep in his arms. He could lie here in this sleeping bag in the middle of the forest with her for a million years and never want to leave. When he held her, everything else seemed to melt away. There was just him and Jess and an overwhelming sense of peace inside him.

And he hadn't known much peace in his life.

She snuggled closer against him, murmuring in her sleep. He couldn't make out the words, but she looked pretty damn peaceful too. Protectiveness welled up inside him. He wanted to hold her so close that all the pain she'd been facing would just disappear. It fucking killed him that he couldn't just kiss her and make it all better. And he was terrified that something serious might be wrong with her.

But one thing was for damn sure: Whatever she was facing, she wouldn't face it alone. He'd be right there beside her, no matter the diagnosis, no matter if she never got a diagnosis. He'd walked away from her once, and he'd step back again romantically if she asked him to, but he would never turn his back on her again.

He lay there and watched the sunrise through the treetops as Jess slept in his arms.

"Good morning," she murmured, her voice thick with sleep.

"Sure is." He tucked her in closer against him.

Her warm, naked body landed flush against his. "It was a good night too."

"Yeah." It sure as hell had been. He'd always enjoyed camping outdoors, and watching the meteor shower with

Jess had been really special. And the sex? Well, he'd been about ready to strangle her while she was torturing him out of his mind, but holy *fuck*, the end result had been amazing. He'd lost control all right, and he'd never come that hard or that long in his life. He had literally seen fucking stars when he lost himself inside her last night.

Just thinking about it made him hard as steel. Or maybe it was the fact that Jess was still pressed against him. She kissed him as she scooted up in the sleeping bag, bringing their bodies into alignment. They kissed and touched as the sky dawned blue overhead. And when he sank into her, he knew nothing else would ever compare.

Because Jess was everything.

Afterward, as they lay there, damp with sweat and panting for breath, he gave her another deep, drunken kiss. "What time do you have to be at work?"

She rolled to her back. "I took myself off the schedule this morning. I have a doctor's appointment at ten."

Reality slammed into him, hard. "More tests?"

She nodded, lines of tension appearing around her eyes. "Lucky me."

He wanted to tell her it would be okay, but he didn't believe in false promises. He knew there were no guarantees, not even that she'd get answers. The human body could be a frustratingly complex, mysterious thing sometimes. "I could come with you."

"That's sweet of you, but I'll be fine."

"Jess..." But he didn't know what to say.

She turned to face him and gave him a gentle kiss. "It's okay. Really. Whatever it is, I'll handle it."

"I don't doubt that for a second."

"But I don't want to talk about doctors or other un-fun things right now, okay?"

"Fair enough." He tugged her in for another kiss.

"Hold that thought," she whispered against his lips. "I need to pee."

He laughed as she slipped out of the sleeping bag. She wrapped a thick, blue blanket around herself, slid her boots on, and walked off into the woods, her brown hair bouncing on her shoulders. He wasn't sure he'd ever seen a sexier or more beautiful sight.

She returned a minute later, still wrapped in the blanket. Now that the sun had risen higher in the sky, he could see the purple smudges under her eyes, a harsh reminder that she wasn't well. She gave him an amused smile as she slid back in beside him. "Seriously, how can you not need to pee when you wake up in the morning?"

He shrugged. "Too many years in the military, I guess. You get used to ignoring it."

"I don't think I'd be very good at that part." She pressed her chilly toes between his calves to warm them.

"You would. You're pretty damn tough, Jess."

She gave him a look but said nothing. They lay together until the sun had risen above the treetops, taking the edge off the chill in the air. "Well, Mr. Tough Army Man, I'm starving, and I didn't pack us any breakfast, plus it's probably time for me to go home and shower and make myself presentable."

"You're already more than presentable."

"You're just saying that because you're the man who ravished me." She gave him a sexy grin as she slid back out of the sleeping bag and scrambled for her clothes. "Crap, it's cold."

He enjoyed the view of her ass while she fumbled with

her panties, then he climbed out of the sleeping back to get dressed himself. Ten minutes later, they were packed up and ready to go.

"Thanks for bringing me out here," he said, knowing his words fell far short of the immense gratitude he felt for having gotten to share this experience with her.

"Thanks for coming and, you know, all the other things." She winked.

He shook his head, fighting a smile. "I'll never see another shooting star without thinking of you."

CHAPTER SIXTEEN

Jessica closed her eyes, wishing she were still out in the woods with Mark, snuggled up with him in their sleeping bag. Because the rest of her day had sucked. After the doctor's appointment from hell, she'd given a massage to an old man with terrible gas and done manicures for a couple of the rudest tourists she'd ever met. By the time she finally made it home from work, it was after eight, and she was dead on her feet and cranky as hell.

And the lights were on in her house.

She frowned as she spotted Nicole's car in the driveway. That's what she got for giving her sister a key...uninvited house guests when she just wanted to be alone. Stifling a groan, she stomped up the front steps and into her house.

Nicole and Brennan sat on the couch, margaritas in hand. A sitcom she didn't recognize was blasting from the TV, filling her living room with its laugh track.

"What the hell?" she said, planting her hands on her hips.

"Sibling intervention," Brennan said. "I drove by here last night to check on you, but you weren't home, and Nicole was texting you all afternoon to ask about your doctor's appointment, but you never replied. So either something's wrong that you haven't told us about or there's a man. Or both. So we're here to find out what's going on, offer our support, and gain any and all juicy gossip." He lifted his margarita with a smile.

"God, you two are nosy." Jessica slung her bags over one of the kitchen chairs and walked to the fridge for a glass of water.

"Guilty as charged." Nicole followed her into the kitchen. "Want a margarita? I already mixed up a whole batch."

"Sure." Jessica poured herself a glass of water and drank half of it without stopping. Truthfully, a margarita was probably the last thing she needed tonight, but it might help make this "sibling intervention" more bearable.

"Have you eaten yet?" Nicole asked as she poured a glass full of the yellowish concoction and handed it to Jessica.

She shook her head as she accepted the drink.

"I knew we should have brought food too. Bren and I both ate earlier. What can I fix you?"

"Nothing. I'll make something later." Jessica left behind her half-empty water glass and walked back to the living room with her margarita in hand.

"We're definitely going to feed you, but first tell us about your appointment this morning," Nicole said.

Jessica sighed as she dropped into the armchair next

to the couch. "Dr. Rimmel drew about a million vials of blood for tests and basically told me that if these tests don't come up with any answers—and she didn't sound very optimistic that they would—that we might be looking at a diagnosis of chronic fatigue syndrome."

Nicole frowned. "Chronic fatigue syndrome?"

"It causes unexplained fatigue, aches, pains...pretty much everything I've been experiencing the last few months."

"So how do you treat it?" Brennan asked.

"I don't think you do, really." Jessica took a sip of her margarita. "There's no cure for it. That's why they call it 'chronic.' You just have to find ways to treat the symptoms and then deal with it."

"Oh, Jess." Nicole put down her drink and came to give Jessica a hug. "That sounds awful. How are you feeling about all this?"

"I'm pissed as hell." She took another drink, waiting for the tequila to numb the sick feeling in the pit of her stomach. "I'm not okay with it at all."

"Does it ever just go away?" Brennan asked.

Jessica shrugged. "I don't know. I didn't ask many questions yet, and I haven't had time to Google search it."

"Don't do that," Nicole said, looking alarmed. "Everyone knows the Internet will convince you that you're dying."

"That's the damn truth," Brennan said. "Last month, Patrick pulled a muscle in his leg, and somehow he convinced himself it was a blood clot. Oh my Lord, he was a mess."

Jessica laughed in spite of herself. Her brother-in-law had always been a bit of a hypochondriac. "I won't let the Internet convince me I'm dying. I promise."

"And surely some of your New Age voodoo stuff will help you feel better." Brennan winked. He liked to tease her about her lifestyle, but he respected it too. A few years ago, when his migraines had gotten bad and the medicine his doctor prescribed made him too woozy to drive, he'd come to her for help. She'd found a combination of acupressure and essential oils that had gotten his pain under control.

"I've been managing my headaches naturally for the last few weeks." She gestured with her glass. "Otherwise I wouldn't be drinking with you guys tonight." She'd also been detoxing her body with mineral baths after-hours at the spa.

"We're here for you, Jess. Whatever you need. Feel free to lean on us any time," Nicole said.

"Seriously. Anything," Brennan echoed, and Jessica knew her siblings were true to their words.

"Thanks, guys." She blinked back the tears welling in her eyes.

"Now tell us about the guy," Brennan said, taking a dramatic sip from his margarita.

Jessica groaned. So much for keeping this thing between her and Mark under wraps. First the girls had interrogated her, and now her siblings were doing it too. There was no such thing as privacy in this town.

"It's Mark, right?" Nicole asked.

Jessica nodded.

"Mark?" Brennan glanced between them, an incredulous look on his face.

"Yes, and I know it's a terrible idea. It just... happened."

Nicole shrugged. "Mom and Dad might be a hard sell, but I say give him a chance. What happened between you guys in high school was a lifetime ago. I assume he's done a lot of growing up between then and now."

"The Army has a way of doing that to a person," Brennan agreed.

Jessica drained her glass, enjoying the fuzzy aftereffects of the tequila. "He's a great guy. He always has been. The problem is, he's just…not there emotionally. And I don't think that will ever change."

"That probably comes from growing up on his own," Nicole said, looking thoughtful.

"I'm sure it does. It's awful what he's been through, but he's got to let me in if this thing between us is ever going to work."

"Well, you know I've always had a soft spot for him," Brennan said. "I don't think I ever told you this, but Mark was the very first person I came out to."

Jessica gaped at her brother. "No, you definitely did not ever tell me that! Why Mark? Why not one of us?"

"I was sitting out back one night, sweating buckets over the thought of telling you guys I was gay."

"Bren, how could you possibly doubt we'd be there for you?" Nicole nudged him with her shoulder.

"It's hard to explain how it felt, but I was fucking terrified. Dad's such a…you know, he's an All-American Guy, watch football, drink beer. At the time, he'd been pushing me to follow in his footsteps and join the Army after high school. I was so afraid he'd be disappointed in me."

"Oh, Bren." Jessica put down her drink to give her brother a hug.

"Anyway, there I was sitting out back, having a mini panic attack, and Mark came outside. He was sneaking off to smoke a joint so I bummed one off him, and then I

just blurted it out. And he just shrugged and said, 'That's
cool, man.' And we smoked a joint together like it was
no big deal, but it was... it was a big deal to me, and I'll
never forget it."

Jessica wiped away the tear that had splashed over her
cheek. "I'm sorry you ever had to feel that way, Bren."
And it didn't surprise her a bit that Mark had reacted the
way he had. He'd never been judgmental, not even in
high school. Still, she felt a new warmth bloom for him
in her heart, for having helped Brennan at such a pivotal
time.

"So Mark's a great guy, but he doesn't open up." Nicole sipped from her margarita thoughtfully. "You could
just keep doing what you're doing, sleeping with him and
hiding your relationship because you're convinced it's
going nowhere..."

Jessica winced.

"Or you could start nudging him in the right direction.
He may need some help, Jess."

"How?" Jessica walked to the kitchen for another margarita, but *whoa*...she needed to think about eating
something too because she was ridiculously wobbly on
her feet right now. She filled her glass and rummaged in
her freezer for one of the TV dinners she kept for just
such an occasion. She warmed up a tray of fettuccine Alfredo in the microwave and brought it back into the living
room with her second margarita.

"I can't believe you eat those things," Nicole said.

She shrugged. "It's organic. Sometimes I get home too
late to bother cooking."

"So back to Mark," Nicole said.

"What do you think I should do?" Jessica spun fettuccine around her fork and took a bite.

"Maybe you could take one of his survival classes."

"And you should give him a spa treatment," Brennan added.

"A spa treatment?" Jessica laughed. "Never in a million years would he agree to that."

"Give him a massage. That's sexy," Nicole suggested.

"And maybe you could get him into one of the spring-fed tubs," Brennan said.

"That sounds great and all, but how is this helping Mark learn to open up?"

"Well, for starters, you guys would be getting familiar with what's going on in each other's lives now, not trying to re-create what you had together in high school, which didn't work out anyway. Maybe you need to leave the past in the past and act like you're newly dating. Go see him in his element, and then let him see you in yours. Plus, it gives you more opportunities to ask him questions about himself. Get to know modern-day Mark," Nicole said.

"Okay, that actually makes sense." Jessica took another bite of her fettuccine Alfredo.

"And then if you really want another chance with him, you're going to have to make it official. Bring him for dinner at Mom and Dad's. Give him a chance to fit back into the family. That's nudging him in the right direction. That's giving him a chance to grow and do better this time."

"Nicole's right," Brennan said.

Jessica stared at the remnants of her dinner as the truth of her sister's words sank in. She'd been holding Mark at arm's length to keep from getting hurt, and in doing so, she was all but ensuring that's exactly what would happen.

* * *

"Heard a rumor you've been holding out on us, man." Ethan grinned like the cat who ate the canary.

"Oh yeah, what's that?" Mark asked, keeping his expression neutral.

"You and Jessica?"

"I heard a similar rumor," Ryan said.

"I don't know where you guys get your intel." Mark shook his head, turning to the lumber he was loading into the back of Ryan's pickup truck. He was not in the mood to discuss Jess with these guys right now. Not in the mood to talk, period.

"You know damn well," Ethan said, still grinning. "And I don't hear you denying it either."

Mark shrugged, continuing to load the back of the truck.

"Kind of a big deal," Ryan commented, "hooking up with your high school sweetheart when, if I'm not mistaken, you hadn't so much as looked twice at a woman in years."

"Yep," Ethan agreed.

"Jess and I have been in touch a lot about the land. That's all." Mark turned his back on the two busybodies behind him.

"Bullshit," Ethan said.

"Yo, Emma already spilled the beans. We know you're sleeping with Jessica." Ryan sounded amused.

Mark bristled. Jess had told her friends, after asking him to keep their relationship quiet? What the hell?

"And Gabby confirmed when I pressed her about it," Ethan said.

"Guess you already know then," Mark said, feeling irrationally pissed. "Good for you."

"Hey"—Ryan clapped him on the shoulder—"we're happy for you, man."

Mark kept stacking wood.

"Seriously, you have nothing to say on the subject?" Now Ethan sounded amused.

"Nope." Mark slung a two-by-four into the truck bed, deliberately allowing it to swing close to Ethan's head.

"Well, now you're just being an asshole." Ethan's smile faded.

"And you guys are acting like a couple of teenagers. Why is it any of your business who I'm sleeping with?"

Ryan got right up in his face, his usual easygoing demeanor nowhere in sight. "Yo, don't be a jackass. You did the same thing to each of us when we started dating again. We were just trying to tell you we're happy for you."

Mark had no idea why he was so angry. Part of it was directed at Jess, for telling her friends about their relationship. Most of it was directed at himself, for being so insecure he didn't want the world to know he was with Jess for fear of losing her. Very little belonged on his friends. "Sorry."

Ryan looked at Ethan, eyebrows raised. "Did he just apologize?"

Ethan grinned. "He sure did. Now we've definitely got to go to Rowdy's after work."

"Count on it," Ryan said.

"Fine." Mark slung the last of the lumber into the truck bed. Heading to Rowdy's with the guys would no doubt result in a friendly ass-kicking, but he'd grin and bear it. He had to because he needed them in his life. They'd become awfully damn important to him since he'd been back in Haven.

With that settled, he hopped in the truck and headed

out to spend the day working on the mountain bike course. Ethan and Ryan were manning the zip-line today. Mark was looking forward to the day spent on his own. It was the best medicine, the best therapy. Because mostly he loved having so many people in his life now, but sometimes...sometimes it was too much. It made him feel claustrophobic and antsy and antisocial. And then he needed to spend a day out in the woods banging nails into wood.

After eight hours spent doing just that, Mark was feeling much better. He was calm and relaxed, physically exhausted but ready to go out for beers with Ethan and Ryan. Jess called as he was loading up the truck to head back to the main building.

"I want to take one of your survival skills classes," she said when he answered.

He raised his eyebrows. "You sure about that?"

"Positive. Lord knows I spend enough time out in these woods. I consider myself pretty well prepared, but that thing with the bears last month shook me up. And besides, I bet you can teach me all kinds of cool new stuff."

"It's valuable for anyone who spends time out in these woods," he agreed. "I teach a few different versions. You want the full class or the short version?"

"The full class, of course." He heard the smile in her voice.

"It's an overnight."

"Overnight?"

"Ethan will drop us off outside town. We get lost in the woods and basically fend for ourselves."

"You really do that?" Jess sounded incredulous. "Like, repeatedly? With strangers?"

"No offense, baby, but a night in these woods is child's play compared to the places I slept in the Special Forces."

"Well, all right then. Sign me up."

He ran a hand through his hair. "You sure about this, Jess? I'm probably going to say this all wrong, but with your health right now—"

"Yep. You can stop right there," she said, her tone gone flat. "There's nothing wrong with me other than some aches and pains. And if I'm going to be dealing with it for a while, all the more reason to know how to handle myself if I ever get lost out in the woods."

He nodded. "Fair enough."

"Mark..."

"Yeah?" He ached to pull her into his arms and hold her tight.

"Thanks, you know, for being so great through all this."

"Don't give me credit for being a decent human being, Jess. That should be a given for any man you're with."

"It should, but... it's a lot for a new relationship."

"Our relationship is anything but new." On the contrary, he felt like he knew her better than most anyone else on the planet.

"But it is new." There was something raw and vulnerable in her voice. "We were just kids before, and then you were gone for ten years. Maybe I still need to get to know the adult version of you. Maybe we should quit thinking about the past and just focus on the present."

"What you see is what you get. I'm not a complicated man."

"I disagree. You're a lot more complicated than you realize."

"How so?" This conversation was starting to feel an awful lot like one they should be having in person instead of over the phone.

"I look at you sometimes, and I don't have a clue what's going on inside that brain of yours."

"Right now I'm just thinking about how damn lucky I am to have you," he said, trying to steer them back onto safer ground. "And if I'm being perfectly honest, I'm hoping I wind up in your bed tonight."

"I'm hoping that too," she said.

"I'm on my way to Rowdy's for a beer with Ethan and Ryan, but I'll call you when I leave."

"No need to call, just come on over."

Yeah, okay, he liked the sound of that. A lot.

He dropped off Ryan's truck, collected Bear from the office, and headed home for a quick shower before Rowdy's—after laying wood all day, he was sweaty and filthy. As he pulled into his spot in front of the condo building, he saw someone standing on the third-floor balcony, next to his front door.

His heart soared for a moment, thinking Jess had come over to surprise him, but this woman was blond, not brunette, and her presence sent his heart plummeting to his toes.

Sharlene.

As he watched, she slipped something under his front door and then hurried down the steps and across the sidewalk without ever glancing in his direction. He waited until she'd rounded the corner out of sight then stepped out of his SUV. With Bear at his heels, he climbed the steps to his condo in quiet fury.

He unlocked the door, and it swung open. Bear trotted inside, pausing to sniff at the white envelope on the floor. *What the hell, Sharlene?*

He picked it up and ripped it open. Inside was a plain, white note card.

Mark,

I'm so sorry. I made a terrible mistake coming here. I thought I could fix things, but it was too late. I'm moving on. If there's ever anything I can do for you, please call.

Mom

A phone number was scrawled below.

Mark's vision blurred. His fist clenched, crumpling the note into a tight wad of paper. His heart beat against his ribs like a fighter in a cage. She'd left. Again. Left him a note. Again. And then she'd had the nerve to sign it "Mom."

She wasn't a mother. A real mother would never walk away. Not once. Sure as hell not twice. He flung the paper across the room, fighting the urge to destroy something with his bare fists. Bear grabbed the crumpled ball of paper and trotted off to chew on it in her bed. He hoped she ate the damn thing.

It was better this way. Better that Sharlene had left before he'd done something extraordinarily stupid like give her another chance.

CHAPTER SEVENTEEN

On Monday afternoon, Jessica swung her backpack over her shoulder and pulled the front door shut behind her. Ethan's red Jeep idled in the driveway. She drew in a breath and smiled. Getting lost in the woods with Mark tonight sounded a little bit scary and a whole lot exhilarating. Maybe it was crazy, but she couldn't wait. It had been almost a week since her "sibling intervention," and she was starting to think Bren and Nicole were on to something with their plan for her and Mark.

"You know you don't have to go to this much trouble to get him in the sack," Ethan said from the driver's seat, grinning at her.

She shot Mark a look, but he kept his eyes straight ahead. No way he'd spilled the dirt on their relationship, which meant Gabby must have done the honors. So much for keeping things under wraps, but after her conversation with Nicole and Brennan, she wasn't sure she cared. "No sacks where we're going, Ethan. Get your mind out of the gutter." She winked at him as she climbed into the backseat of the Jeep.

Ethan laughed himself silly while Mark remained stony-faced. Jessica just shook her head as she buckled her seatbelt. They drove out of Haven, not so far from the spot she and Mark had camped beneath the stars to watch the meteor shower. Ethan guided the Jeep down a dirt road that became little more than two tire ruts in the earth, pulling to a stop when they reached the end.

"Have fun, kids," Ethan said. "Don't do anything I wouldn't do."

Mark shot him a look before stepping out of the Jeep. Jessica climbed out of the back, slinging her backpack over her shoulders. Mark had brought a pack of his own, larger than hers and with a tent rolled beneath.

"Isn't that cheating?" she asked as they stood there, watching Ethan drive away.

He shook his head. "Many hikers who get lost have basic camping supplies. We'll go over how to build a shelter, but we'll be sleeping in the tent tonight."

"Okay." She wasn't going to argue about spending the night in a tent with Mark versus lying on a bed of leaves and sticks. "So how does this work?"

"Well, we're going to operate as though we're lost hikers, more or less, although I'll know where we are the whole time, and I've got a sat phone in my pack that could bring the cavalry our way should we need it for any reason."

"That's good to know."

"So the first thing we'd want to do in any version of this scenario is take stock of our supplies." He set his backpack on the ground. "I'll also go over a few things that are helpful to have, things you might not usually keep with you, but after you've spent the night roughing it without them, you'll remember to pack in case you ever face this scenario in real life."

"Okay." She crouched beside him, watching with interest as he went over all the things he had packed—and she wasn't sad to discover he'd brought food for them either. She hadn't exactly been looking forward to foraging for leaves and berries for dinner.

"One thing you always want to keep in your backpack is a compass," he said, holding his up. "And make sure you know how to read it."

"I know how to read a compass."

"You'd be surprised how many people don't. It's easy to get turned around out here. If you've got a compass, you can at least keep yourself walking in a straight line. What you don't want to do is wander around in circles while search and rescue are trying to track you. Generally, you want to locate a water source—which is never too far away out here—make shelter, then stay put and wait for rescue."

Jessica nodded. "Got it."

"I've packed us enough water for the trip, but we're going to start by searching for water because if this were real, you wouldn't know how long you're going to be out here. Now where do you think we should look?" He paused and looked up at her.

"Um." She looked around. Aside from the barely visible path Ethan had taken to drop them here, all she could see were trees in every direction. Dense trees, and lots of them. "We could look for someplace with better visibility, like a hillside. Or climb a tree."

"Good thinking," he said. "And be on the lookout for the type of terrain where you find water, often a ravine or a valley. Also worth mentioning, always tell someone before you go hiking. Let them know where you're going and when you expect to be back. If no one knows where you are, no one's going to come looking for you."

"Right." She followed him into the woods, cringing inwardly as she thought of how often she struck out alone in these woods without telling anyone. With the dizziness and other problems she'd been having lately, she needed to put an end to that practice.

"If no one's looking for you, and you're not in a well-hiked area, then staying put probably isn't your best option. You want to find water and follow it. Streams and rivers always flow downhill, and people tend to build stuff near them so chances are, if you keep following the stream, you're going to find help sooner or later."

"Makes sense," she said.

Mark kept talking, pointing things out as they walked. He showed her deer tracks that might indicate they were near a water source and what kind of vegetation to look for.

"Are we going to eat any of this stuff?" she asked with a smile, fingering a leafy bush as she walked past.

"The best rule of thumb out here is that if you aren't one hundred percent sure what it is, you shouldn't eat it. You can survive a long time without food, and you can cause a lot more harm than good when you start foraging for yourself. But yeah"—he turned and gave her a smile—"I can show you what to eat if you want to be adventurous."

"I do," she answered without hesitation. Both on this excursion and with Mark. She was counting on tonight bringing them closer, in more ways than one. He'd been distant the last few days, spending more and more time out here in the woods by himself. Maybe coming out here with him today would help her better understand this side of him. They walked on, crunching through the thick bed of fallen leaves. The air was crisp and cool today, and she was comfortable in her fleece jacket and knit hat.

Mark stopped. "Listen."

She did. The wind rustled through branches overhead, and a bird squawked somewhere nearby. But there in the background...the faint babbling of...

"Water!"

He nodded. "Little creek up ahead."

She smiled softly. "You knew that the whole time, didn't you?"

He gave her an amused look. "Course I did."

"It's hard to even pretend to be lost when I'm with you." She stepped forward and slipped her hand in his.

He tugged her up against him. "Pretending you're lost isn't as important to what we're doing as learning valuable skills to use if you ever find yourself in a real survival situation in the future."

"True." She kept her hand in his as they walked, enjoying the warmth and strength of his grip. They reached the stream, and Mark spent the next hour showing her how to hunt for crayfish and other potential food sources in the water before turning his attention to shelter for the night.

"We'll build a shelter for practice, then I'll pitch the tent," he said.

"Great." Building a makeshift shelter sounded fun, especially knowing she'd be sleeping in the relative luxury of Mark's tent tonight. They gathered pine straw and leaves for the flooring.

"Ideally, you want several inches of this stuff underneath you this time of year," he said. "It's good insulation.

The ground gets cold at night. Hypothermia is a real danger for lost hikers."

They selected a spot near a fallen tree, using its trunk as one side of the shelter. They wove pine branches together to form a protective canopy, and then their shelter was complete. Jessica crawled inside, looking up at the pine boughs overhead. Beneath her, the bedding was thick and soft. She couldn't sit up without poking her head through the roof, and it was just wide enough for the two of them, but somehow the tight quarters felt cozy instead of claustrophobic. "You know, this isn't half bad."

"Not at all." Mark leaned back, resting his hands behind his head.

"You've slept in worse places." She lay beside him.

"Yeah."

"Tell me," she said softly.

"The desert's a tough place," he said, staring into the branches above him. "Your mouth gets so dry you can taste the sand. Sometimes I still taste it."

She slid closer, silently urging him to keep talking.

"Can't sleep out in the open. We'd look for caves, places like that."

"You've slept in a cave?" For some reason, that creeped her out. She imagined bats swooping overhead and spiders crawling over them as they slept.

"A cave was the best-case scenario. Protected from the elements, and the enemy. We'd take turns standing guard. But there was one night..." He paused, glancing over at her.

She curled herself against his right side. "Yes?"

"Whole mission went to shit. Me and a couple guys were stranded overnight in hostile territory with no cover. We had to burrow down in the sand with our combat helmets over our faces and pray like hell we'd make it until morning."

She blew out a breath. "I can't imagine what that's like. I really can't."

"You aren't supposed to. You shouldn't." He wrapped his left arm around her, drawing her in closer.

"You were a natural, weren't you? The danger, the adrenaline, all of it." She could feel the steady thump of his heart beneath her cheek.

"Yeah."

"You never would have left if you hadn't been injured."

"No." It was a simple answer to a loaded question. If he hadn't been injured, they never would have gotten this second chance.

"Do you miss it?"

He nodded. "It was the first time I'd been part of something like that, a team, a unit. Someplace I really belonged."

Oh, Mark. Her throat tightened painfully. He'd always seemed to prefer to be on his own, but had it been by choice or simply because he'd never felt like he truly belonged anywhere else? "Your unit was like a family to you."

He didn't respond, still staring up into the pine boughs overhead.

"And then you lost them too." She blinked back tears. For the first time, she felt like she understood some of what he'd been through, what it had been like for him growing up on his own. Never to have a place or a family to call his own. "I'm so sorry."

"No reason to be," he said, his voice slightly gruff. "No one on my team lost their life, which was damn

near miraculous. I'm still in one piece...well, mostly."
He cracked a small smile.

"You must have felt so alone again though, having to
leave your team behind."

"That was tough," he admitted.

Jessica watched him for a moment in silence, her heart
bursting with all kinds of emotions. Huge, powerful
things she'd felt only once before, and only for the man
beside her. "Thank you for sharing this with me. It really
means a lot."

"You mean a lot, Jess. You always have." His arm
tightened around her.

And dammit, there was no denying it. She was in love
with him. Maybe she'd never stopped. "You too, Mark.
So much."

"When things were tough, I'd think about you." His
voice was gruff.

And she had officially turned to mush in his arms.
"Really?"

"You got me through a lot of long nights."

She blinked back more tears. "I don't...I don't know
what to say."

In answer, he tugged her on top of him, lifting his head
to kiss her. She met his lips, kissing him back with a hunger
that bordered on desperation. He'd opened up to her in a
way he never had before, in a way that maybe he hadn't
with anyone else before. And in doing so, he'd given her
hope that there might be a future for them after all.

She lay sprawled across him, his hard contours softened by the layers of clothing between them, but there
was no mistaking the bulge in his jeans, pressing urgently
against her. They kissed as their hands explored and the
air grew thick and hot between them.

"Mark," she whispered. A shiver ran through her as he kissed her neck, his scruff teasing her delicate skin.

He shifted her to the side and reached outside their shelter for his backpack. "You don't want to get naked in pine straw. Trust me."

She pressed her hand against his heart. "I trust you."

* * *

Mark lay tangled in Jess's arms inside the sleeping bag. One of her thighs rested between his. Her face was pressed against his neck, and she was breathing just as hard as he was.

"Wow," she whispered.

"Yeah." He tightened his arms around her. *Wow* seemed to describe everything between them these days. He'd been lost, adrift on his own, for most of his life. But when she was in his arms? He was home. It didn't matter if they were in a makeshift shelter in the middle of the woods or her bed, as long as he had Jess.

"I don't want to move…like at all," she murmured. "But I'm starving."

"Same." As if to prove his point, his stomach rumbled like a hungry animal.

Jess laughed, still making no move to leave the sleeping bag. "So what's for supper, Mr. Survival Expert?"

"PB and J sandwiches and beef jerky, and if you're still feeling adventurous, I can show you how to get to the edible part of pine bark."

She lifted her head to give him a funny look. "Pine bark?"

"It's surprisingly nutritious."

She smiled, looking so goddamn beautiful, all glowing

and mussed from sex. "I'm definitely feeling adventurous today so let's do it."

"After you," he said, since she was still lying on top of him.

"Fine, fine," she grumbled as she reached behind him to unzip the sleeping bag. She slid out, reaching for her clothes as the outside chill reached their overheated skin. She winced, reaching for her left knee. "Ouch."

He reached around her and grabbed his boxers. "You okay?"

"Tweaked my knee again." She was already scrambling into her clothes, distracting him as she pulled on her bra and panties, then covered them with the green shirt she'd been wearing earlier.

"Hold on a minute." He stopped her as she reached for her jeans.

"I'm hungry, Mark. Can't you wait until after dinner?" she teased, pushing his hand away.

"Your knee." It was visibly swollen, and as he reached for her, he discovered it was hot to the touch. "Did you ever get this looked at?"

She shook her head. "It stopped bothering me before I ever got around to it."

He reached into his backpack for the Ace bandage in his first aid kit. "Next lesson: Always have a first aid kit in your pack."

"Got it." She nodded. "Wish I'd had one that day we were scoping out the new land."

"The day you came down with the flu." He began to wrap the bandage around her swollen knee. "Jess, what if you didn't sprain your knee that day? What if this is another symptom?"

She froze, eyeing him warily. "A symptom of what?"

"I don't know." He thought for a minute. "Did you mention joint pain to your doctor?"

"I...I can't remember. I think I did, back when this all started."

He finished with the bandage. There was something nagging at him, but he couldn't quite put his finger on it. "Well, make sure you mention it the next time you go in, okay?"

She nodded. "I will. Thanks."

They finished getting dressed and crawled out of the shelter. The sun dipped low over the trees across the valley, casting the hillside in its amber light.

"It's beautiful," Jess said from behind him.

He nodded. "How's the knee?"

"Sore."

"Maybe we should head out now before it gets dark."

She shook her head. "It'll be sore whether I'm here or at home, and I've got to hike out of here either way. I don't want to leave, Mark."

He didn't like it, but he couldn't argue with her either. "It's illegal to build a campfire out here. Even though I've got a special permit from the park service to camp overnight with clients as part of the course, they still won't let us start a fire. But if you were in a true survival situation, you'd need to break that rule to stay alive so we're going to prep a fire we're not going to light."

"Okay."

He showed her how to build a fire-safe perimeter and gather the necessary kindling and wood to get started. "Best-case scenario, you've got matches in your pack."

"Worst case?"

"You can use the battery in your cell phone, or any battery really." He demonstrated with an old battery he kept in his backpack for just this reason, creating a spark but extinguishing it before it caught fire.

"Whoa," Jess said, looking impressed. "That looks so much easier than rubbing two sticks together."

"Yeah, that doesn't really work, not for most people anyway. I'll show you a few more fire-starting tricks after we eat."

They sat and ate their dinner—such as it was—on a rock beside the stream. Then he stored their trash in a bear-proof container inside his backpack.

"Something else I should have?"

"If you've got food and plan on camping in one place for a few days. Black bears don't usually mess with us, but if you leave food or trash around, they're going to come investigate, and that's not something we want."

"So are you going to show me how to eat tree bark now?" she asked with a smile.

"Sure thing." He walked to a nearby pine tree. "What you want is the inner bark." He pulled out a pocket knife and cut away a rectangle of brown bark, revealing the soft, yellowish layer beneath. "This stuff." He cut away a piece and handed it to her. "It's got protein, carbs, and some other nutrients too."

"Hmm." She sniffed it and then gave him a funny smile as she put it in her mouth.

"Chew it really well before you swallow," he told her before popping a piece in his own mouth. The bark was thick and chewy, without much flavor. He chewed it until it had softened then swallowed.

Jess did the same. "That tasted like . . . well, like tree bark," she said with a laugh.

"But if you were starving, it would fill you up and give you some decent nutrition in the process."

"And I had no idea it was edible."

"You can eat acorns too."

Her eyes widened. "Really?"

"Yep. Not raw, though. They'll give you an awful stomachache...or worse. You've got to shell them, then soak them in warm water for a few hours until they've lost their bitterness. Boiling them is best, if you have a fire going. If not, you can set them in some water in the sun, but it will take longer and your results won't be quite as good. Once you've done that, you can roast them. They're not half-bad."

"Huh. You learn something new every day." Jess glanced around at the many acorns littering the forest around them.

He spent the next hour showing her more food sources and other survival tips. She was limping—just slightly—but even so, it was all he could do not to use the sat phone to call Ethan and have him meet them out here with the Jeep.

"You ready to pitch the tent?" he asked after he'd finished teaching her everything she needed to know.

She nodded, her cheeks flushed from the cool mountain air. "You don't share a tent with your other students, do you?"

"Never."

She took his hands, going up on tiptoes to kiss him. "Good."

"And just so you know, nothing else I have planned for tonight is anything I do with my other students either."

CHAPTER EIGHTEEN

They got home midmorning on Tuesday. Rather than using their compass to hike over to the main trail in Haven like they'd planned, they'd backtracked to the access road where Ethan had dropped them off yesterday to get picked up. Mark had insisted.

And even though Jessica wanted to protest, she hadn't. The truth was that her knee hurt. It was still swollen, and Mark's words yesterday stuck uncomfortably in her gut. What if her joint pain was another symptom? What if she'd never injured her knee at all?

Ethan and Mark dropped her off at home before heading to Off-the-Grid. Since it was her day off, she went inside for a nice hot shower and a nap. When she woke, it was past noon, and she was in no hurry to get out of bed. Instead, she opened her laptop and went over the proposals from the three contractors she'd seen for her spa cabins. Melissa Gormier's quote had fallen in the middle, cost-wise. But her rendering for the spa cabins was Jessica's favorite, and her quote was within the budget. Plus Jessica felt like Melissa really got her vision for the cabins.

Okay, apparently she'd already made up her mind. She called Melissa and left a voice mail. Then she spent the rest of the afternoon running errands and catching up on all the other chores she'd fallen behind on.

The next day, she worked a full day at the spa. At lunchtime, she caught up with Melissa and made things official. The excitement over taking this next step put a spring in her step for the rest of the day. She was still tired, still achy, but these were things she was going to have to get used to. She could work through it. She had no other choice. Even if it meant ignoring that little voice in the back of her mind that said she was being foolish to move forward with the expansion while her health was still up in the air.

By seven o'clock, she was in her office, finishing up paperwork. When she peeked out, she saw that the lights up front were off. She was the last one here. And Nicole's advice was still ringing in her ears. *Give him a spa treatment.* She *was* in the mood to celebrate after hiring a contractor to build her cabins. And she hadn't seen Mark in more than twenty-four hours.

She pulled out her phone and texted him. You busy?

No, he replied. As succinct in text messaging as he was in person.

Meet me here at the spa in fifteen minutes. She tucked her phone back into her purse and went down the hall to get a room ready for him. She lit some frankincense in the incense burner, set towels and oils to warm, and started the music. She'd never given a "happy ending" massage before, but tonight...

Oh, tonight, she'd make sure Mark finished happy. *Very* happy. And then they'd soak in one of the natural hot tubs together. Grinning like a fool, she headed toward the front door.

Mark stood outside, wearing jeans and a black jacket, his expression guarded. "Everything okay?"

"Everything is great." She tugged him inside and locked the door behind him. "You got to show off for me with your survival skills class. Now I'm going to show off my skills to you."

His expression turned wary. "How so?"

"I'm going to give you a massage."

"Nope." He made to turn around and leave, but she grabbed his hand, dragging him away from the door. And he let her. She was under no illusion that he couldn't have pulled free and left at any moment if he'd truly wanted to.

"No one's here. We have the whole place to ourselves, and I'll make sure you enjoy yourself. I promise."

"The spa's not really my thing."

"I know that." She went up on her tiptoes and gave him a kiss. "You trust me, right?"

"Of course."

"Okay then." She led him down the hall to the room she'd prepared. "You're going to strip down, climb up on that table, and cover yourself with the sheet. Or, you know, leave the sheet off if you prefer." She winked.

Mark stared at her, hands in his pockets, expression unreadable.

"I'm going to get ready." She turned and went to the back of the room. Normally, this was when she'd leave her client alone to get undressed. But this was Mark, and he didn't need privacy to undress. The question was, would he undress?

Sure enough, as she prepared her oils, she heard him shuffling around behind her and then the creak of the massage table as he climbed on.

Yes.

She rubbed the warmed massage oils into her hands and turned. Mark lay facedown on the table, the sheet thrown loosely over his lower half, hiding his bare ass from her view. She dimmed the lights and walked over to him. She could feel the tension vibrating off him before she'd even touched him. "Relax, Mark. You're going to enjoy this."

He made a noncommittal grunt.

She smiled as she touched her fingertips to his shoulders. Oh yeah, he was tense. She feathered her touch over his shoulder blades, gradually increasing the pressure as she located the knots of tension in his muscles.

He said nothing, made no sound at all as she worked, but after a few minutes massaging his neck and shoulders, he was feeling pretty relaxed, if his muscles were any indication. There was no faking the fact that the tension had leaked out of him. The knots in his muscles eased. His breathing grew slow and deep as Jess made her way down his back.

She took her time on his lumbar muscles, kneading deep into the soft tissue there, admiring his strength as she released his stress. She allowed her fingers to slide below the sheet, skimming over his ass as she headed for his quads.

Mark sucked in a breath. "You touch all your clients this way?"

"Only you," she whispered as she sank her fingers into his hamstrings. She worked her way down the backs of his legs.

Mark had lapsed back into silence, his breathing slow and deep, his muscles loose and relaxed.

"You can roll over now."

He moved slowly, turning over on the table. She handed him a pillow to put below his head and another to go below his knees. As he settled into position, the sheet still covering his hips, she broke into a huge grin. There was no hiding the tent in the sheet.

Mark was already fully aroused.

A warm ache settled between her thighs as she worked her way over his chest, moving ever closer toward the promised land. She massaged her way over his pecs and slid down his abs, allowing her fingers to skim over the sheet. He was rock hard beneath it.

She bent her head and traced her tongue over his length. His cock jerked beneath the sheet, surging harder still. Smiling, she tugged the sheet down, letting it fall to the floor.

The sight of Mark on her table, naked and hard as steel, was possibly the most erotic thing she'd ever seen. "I'm going to enjoy this so much," she whispered as she took him in her mouth.

He let out a groan, and his hands fisted in her hair.

She traced her tongue over the head of his cock and then sucked him in deep. Mark's hips rose up off the table, and she would have given anything to see the expression on his face right then. She sucked hard, sliding up and down his shaft, taking him all the way to the back of her throat. Her tongue pressed against the vein that ran below his cock, pulsing with his arousal. She kept going, sucking harder each time, reveling in the way his hips thrust against her, his breathing grew ragged, and his fingers clenched in her hair.

Yes. Yes. Yes.

He tensed beneath her. She took him all the way in and sucked, hard. His whole body jerked as he came in a hot, salty spurt. She stroked him with her tongue and swallowed, urging him on.

"Fuck." His hips jerked again, and he was still coming.

She sucked out every drop of his pleasure, finally releasing him after he'd collapsed in a limp heap on the table.

"Holy shit, Jess."

"Good?" she asked, kissing her way up his stomach and over his chest.

"Guess now I get the fuss about those happy ending massages." He smiled, hauling her up on the table beside him.

"I've never given one before," she admitted as she sprawled awkwardly across the top of him. These tables were definitely not made for two.

"Good." His arm tightened around her, so possessive and secure.

She pressed her cheek against his chest, feeling the steady beat of his heart as it gradually slowed from a gallop to a trot.

"Gotta say, I'm not sure I've ever been this relaxed," he said finally.

Indeed, as she traced her hands over him, his muscles felt like butter beneath her touch. If only the same could be said about her... That restless ache still throbbed inside her, and oh, she couldn't wait to get him in the hot tub.

His hand slid down her side and inside her pants. Now it was her turn to squirm.

"Christ, Jess. You're so wet," he rasped as he stroked her with his fingers.

"I enjoyed your happy ending massage almost as much as you did." Her hips moved in time with his fingers as the slow burn inside her burst into flames.

"Almost isn't good enough."

"No?" She gasped as the pad of his thumb scraped over her clit, sending a shockwave of sensation through her.

"No." And he made good on his word as his fingers stroked and plunged, driving her right over the edge.

She tensed as the orgasm ripped through her, rocking her with waves of blissful release.

"That's more like it," Mark said, his voice low and gruff.

"Yes," she whispered, breathless.

His cock pressed into her thigh, already semi-hard again. "Okay so the spa isn't all bad."

"Wait until you see what's next." She lifted her head to smile at him, and her heart melted at the expression on his face.

Fierce. Protective. Smoldering hot.

"There's more?" His smile was wicked.

"Much more."

* * *

Mark walked across a covered patio behind the spa, following Jess as she led him past a row of hot tubs. Privacy screens were set up on either side of the tubs, which would offer guests a private setting to soak while still enjoying uninterrupted views of the spa grounds beyond. Tonight, he didn't give a shit about privacy because he and Jess had the place to themselves. And after the way his massage had turned out, he was more than happy to indulge whatever she had planned for him next.

"You know what makes these hot tubs special, right?" she asked, glancing at him over her shoulder.

"You?" Because anything Jess created was special, as far as he was concerned.

She swatted at his arm with a smile. "The natural hot springs."

"Oh. Right." He had known that, and it was pretty cool that she'd been able to tap into the hot springs.

"They're full of all kinds of minerals and natural elements that help cleanse and heal your body." She kept walking once they'd reached the end of the patio, following a flagstone path that led toward a gazebo at the back of the spa's grounds.

He followed her, somewhat disappointed that they wouldn't be sharing one of the natural hot tubs together even though, an hour ago, he would have sworn on his life that he'd never voluntarily step foot inside a spa let alone want to soak in one of its tubs. Apparently, Jess could convince him to do just about anything.

They walked to the gazebo, which turned out to be some sort of seating area with robes, towels, a private changing area, and even a bathroom. On the far side of it, facing the forest beyond and hidden from view of the rest of the spa, was a natural rock formation. It was hard to make out in the dim light, but it seemed to form a sort of natural pool.

"This," Jess said, turning to face him, "is the Crown Jewel of my spa tubs."

"I'd say so." He stepped past her for a closer look. The stone was hollowed out, forming a natural pool that beckoned under the silvery light of the moon. "Was this already here?"

She nodded. "I improved on what nature had given us.

We enlarged the pool, smoothed it out, and carved some seating around the perimeter, but Mother Nature keeps it full. Ready to take a dip?"

"Yeah." He pulled her up against him for a lengthy kiss, helping her scramble out of her spa uniform. He wore only his jeans, which he'd hastily buttoned to follow her outside. She released them now, sliding them down his legs.

"Will this be your first time?" she asked with a playful wink.

"Huh?" He was distracted by the feel of her naked body against his.

"In a hot tub."

He nodded. He'd never been anywhere that had them, nor had he ever felt any inclination to sit in a tub full of swirling hot water. But right now? It sounded like heaven.

Jess led him over to the side of the rock, and together they climbed in. The water swirled up over him, hot and bubbly. It didn't have the chlorinated smell of pool water. This tub smelled fresh and clean like the mountain spring that fed it.

"What do you think?" Jess asked as she settled in beside him.

"I like it." The edge of the rock had a bench seat carved into it, and he sat.

She twisted her hair up on top of her head, tied it, and then sank down onto the seat next to him. The water reached her chin. She closed her eyes and leaned back, a blissful look on her face. A light from the gazebo area provided a faint glow over the rock tub, but not enough to illuminate their bodies beneath the black surface of the water.

Mark wished for daylight so that he could have seen

her better, but daylight meant the spa would be open to the public. So he'd take the darkness because it meant he got to have the spa, and Jess, all to himself.

"It's so peaceful," she whispered, her eyes still closed.

It really was. The water here didn't pound out of man-made jets. It swirled gently over him, steadily moving, leaving behind a misty spray on his face.

"I've been doing this a lot at night," she said softly. "Kind of a natural detox for whatever's going on inside me."

"That's a good idea." He wasn't as holistic as she was, but he believed in the healing power of nature, and the mineral water swirling around them couldn't be anything but good for her.

"Might be wishful thinking, but I always feel a little bit better after a long soak."

"How's the knee?" he asked.

"Still sore. I'll mention it to my doctor the next time I go in."

He tightened his arms around her, wishing more than anything that he could take it all away and make her better. Unfortunately, life didn't work that way.

She scooted closer, and her hand skimmed up his thigh. "I've always wanted to have sex in here."

"Is that allowed?" His dick surged from half-mast to full attention at the proximity of her hand.

"No." She laughed softly. "But I'm the owner, and I also happen to know the cleaning crew will be here later tonight to scrub all these tubs out thoroughly so, if there were ever a time to break the rules, it's right now."

He reached over and lifted her into his lap. She settled against him, her skin hot from the tub, her lips demanding as they met his. They kissed, touching and teasing as the tub swirled around them, steady and hot like the need pulsing in his veins.

"I can't seem to get enough of you," she whispered against his lips.

"That makes two of us." He thrust his tongue against hers. It wasn't enough. Never enough. He'd settled her sideways across his lap because of her knee, but their current position kept them from going any further.

Jess shifted, swinging one leg around to straddle him, bringing their bodies into alignment just right, but...

"Your knee," he said, because right now she was basically kneeling on stone, and that wouldn't do.

"It's fine." She pressed her hips against his cock, reminding him that it would take only one thrust to be inside her.

"Hang on. Let's find a position that's better for your knee." He tested the water around them. The center of the tub was too shallow for him to stand with her in his arms, but too deep for him to sit or kneel without submerging Jess.

"Mark," she whimpered.

"Don't worry, babe. I can be creative when I need to be."

"Then be creative now." She rocked her hips against his.

"Working on it." He spun them so that Jess was seated on the underwater ledge and knelt between her legs. Awkward, but fuck yeah, he could make this work. He reached behind her for his jeans, fishing out the condom he'd taken to carrying in his wallet.

"Hurry." She wiggled beneath him.

He sat back and rolled on the condom and then positioned himself against her. The feel of Jess's heat, combined with the heat of the tub...his dick was already pulsing so hard he could hardly hold himself back.

He filled her with one long, slow stroke. Jess moaned,

her body gripping him, urging him on. His feet slipped on the bottom of the tub, and then he was floating, anchored only by his dick, nestled balls-deep inside her. He placed his hands on the underwater ledge, one on either side of her. "This is me being creative," he said through gritted teeth as he hovered above her.

"You work well outside the box," she murmured, lifting her hips to take him even deeper.

Necessary trait in his line of work. He pumped his hips, thrusting inside her as the water buffered him, raising the temperature in his blood from hot to molten. Unable to find purchase against the smooth bottom of the pool, he balanced on his hands, kicking out with his feet with each thrust of his cock into her body.

He felt like some kind of aquatic superhero because each stroke felt so fucking good. Jess moaned beneath him, the look on her face letting him know she was as far gone as he was.

"No holding back," she whispered, wrapping her arms around him to draw him in closer.

Oh, he wasn't holding anything back. Not anymore. He moved inside her, as hard and fast as the water around them would allow. Jess had freed him of his constraints, let him see the beauty of losing control. Now that he knew what it felt like to let himself go inside her, he could never hold back.

He moved faster, deeper, harder, kissing her as the need inside him roared like a hungry beast, searing through his veins, burning deep inside him with a pleasure that bordered on pain. Jess gripped his ass, hauling him even deeper.

"Now, Mark, oh!" Her body clamped down on him as she came.

He kept moving, urging her on as he felt the tingling

at the base of his spine that signaled the start of his own orgasm.

"Yes," Jess panted as she writhed beneath him.

Release tore through him in a series of blazing hot waves. He ground himself against her as they both lost themselves in their pleasure, clinging to each other and moving frantically.

Finally, she flung her head back, a blissed-out expression on her face. "Every time, I think it can't possibly get better, and then it does."

"Yeah." He dropped his head to hers, panting for breath as his dick still pulsed inside her.

"Mark..." She tightened her arms around him. Tears streaked her cheeks.

He froze as fear dropped like a bucket of ice water over him. "What's wrong?"

"Nothing." She smiled through her tears. "Just the opposite, really. It's so good, it's almost *too* good. Does that make sense?"

"Yeah, it does." He felt it too. This thing between them had grown so big so fast; it was fucking terrifying when he stopped to think about it.

She looked straight into his eyes. "Promise me you won't run this time, Mark. Whatever happens between us, we'll face it together."

He braced himself above her, his dick still buried inside her, his heart bursting with all the emotions charging through him. "I promise."

"If something's going on in your life, whatever it is, you need to talk to me about it. That's what people do in relationships, Mark. I don't care what it is or how hard it is to talk about. You can't shut me out this time. Promise me you'll never do that to me again."

Is that what he'd done? He pulled out and flipped them, settling her back in his lap. "I never meant to make you feel that way, Jess."

Fresh tears streaked her cheeks. "I know you didn't. I know that."

"I'm sorry." He bent his head, inhaling the scent of her hair. She smelled like some kind of flowery shampoo and incense.

"Don't be sorry. You were a kid. *I* was a kid. But we're adults now, and I'm telling you, because I know you don't have a lot of experience with relationships. This...you and me...we're in a relationship now, Mark. And that means we're part of each other's lives. If something's going wrong between us, you need to let me know. Talk to me so we can try to work it out. And if we can't work it out, if it's time to call it quits, we talk about that too. Okay?"

He nodded as he wiped the tears from her cheeks. "I promise you, Jess."

"Good." She kissed him again. "Because you mean a lot to me, and this thing between us is more than just sex. You know that, right?"

"It was never just sex." He tightened his arms around her. "Not for me. You've always been so much more important to me than that."

"I'm not naïve. I know we're going to hit some bumps, maybe even huge bumps, but I don't want to hide our relationship anymore. I want to make you a full-time part of my life, which means reintroducing you to my family, for one thing."

"Okay."

"Nicole and Bren are totally on board with this, by the way. And my parents will come around too."

"If you say so." He couldn't blame them if they didn't. If he put himself in their shoes, he'd want to kick his own ass too.

"They will." She snuggled closer in his arms.

His heart thumped against his ribs. This was a big deal, a huge step in their relationship. It was what he'd wanted, what he'd always wanted. A second chance with Jess. He still wasn't sure he deserved it, and he was terrified he'd somehow manage to fuck it up anyway, but he was going to do his goddamn best not to.

CHAPTER NINETEEN

$\mathcal{I}$ have the results of your blood work. Please give my office a call at your earliest possible convenience."

Jessica replayed the message from her doctor as fear ping-ponged around inside her. Was that a routine message or did it mean they'd found something? She'd already called and left a message, but as she was booked solid with clients all day, she and her doctor had been playing phone tag.

Which left Jessica a nervous wreck. A headache grew behind her eyes, and her left knee was still swollen and sore, not to mention the fatigue that constantly pressed over her, slowly smothering her with its pressure.

By five o'clock, she was about to jump out of her skin as she dialed Dr. Rimmel's line again. This time, the receptionist put her on hold, and a moment later the doctor's voice came over the line.

"Glad I finally caught you," Dr. Rimmel said.

"Yes." Jessica blew out a breath as her heart pounded and sweat slicked her palms. "This feels like more than a call to let me know the blood work didn't turn up anything new."

"You're right," Dr. Rimmel said. "I ran a few extra tests on a hunch, and one of them came back positive. You have Lyme disease, Jessica."

"Lyme disease," she repeated, sagging back in her chair. "Is that...is that good news or bad news?"

"Well, it's hard to say. The good news is that we have a diagnosis, and we can begin treatment right away. I'll need you to come into the office to go over all the details, and we'll start you on a round of antibiotics to treat the infection. The bad news is that, as is often the case with Lyme disease because it's so hard to diagnose, yours has gone untreated for several months. The infection has likely spread throughout your system, which means it won't respond as well to treatment now as it would have if we'd begun antibiotics when you were first infected."

Jessica took a slow, deep breath and blew it out. "What does that mean?"

"It means I want to run a few more tests when I get you back in here, try and see what we're working with. Lyme disease is one of these Pandora's box conditions. It can cause a wide variety of problems. You might be completely cured after your first round of antibiotics, or you may struggle with your current symptoms and even new, more serious symptoms for months or even years to come."

And that didn't sound like good news to Jessica. Not at all.

* * *

"Lyme disease?" Mark pulled her into his arms and held her tight. Jess had showed up at Off-the-Grid a few minutes ago, her eyes wide and haunted.

She nodded against his chest. "I did a little research on my laptop after I got off the phone with my doctor, and I don't think I ever had the flu. I think that was the initial Lyme infection, which means I probably got bitten by a tick sometime in September, maybe even as far back as August. I never got a rash. You always think of the bull's-eye rash with Lyme disease, but I guess it's pretty common not to get the rash too. I didn't know."

This was what had been nagging at him in the back of his mind since he'd made the connection with her knee last week. "And your knee. That was joint pain from the Lyme disease?"

"Yes."

"God, Jess, I'm sorry." He held her tight as emotions battled inside him. Relief that she had a diagnosis, a real diagnosis, and fear that she still had a long road ahead of her. "Whatever happens, we'll face it together. I am right here with you, every step of the way."

"Thank you," she whispered.

They stood like that for a long time, holding on to each other as if their lives depended on it. He felt a surge of protectiveness so strong it almost swallowed him whole. He'd do anything for Jess, absolutely anything.

Finally, she pulled back and looked at him. "The antibiotics they're going to put me on are supposed to be pretty brutal, and I don't have any guarantee that I'll feel better once they're finished. I might be sick for a while. I might get even sicker than I am now."

What was she saying? "If you think any of that

changes the way I feel about you or the promises I made to you last night in that hot tub—"

"No, I know it doesn't. And thank you for that." She pressed her lips to his. "But the land...what if I'm in over my head taking on a spa expansion right now? Maybe I should just have you guys buy me out before things go any further."

He was already shaking his head before she'd even finished speaking. "No. Don't give up on your dreams because life's thrown you a curveball. We'll help you, Jess. Whatever you need. Ethan and I are good with our hands. We can help out, keep your construction costs down. And if you need us to cover mortgage payments for a few months until you're back on your feet, you can pay us back once your new spa's up and running."

"I can't ask you guys to do that," she said, wiping a tear from her cheek.

"Jess, we'd do it for any business partner, but especially you."

She pulled away, shaking her head. "I just don't know what to think right now."

"Which is why you shouldn't make any rash decisions. You've been managing the expansion on top of your illness just fine up until now."

"It's just...I watched my parents go into debt after a bad investment. They had to take out a second mortgage on the house and max out their credit cards to make ends meet. It took them years to dig their way back out of debt. I don't want that to happen to me."

"It won't." He drew her in and held her close. "You can do this. And if you need a helping hand, you can count on us to back you up."

* * *

Jessica chugged a glass of water laced with probiotics and then slumped back against the kitchen counter. She'd started treatment last week, and it was taking its toll. Now, on top of the aches, pains, and fatigue caused by the Lyme disease, she also felt nauseous from the antibiotics. And she was about to bring Mark over for Thanksgiving dinner at her parents' house.

Not quite "meet the parents," but it would be the first time he'd seen her parents since Jessica and Mark were teenagers. And they might not welcome him with open arms. Her mom had been lukewarm at best when Jessica filled her in about her relationship with Mark. Her dad hadn't had anything at all to say on the subject. He was a lot like Mark in some ways. They were both men of few words, both Army veterans.

Surely Mark could win him over, and her mother too. Her parents were reasonable people. Once they'd spent some time with him, they would see what Jessica saw: a good, honorable man who screwed up when he was a teenager but had more than made up for it since.

But what if they didn't?

There was a knock at the door. She put her empty glass in the sink and walked to answer it. Mark stood there in jeans and a blue Henley shirt, and if she didn't know better, she could swear he actually looked nervous. She pulled him in for a kiss. "Hey."

"Hey yourself." He wrapped his arms around her as he kissed her back.

"You ready for this?" she asked.

"I haven't been to a family dinner since…well, since the last time your parents had me over for dinner."

"That's a long time." It made her unspeakably sad that he hadn't sat around the dinner table with a family—any family—in over ten years. No wonder he had trouble sharing himself with her. He'd been on his own for so very long. She honestly couldn't even imagine what that was like.

The thought of going through life, especially all the crap she'd been through the last few months, without her family behind her, supporting her? It made her want to wrap her arms around Mark and never let him go.

"You ready?" he asked.

She walked to the kitchen for the apple pie she'd baked earlier and then grabbed her purse from the table beside the door.

"How are you feeling?" he asked as they walked to his SUV.

"Tired. Gross. Same old." She scrunched up her nose. She was as tired of feeling this way as she was of answering questions about how she felt.

"I read a few articles online. You know some people go years before they get diagnosed? Yours was only a few months. I think there's a good chance that you'll be feeling much better by the time you finish these antibiotics."

He'd researched Lyme disease online for her? She was so screwed where he was concerned. Yep, she was totally done for. "I hope so."

"And I still think you should get started on the spa expansion. We'll back you up if you need it, and if you *are* still feeling lousy for a while, don't you think it would be better to have this project to keep your mind off things? By the time the cabins are finished, you should be as good as new and ready to jump in full force."

"But Mark...I may not ever be as good as new," she said quietly. Because she'd done her research too, and there was a lot that doctors still didn't understand about treating and curing Lyme disease. Chronic Lyme disease was a thing, and it could affect people for the rest of their lives. There could be complications—serious complications—with her heart, her immune system...the possibilities were endless, and overwhelming.

"I know that." He reached over and took her hand. "And I'm here with you, no matter what."

"Thank you." She tried not to read too much into his words, but still, it made everything less scary having him at her side. "It feels good to have a diagnosis though. No more wondering. The not knowing was driving me crazy."

He smiled. "It was driving me crazy too."

He turned into her parents' driveway, pulling in behind Brennan's car.

Jessica sucked in a breath. Okay, even she was a little bit nervous about the evening ahead. "Let's do this."

He nodded as he shut off the engine and stepped out of the SUV. She picked up her pie and followed him out. He walked around the front to meet her, taking her hand in his as they walked toward the front door together.

Her mom pulled it open as they reached the front porch. "There you are! How are you feeling? Are the antibiotics making you sick? Let me get you inside and have a good look at you."

"Oh boy," she muttered under her breath.

Mark gave her hand a squeeze.

"I'm okay, Mom. Taking lots of probiotics like you suggested. It's not so bad."

"I know, it's just...I worry." Her mother gestured them inside. "Mark, it's good to see you again."

"You too, ma'am. Thank you for the invitation."

Her mother gave him a startled look. While Mark had always been polite, and especially in her parents' presence, he hadn't picked up the "ma'am" and "sir" habit until he joined the military. In high school, he'd called her parents Mr. and Mrs. Flynn.

"Please call me Paula," her mom told him.

"Yes, ma'am...Paula." Mark looked as uncomfortable as Jessica had ever seen him.

"Need any help in the kitchen?" she asked her mother.

"Always," her mom said with a laugh. "The turkey's almost finished roasting, but everything else is a work in progress. Nicole and I have got it under control for now. Why don't you and Mark go on into the living room for a bit? The guys are watching the game."

"Okay," Jessica agreed. She'd rather go help her mom and sister in the kitchen, but she needed to make Mark comfortable first. "It smells amazing in here."

"My favorite meal of the year," Paula said.

"Mine too," Jessica agreed, although she doubted she'd be able to eat much of it this year. Her stomach lurched at the thought.

Mark had gone noticeably silent, hanging back as she talked to her mother.

"Mark, there's beer in the fridge in the garage. Help yourself to whatever you'd like," Paula told him.

He nodded. "Thank you."

Jessica smiled as she took him through the kitchen—dropping off her pie and saying hello to Nicole as they passed—to the garage. She went up on her tiptoes to give him a quick kiss. "You okay?"

"It's weird having your mom offer me beer," he said, and she laughed.

"It's probably weird for her too, but tonight's all about introducing them to the adult version of you."

He grabbed a beer from the fridge, and she led the way into the living room, where her father, Brennan, Patrick, and Dennis sat watching football. "Dad, Bren, you remember Mark. Mark, this is Nicole's husband, Dennis, and Brennan's husband, Patrick."

They raised their hands in greeting. All of the younger men wore wide, friendly smiles. Her father simply tipped his head in acknowledgment of her introduction. Jessica's stomach tightened. Her dad had never approved of her dating Mark, and he'd been outraged by the way Mark dumped her when he enlisted. Could he find his way past it to accept Mark back into the family?

CHAPTER TWENTY

Mark chewed and swallowed the last bite of Thanksgiving turkey on his plate. He'd never paid so much attention to his manners in his damn life. Never tried so hard to make a good impression. Jess's family had seen him at his worst back in high school. Tonight they needed to see him at his best.

"Go ahead and have seconds if you'd like," Jess's mother told him, a warm twinkle in her eye. She'd spent most of the time before dinner grilling Jess about her health. Mark had tried to stay out of the conversation, but somehow she seemed to have warmed up to him anyway.

"Thank you. Everything is delicious." He scooped another helping of mashed potatoes onto his plate and then reached for the turkey.

"So unfair," Nicole said with an unconvincing scowl. "Guys can have seconds and never gain an ounce."

"Because we weigh more in the first place," Dennis commented, reaching for another dinner roll.

Mark glanced over at Jess. She'd been quiet during dinner and hadn't eaten much. He suspected the only reason she'd eaten as much as she had was to keep her mom off her back. Paula loved to fuss over her kids, and Jess hated to be fussed over.

That much hadn't changed since the last time he'd had dinner with the Flynns. He enjoyed watching their banter, but he never knew what to say to join in the conversation. He'd spent plenty of holidays with his Special Forces team, but sharing a table with a bunch of rowdy soldiers was nothing like this. So he did what he did best, sat back, and watched.

Patrick told them about his newest exhibit—he owned the art gallery in downtown Haven—while they finished up their meals. Afterward, they all carried their dishes into the kitchen, and Jess and Nicole hung around to help their mom clean up while the men headed back into the living room.

"Scotch?" Jack Flynn asked Mark, holding up a bottle.

Mark nodded. "Thank you, sir."

"Let's walk," Jess's dad suggested, handing Mark a glass.

Mark followed him onto the back patio. The night was cold and clear, the sky above filled with stars. The Flynns' house faced into the woods with a small grassy yard currently blanketed in fallen leaves. Mark remembered sneaking into the woods behind their house on more than one occasion to smoke a joint.

Standing here with her father now, he was ashamed of the man he'd been then.

"Jessica tells me you were in the Special Forces."

"Yes, sir. Eight years."

"Honorably discharged?" Jack rested his elbows on the railing, staring off into the darkness.

"Yes, sir."

"Gotta say, Mark, I didn't expect you to take me at my word that night." Jack kept his gaze straight ahead. That night had been the last time they'd seen each other, until tonight. Jack had lectured Mark within an inch of his life and then given him a scrap of paper with the address for the local recruiting office written on it, told him to enlist and come home a man.

"You didn't?" Mark took a drink of scotch, feeling the burn slide all the way to his stomach.

"Nah. Figured you'd toss that piece of paper in the trash and keep right on smoking pot in my backyard and running your future into the ground."

Mark flinched. "Thank you for what you did. You turned my life around."

Jack looked at him then, his brows knitted. "You're thanking me? I kicked your ass that night."

"It needed kicking, sir."

"It did." Jack barked out a laugh. "It sure as hell did. You were headed down a bad path, a path I didn't want my daughter to get dragged down with you."

"It's true," Mark agreed. Even at eighteen, he'd seen the truth of Jack's words, and he'd known what he had to do. And he'd never once regretted his decision.

"The thing is, I was trying to help you turn yourself around for Jess's sake, and then you went and dumped her anyway." Jack gave him a cutting look.

"I never wanted to hurt her, sir. I didn't see any other way." He still didn't.

"There's always a way, son. To be frank, I half expected

you two to try to elope before you shipped out. That's what Paula and I did."

Mark was silent. Elope with Jess? The thought had never crossed his mind.

"I was prepared to raise hell about it, mind. But you didn't even try." Jack looked out over the backyard. "So, in the end, I figured she was better off without you."

"You weren't wrong," Mark said, polishing off his scotch.

"I wasn't." Jack nodded. "Not then. But I can see that the Army turned you into an honorable man, and I can also see that you and my daughter are still crazy about each other. You have my blessing this time around, Mark."

Mark nodded. "Thank you, sir. That means a lot."

Jack's eyes narrowed. "Hurt her again and you'll wish you never met me. Clear?"

* * *

Jessica reached for her apple cider, wishing it were something alcoholic. This had been an exhausting Thanksgiving, and if she was feeling overwhelmed by it all, she could only imagine how Mark felt. After dinner at her parents' house, they'd come to Ryan and Emma's for dessert. Carly and Sam were here too, and while Jessica loved spending time with her friends during the holiday, the dynamic today was completely different.

This was the first time she and Mark had hung out with their friends as a couple. And to be perfectly honest, it was a little weird. This was a huge step forward in their relationship, no two ways about it. She leaned in to whisper in Mark's ear. "How are you holding up?"

He turned to give her an amused smile. "I'm good."

"Who's ready for more?" Emma asked, gesturing to the half-eaten desserts spread on the table in front of them. "Seriously, we have so much food left. Eat up, you guys."

Ryan reached for the pumpkin pie, cutting himself another slice.

"I'm stuffed," Jessica said. She'd had a small slice of apple pie at her parents' house and a small slice of Emma's pumpkin cheesecake, and already she felt sick to her stomach.

"You barely ate anything," Carly protested. "You haven't even had one of my pecan pie tarts yet, and you're the one who requested them." As she spoke, Sam slid two more tarts onto his plate with a sly smile.

Jessica frowned. "I'm sorry. Blame the antibiotics."

Beside her, Mark was loading up a plate with second helpings of pie, cheesecake, and one of Carly's tarts too. The man had a serious sweet tooth.

"I still can't believe it," Emma said. "Lyme disease?"

"I didn't think we even had to worry about Lyme disease here in North Carolina," Carly said.

"I didn't either," Jessica said. "It's less common here than other parts of the U.S., but apparently the rates are going up."

"That's scary," Emma said. "Especially considering how much time we all spend in the woods. And Jess, I'm just so sorry you're going through this. I had no idea you'd been so sick."

"I know. I just got tired of hearing myself complain about it." She leaned her head against Mark's shoulder. "Poor Mark had to endure all my griping."

"You never griped," he said, taking a big bite of pie.

"We hate that you're sick," Ryan said, "but I can't tell you how much I'm enjoying watching you and Mark be all snuggly together tonight."

"Snuggly?" Mark's expression was stony.

Emma giggled. "You guys are all kinds of sweet together, and we love it."

"But I wish you had told us you weren't feeling well before the Adrenaline Rush," Carly said. "I feel so bad about that."

"You shouldn't," Jessica said. "I had fun, and I'm glad I ran."

"Well, don't hesitate to lean on us for anything you need," Emma said. "Seriously, we're all here for you."

A murmur of agreement ran around the table.

Jessica pressed a hand to her chest. "I appreciate it, you guys. Really."

After everyone had stuffed themselves on dessert, the women drifted into the kitchen to chat while the men took beers with them into the living room to watch football. Some things were the same no matter whose house you visited.

"So"—Emma turned on her as soon as the men were out of earshot—"I know we only have half our girls' night group here tonight, but Carly and I are dying for an update."

Carly nodded, her eyes sparkling. "Did you unleash Mark's wild side?"

Jessica grinned. "As a matter of fact, I did."

Emma squealed. "Oh my God, we need details."

Jessica glanced toward the door to the living room, keeping her voice low. "Well, I had to torture the poor man in all kinds of sexy ways before he finally broke, but holy shit, you guys…" Warmth crept into her cheeks at the memory. "Once he cut loose, it was ah-mazing. Mark has set the new gold standard for best sex ever."

"Whoa." Carly's eyes were wide.

Emma was grinning like a fool. "I'm never going to be able to look at him with a straight face again."

Jessica pointed a finger at her. "Don't you dare repeat any of this to Ryan."

"I would never!" Emma exclaimed.

"Oh yeah? Well, you spilled the beans when I first told you Mark and I were sleeping together, and you promised then too."

Emma hung her head. "Okay, I did slip and tell Ryan you guys were hooking up, but I swear, I would never share details. For that matter, I'm pretty sure Ryan has *no* desire to know that much about Mark's sex life." She dissolved in giggles.

Even Jessica was smiling now. "Let's hope."

Carly waved her cell phone. "But I do think we need to tease Gabby and Mandy about what they missed."

Jessica rolled her eyes. "You ladies are terrible."

And she loved them so much.

* * *

The sound of women's laughter drifted into the living room. Ryan's eyebrows rose. "Ten bucks says they're talking about us right now."

"No doubt about it," Sam agreed.

Mark said nothing. Did women share that much with each other? He remembered how news of his relationship with Jess had gotten back to Ethan and Ryan through Gabby and Emma, and for some ridiculous reason, it got his hackles up all over again.

"Welcome to the club, man," Ryan said, tipping his beer in Mark's direction. "Now you too can wonder how many details have been shared about your sex life."

Mark choked on his beer.

"I think you're scaring him," Sam commented.

"Don't stress, bro," Ryan said. "Unless you have problems, you know, in the sack..."

Mark sent him a murderous look that had Ryan doubled over with laughter.

"Who would've thought though?" Ryan sobered. "If you'd told me last year this time that I'd be hosting Thanksgiving dinner today with my *wife*, I'd have laughed in your face. And here I am all domesticated. All of us are pretty damn domesticated these days."

"It's true," Sam agreed. "I never thought I'd settle down and get married, certainly never meant to end up living part-time out here in the Smoky Mountains."

"Never thought I'd have friggin' Sam Weiss in my living room," Ryan said with a wide smile.

"It's been good for me though," Sam said. "It balances out the insanity of Hollywood quite nicely. In fact, lately I've been spending more time here and less time there."

A prickling sensation crawled across Mark's skin. He wasn't domesticated, far from it. This thing between him and Jess...it was intense and overwhelming. Half the time, it scared the shit out of him. Maybe it was the combination of Thanksgiving dinner with her family and dessert here with their friends, but right now he felt like he was suffocating.

He needed to be alone, needed space, needed fresh air.

Jess came through the doorway from the kitchen, and her eyes locked on his. She smiled, and it was like the sun coming out from behind a cloud. His chest loosened, and he drew a deep breath.

"You ready to get going?" she asked.

He nodded, standing.

They said their good-byes and headed out into the night. He wrapped an arm around her shoulders as they walked to his SUV. He could have asked her to come up-stairs with him to his condo, but he didn't. He needed to take her home. Tonight, he needed to be alone.

CHAPTER TWENTY-ONE

The last week of November passed in a fog. Jessica kept her head down, immersed in work at the spa, too tired and too sick to think of much else. Despite her better judgment, she'd gone ahead with the expansion, and construction was in full swing in the woods behind the spa.

December brought with it a new chill in the air and Christmas music on the breeze. Fall had always been her favorite season, but she couldn't help a sense of excitement over the upcoming holidays too. She had only days left on her antibiotic treatment, and maybe she was just being optimistic but she could swear she was feeling a little bit better.

She already had a girls' night out planned for next week once she could drink again. In the meantime, she finished up with her last client and headed home for a shower and a hot cup of tea. Today was Mark's birthday, and since he'd confessed a few days ago that he couldn't remember the last time he'd celebrated, she felt compelled to change that for him this year, especially with this being a milestone birthday for him. She wanted to give him the kind of perfect birthday he hadn't had in way too long, if ever.

Rather than throw him an elaborate surprise party—which she knew he'd hate—instead she'd rallied the group for dinner at Rowdy's. And afterward, she would have Mark all to herself for a little private celebration. Simple, but meaningful.

The hot shower and tea revitalized her. She swallowed her next antibiotic pill and went into the bedroom to get ready. Mark was going to have to wait to open his present until they were alone because he'd have to undress her to get to it. She'd bought a skimpy red lingerie set, and she couldn't wait to see the look on his face when he discovered it.

She slipped into a pair of dark-wash skinny jeans, a slinky red top, and black leather boots. And just for fun, she even jazzed up her makeup for tonight, accenting her eyes with a smoky eye shadow that shimmered and going for the red lipstick that she seldom wore. She'd just finished when she heard Mark knocking at the door. She gave herself a quick spritz of perfume and hurried to let him in.

"Happy birthday," she said as she pulled open the door.

Mark's gaze went from wide-eyed to smoldery as it traveled the length of her body. "Thanks," he said finally. "You look…" He crushed her against him, finishing the thought with a kiss that heated her up until she'd melted in his arms.

"Is that a good thing?" she asked, breathless and teasing.

"Change of plans." He kicked the door shut behind them. "We're staying in tonight."

"No way." She smiled against his lips. "Not after how long I spent getting ready, and besides, all our friends are waiting at Rowdy's to celebrate with you."

"Don't care." He hauled her up against him, letting her feel how hard he already was for her.

"I'll make it up to you later," she whispered. "Repeatedly."

"I don't know what I ever did to deserve you," he said, his voice all low and gruff.

Her heart thumped painfully against her ribs. "Just be yourself, Mark. That's more than enough." She wanted so badly to tell him she loved him, but she didn't want to say the words too soon and freak him out. He'd been on his own for a long, long time, and while he seemed to be settling comfortably into their relationship, she still caught him sometimes pulling back. He still spent entire days on his own, prowling around in the woods and shutting out the rest of the world.

She didn't mind. She didn't want to change a single thing about him, but she couldn't help thinking that, if she rushed their relationship too quickly, he might take off like a startled deer and run for the hills, never looking back.

"Sure I can't convince you to stay in?" He slid his hands inside her blouse, encountering the lacy surprise she was hiding. "Fuck. *Me.*"

She grabbed his hands before they could explore any further. "No peeking. You can unwrap your present when we get home."

"You're my present?" The expression on his face was tortured. "You can't do that to me, Jess. You've got to at least let me have a peek."

"Nope." She grabbed her purse and led the way to the front door, turning to wink at him over her shoulder. "I'm going to let you fantasize about it until we get back here later tonight."

* * *

Mark leaned back in his chair, stuffed full of beer and wings, happier and more content than he could remember feeling...pretty much ever. And he had Jess to thank. All of these guys really, but even after he'd started working with Ethan and Ryan, he'd still felt empty and restless until Jess came back into his life. He still got twitchy from time to time—probably always would—but the more time he spent with Jess, the more right it felt.

She squeezed his hand under the table, looking so god-damn gorgeous it was all he could do not to haul her into his lap and kiss her senseless right here in the middle of the restaurant.

"So this is the big one for you, huh, old man?" Ryan tipped his beer in Mark's direction.

"Who are you calling old?" Mark asked. He was the youngest of the three of them, and they all knew it.

"You walked right into that one," Emma agreed with a grin, ribbing her husband.

"I'm loving my thirties so far," Ryan said, slinging an arm around Emma's shoulders. "Never been happier."

"Same," Ethan said, leaning in to give Gabby a kiss.

Trent—Ryan's teenage brother—made a gagging sound from the end of the table. "Don't kid yourselves, you guys are *all* old."

This sent the entire table into a round of laughter.

"Thirty's no big deal," Mark said, shrugging. Truthfully,

he'd never been all that hung up about age, and while thirty did seem like a milestone, he didn't mind it.

"Here, here." Ethan lifted his beer mug in the air for a toast.

"I don't know." Jess gave him a teasing look. "I'm glad I have a few years before I cross over to the dark side."

"Ooh." Ryan laughed, elbowing Mark in the ribs. "Your girlfriend's feisty tonight."

Mark glared at him. "You're just pissy because you're the oldest. Wait until we're back here in a few years, cheering for you when you turn forty."

Ryan jeered at him good-naturedly. "Yo, we've got nine years before that celebration, and who knows how many kids will be at the table by then? Can't fuckin' wait."

"Me either," Emma said, giving her husband a kiss.

It was strange to think about. Mark had once been so sure he'd stay in the Army until they shipped him home in a flag-draped coffin. But now...well, the thought of sitting around the table with these guys and their kids in nine years sounded pretty damn okay.

Even better if Jess was still beside him.

They kept talking long after the table had been cleared, laughing and joking and reminiscing about their adolescent misadventures. Hell of a thing, having all these people around who'd known him since he was a kid. Felt an awful lot like what he imagined family might be like.

Jess bent over to reach for something in her purse, revealing a flash of red lace beneath her top that set Mark's blood on fire. He'd copped a feel of that lace earlier, and whatever she was wearing under her jeans tonight was killing him in the best possible way. He could hardly wait to get his hands on her later. He was going to get to know every inch of that lace in intimate detail...

"How's construction coming?" Emma asked Jess.

"They're starting to look like cabins," she said, a sparkle coming into her eyes. "It's coming along really well."

"Well, you can reserve the best one for us sometime next fall when we're ready for our first night away from the baby." Emma rubbed a hand over her belly affectionately.

"Oh yeah?" Ryan gave her an amused smile. "And who's going to watch her for us while we spend the night in a spa cabin?"

"Me," Gabby said, practically bouncing in her chair.

"Say what now?" Ethan raised his eyebrows.

"I volunteered us to watch Lily while they take a night off," Gabby told him.

"Uh." Ethan looked slightly horrified at the thought.

Mark laughed under his breath at the look on his buddy's face.

"So, the baby fever has hit, huh?" Jess winked at Gabby.

Gabby blushed. "Maybe a little."

Baby fever? Mark had never heard the term before, but he thought he could guess what it meant. Was this something women talked about? Getting married and then lusting after babies? Did Jess want that too?

He glanced at her. She was whispering something in Gabby's ear, and they were both giggling. Marriage. Babies. They weren't things Mark had ever thought about. Not things he'd wanted or imagined for himself.

But he wanted Jess, wanted her more than anything in the world, and the idea of his ring on her finger or their baby in her arms didn't exactly send him into a cold sweat. In fact, it felt like something he might want...someday.

He lifted his beer and took a long drink. This milestone birthday must be going to his head.

"You're quiet tonight," Jess murmured in his ear. "Still thinking about your present?"

Hell. He'd actually forgotten about it for a few minutes with all the talk of babies, but now... "Yes."

"I think I'm ready to be unwrapped."

He stood, his chair scraping loudly over the tile floors as everyone at the table turned to look at him. "Ah, we're heading out."

Jess watched him with an amused smirk on her face. Emma leaned across the table to whisper something in her ear, and Jess nodded, still smiling. Fuck it. He didn't even care if they were gossiping about his sex life.

He just needed to get Jess home and in his bed. Now.

She stood, grabbed her purse, and followed him out. "Gee, in a bit of a hurry, are we?"

"Yes." He grabbed her hand and strode down the street toward where they'd parked.

"You do realize they're going to tease you about this for, well... forever." She still looked amused... and aroused.

"Don't care." He pushed her up against the side of the SUV and kissed her, seizing the opportunity to explore the lacy thing beneath her clothes a little more intimately. It was delicate and soft and feminine. "I love my present so damn much."

Jess blinked up at him from those big, brown eyes.

She'd told him *she* was his present.

And he hadn't meant to say...

Or had he? Hell, he didn't even know. He bent his head and kissed her again, until they were both panting, his dick straining against the front of his jeans.

"We should go home now," she whispered.

"That's a definite." He unwound himself from her reluctantly, giving her one last kiss before he unlocked the SUV and climbed inside.

Jess climbed into the passenger seat, her hair mussed, lips swollen from his kisses. Absolutely gorgeous.

"My place or yours?" he asked.

"Mine. I have dessert for you." She grinned, and he didn't even care if she meant that literally or not. "Should we stop at your place on the way and get Bear?"

"Maybe Trent can keep her tonight." He pulled onto Main Street, hell-bent on getting her home and naked as quickly as possible.

"That's silly," Jess said. "We're right here. Go get her."

Mark gave her a look.

She rolled her eyes. "You can lock her out of the bedroom if you want."

"Fine." He swung a left and pulled into his spot in front of the condo building. Leaving Jess in the car, he jogged up the stairs to retrieve Bear, who was overjoyed at the prospect. "Any attempt at cock-blocking tonight and it'll be the last time you sleep over at Jess's. Got it?"

Bear wagged her tail, jogging down the steps beside him.

"Hey, Bear." Jess turned in her seat to greet the dog after he'd loaded her into the car. "Have you seriously not bought her a collar and leash yet?"

"Been meaning to." He pulled back onto Main Street, headed for Jess's house.

"She'd follow you anywhere." Jess was still turned sideways in her seat, kissing and petting Bear.

And damned if he wasn't jealous. Of his dog. He shook his head at himself. Absolutely ridiculous. Ten minutes later, he pulled into Jess's driveway. He hustled her toward the front door as Bear trotted along beside them.

"She's staying in the living room for now," he said as he stepped Jess backward into her bedroom and closed the door behind them.

"Fair enough." She went up on her tiptoes, wrapping her arms around his neck. "Happy birthday."

He kissed her, slow and deep and thorough. And this time, when he reached for her top, she made no move to stop him. He lifted it over her head, revealing the red bra beneath. Or at least he supposed it was a bra, but this was more like a scrap of red lace, and it was connected to her panties, or whatever else she wore beneath those jeans, and it was sexy as fuck.

He palmed her breasts, skimming his thumbs over the pink buds of her nipples. They beaded beneath his touch, pressing into that red lace. He drew her in against him as he slid his hands inside her jeans, exploring what lay beneath.

More lace. And not much of it.

"You approve?" she asked, breathless.

"Hell yes." He unbuttoned her jeans, and she kicked them off, baring the lace in its entirety.

"Your turn," she whispered, helping him out of his clothes.

Then he was naked, and Jess was in nothing but red lace, and he couldn't keep his hands off her. They kissed while he touched every inch of that lace, paying special attention to the narrow strip between her legs where she burned so hot for him. He pushed it aside, stroking her with his fingers.

Jess gasped. "No...wait. You first on your birthday."

"Baby, I'll enjoy it even more if I get to watch you come first." He thrust two fingers inside her, letting her pleasure fuel his as she panted in his arms.

"If you insist," she whispered, her eyes shut, hips still moving against his hand.

"I do." He kissed her, drinking her in while he stroked her toward her release. She was so fucking spectacular. He allowed the lace of her lingerie to scrape over the sensitive head of his dick, driving him out of his mind with pleasure. He thrust in rhythm with his fingers, harder, faster.

Her hips rocked against his, fueling his need as he pumped his fingers inside her. Jess was mumbling incoherently, her eyes closed, cheeks flushed. He pressed his thumb against her clit, letting her ride him right over the edge, and boy, did she.

She bucked against him, and he held her tight, completely lost to her pleasure.

"Wow," she panted, resting her head on his shoulder. She stayed like that for several seconds while he held her. Then she lifted her head. "Now it's your turn, Birthday Boy."

She pushed him back onto the bed, looking like a goddess above him in that red lace. A harsh groan escaped him as she kissed her way down his chest, stopping just short of his aching cock. He held his breath.

And then she took him in her mouth.

CHAPTER TWENTY-TWO

Jessica lay sprawled in bed with Mark, boneless and completely blissed out. He had definitely enjoyed her lacy lingerie, and once he'd finally taken her out of it, they'd had even more fun. Now they lay together, arms and legs entwined, the sheet tangled around them. "Ready for dessert?" she asked.

He cracked open an eye and peeked up at her. "That wasn't dessert?"

She shook her head. "I got you a cake."

"Yeah?"

She nodded. When was the last time he'd had cake on his birthday? "Chocolate."

He grinned. "My favorite."

"Want to eat it in bed?"

"Hell yes, I do." He lay back, all naked and satisfied and so masculine she was practically drooling at the sight.

"Don't move a muscle." She slipped his shirt over her head, breathing in his scent as she left the bedroom and walked to the kitchen. Bear hopped off the couch and came trotting over, tail wagging. "Sorry we've been ignoring you," she told the dog. "I'll convince him to let you in later, okay?"

With Bear at her heels, she walked to the pantry and pulled out a serving tray. She set the cake on it, along with two small plates, forks, and a serving knife. Balancing it all on the tray, she headed back toward the bedroom.

Mark climbed out of bed to shut the door behind her, leaving Bear in the hallway. The dog whined.

"Aww, she's lonely," Jessica said.

"She'll survive." He looked down at the cake on the platter. "All that for us?"

"Just us. Go nuts." She grinned as she set the platter down on the end of the bed.

Mark sat beside her. He picked up the serving knife and cut two enormous wedges of cake, putting one on each plate. He handed one to her and leaned back in bed with the other plate in his hand. "Looks good."

"It's from the bakery." She eyed the huge piece of cake on her plate.

Mark took a big bite. "Oh yeah. It's good."

She scooted over next to him and took a bite of her own. Flavor exploded on her tongue, rich and chocolaty. "Yum."

True to his word, Mark devoured his slice and went in for seconds. She picked at her slice, but she still didn't have much of an appetite and honestly chocolate cake had never been her thing. She much preferred apple pie, but it was more than worth it to see Mark enjoying his cake so much.

"Not hungry?" he asked as she set her plate aside.

She shook her head. "Only a few days left on the antibiotics."

"You've lost weight." His gaze dropped to her hips.

She tugged self-consciously at his oversized shirt that she wore, nodding.

"You know I like you the same no matter how you look," Mark said, "but I kind of miss your curves."

A smile tugged at her lips. "Then you'd better feed me lots of cake once I finish these antibiotics."

"That is a definite 'can do.'" He leaned in to kiss her, still sitting there gloriously naked in the bed, holding a plate of half-eaten cake.

"You look really hot right now," she murmured against his lips.

"That so?" He set his plate aside and tugged her into his lap. He kissed her again, slow and deep, as rich and decadent as the chocolate cake he'd just finished. They kissed, touching and groping until her body was burning up with need.

When Mark pushed inside her, he made love to her with the newfound freedom she'd unleashed in him. No more holding back. He took her completely—wild and passionate and intense. Afterward, they lay together, holding on to each other and panting for breath.

"Thank you," Mark said in that low, gruff tone he used right after sex. "I don't have a lot of experience with birthday celebrations, but I can't imagine anything topping this one."

Oh, Mark. She had it so bad for this man. "I hope this is the first of many great ones for you." And she hoped she would be there with him to celebrate every single one of them.

* * *

Mark woke to the sound of his cell phone ringing, momentarily disoriented until the swirling purple light from Jess's lava lamp reminded him where he was. And the absolutely fucking amazing birthday she'd given him.

He squinted at the screen on his cell phone. Why was Ethan calling him at four o'clock in the morning? A prickle of unease ran between his shoulder blades. He grabbed the phone and headed for the hall so he wouldn't disturb Jess, connecting the call as he pulled the door shut behind him.

"Off-the-Grid's on fire," Ethan said.

"What?" Mark straightened, instantly awake and alert.

"The fire department just called. The building is on fire." Ethan paused, his voice taut and rough. "I don't know how bad yet. I'm on my way there now."

"I'll meet you there." Mark turned and went back into the bedroom, reaching for his jeans where they lay on the floor.

"Who was that?" Jess asked sleepily from the bed. "Everything okay?"

"There's a fire at Off-the-Grid."

She sat up, the sheet clutched against her chest. "Oh my God! What? How?"

"I don't know. I'm heading over to meet Ethan and Ryan." He finished dressing and sat on the edge of the bed to put on his shoes.

"I'm coming with you."

"Stay in bed." He leaned back to give her a kiss. "If too many of us are there, we'll only get in the fire department's way. I'll call."

She looked uncertain. "Okay. Let me know if there's anything I can do."

"I will." He gave her another kiss and headed for the door.

Fifteen minutes later, he pulled up to Off-the-Grid. Couldn't miss it tonight. The street was completely blocked with emergency vehicles, illuminating the night with red flashing lights. He pulled over behind Ethan's Jeep on the side of the road. Up ahead, he could see Ethan and Ryan standing behind the nearest fire truck.

He strode toward them.

"Looks like an electrical fire," Ethan said when he reached them. "It's mostly out now."

Mark looked at the little white house that served as their office building, dwarfed now by the fire trucks surrounding it. Smoke rose from the rear of the building, but no flames were visible. "How much damage?"

Ryan was shaking his head. "Too soon to say. I'll get on the phone with our insurance company as soon as they open to get a claim started."

"Bad fucking news either way," Ethan said, staring at the house.

Mark knew it was true. They'd only been in business a year, had just started turning a profit. And now, with the added expense of the mortgage on the new land, this was the worst time for something like this to happen.

* * *

Jessica tossed and turned in bed. What was going on at Off-the-Grid? How bad was the fire? Should she go after Mark even though he'd told her to stay here? She rubbed Bear's furry ears. The dog had jumped up in bed with her as soon as he'd left and now lay sprawled across his side of the bed, her head on his pillow, snoring loudly.

Giving up on sleep, Jessica went into the kitchen and fixed herself a cup of tea. Why hadn't he called yet? Did that mean the fire was still burning?

Finally, just past six o'clock, her cell phone rang.

"What's going on?" she asked Mark.

"Fire's out. Looks like it was an electrical fire. We're waiting to be cleared to walk through the building with the fire marshal."

"How bad is it?" she asked, clutching the phone to her ear.

"The house is still standing. Beyond that I don't know yet."

"Well, that's good news, I guess. Is there anything I can do?"

"There's not really. We're just standing around out here. After we walk through the building, we're going to head over to the condos to make phone calls, reschedule today's appointments, insurance, all that stuff."

The knot in her stomach loosened. This fire was bad news for them, certainly, but it wasn't disastrous. The building was still standing. No one had been hurt. All their classes were conducted outdoors so they'd only lost their office space. "I'm so glad it wasn't worse."

"Me, too." Mark sounded tired. "What time are you working today?"

"Nine to closing." She was booked solid today. And while she would shift her schedule around in a heartbeat to help Mark and the guys if they needed her, it would really hurt to do it. She'd already taken so much sick time in the last few months.

"Could you do me a favor and drop Bear at my place on your way in?"

"Sure. Or she can stay here. I don't mind." Jessica rubbed the dog behind her ears.

"I know, but you're going to be gone all day, and I'll wind up at my condo by midmorning. But if you're running late or anything, don't worry about it. She'll be fine."

Jessica laughed softly. "I've been up for hours already, Mark, I've got plenty of time to drop her off before work, and you're right. She'll be much happier with you than here all day by herself."

"Trent has a spare key. Just knock on your way up."

"Will do. Keep me posted."

After she'd hung up the phone, she went down the hall to shower and get ready for her day. An hour later, dressed in her spa uniform and with Bear in tow, she stepped outside. The early December air slapped her in the face, shocking away the last of her fatigue.

She'd let Bear outside earlier to do her doggy business so now she led the way straight toward her car. The dog walked beside her for a few steps and then trotted off across the yard and into the woods behind the house.

Dammit. Why hadn't Mark ever gotten her a leash and collar?

"Bear, come back here, girl," Jessica called, keeping her voice light and friendly.

No response.

She walked to the tree line, looking around for any sign of the dog. "Bear!"

Nothing.

"Bear? Come here, girl. Where are you?" She walked into the woods, grateful that the leaves were off the trees now, making it easier to look for Bear.

The dog trotted into view a few yards away, tail wagging. She watched as Jessica walked toward her and then took off, running farther into the woods.

Jessica huffed a breath. "Bear!"

She was not going to lose Mark's dog this morning. Nope. Wasn't going to happen. She zigzagged through the woods behind her house, looking in vain for the dog. She was just formulating her next plan of action when Bear came trotting toward her, still wagging her tail. "You're a real diva when Mark's not around, aren't you?"

The dog fell into step beside her, walking back toward the house.

"Okay, let's get you home." Jessica walked to her car and opened the back door, motioning for Bear to hop up.

Bear gave her a look, wagged her tail, and then ran across the street and disappeared into the woods on the other side.

"You know, I think I'm starting to get an idea of how you wound up all alone in the woods in the first place!" Jessica called after her, exasperated.

What should she do? She knew absolutely nothing about dogs or how to catch one who had decided to play hard to get. Thinking on her feet, she raided the lunch she'd packed for herself, pulling a slice of roast beef out of her sandwich. And dammit, she needed a leash. She poked around in her shed until she found a short length of rope, which she coiled and stuffed into the pocket of her jacket.

Sorry, Bear, but a girl's gotta do what a girl's gotta do.

Holding the roast beef out in front of herself, she crossed the street and stepped into the woods on the other side. "Bear! Come here, girl. I've got roast beef. I've seen you share a sandwich with Mark. I know you love meat. Come and get it."

She walked along, waving the meat like a lure in front of her, looking everywhere for Bear. Where was she? Oh

God, what if she'd actually lost Mark's dog? On the same morning his business burned down. This was a nightmare!

"Come on, Bear. Come and get this yummy roast beef!"

Bear materialized out of the woods beside her, tail still wagging as she eyed the tasty treat in Jessica's hand.

Relief flooded through Jessica's system. "Oh, thank goodness. Come here, you." She waited until the dog had leaned in to snatch the meat out of her hand before she whipped the rope out of her pocket and looped it around her neck.

Bear drew back, startled.

"Sorry, girl. Just making sure you don't run off on me again." She tied a slip knot in the rope, just tight enough to keep it from coming over her head. Once the rope was in place, she fed her the piece of roast beef, which the dog gobbled down hungrily. "Okay then. Let's get you home before you cause any more trouble."

She led the way back across the street, and Bear followed obediently now that her freedom had been revoked. "I'm buying you a real collar and leash later today, just so you know," she told the dog as she loaded her into the car.

Bear panted from the backseat, looking as innocent as could be with those big, fluffy ears and wide brown eyes.

"Good thing you're so cute." Jessica started the car and headed for downtown. She wanted to get Bear dropped off quickly so that she might have time to stop by Off-the-Grid on her way to the spa and at least get a look for herself at how bad the damage was. She parked in Mark's spot in front of the condo building and climbed the stairs to the second floor with Bear at her side. She knocked on Trent's door.

He opened it a minute later, his black hair disheveled

like he'd just rolled out of bed. "Oh, hey. Here you go." He held out a silver key.

"Thanks, Trent."

The teen glanced down at Bear, still wearing her makeshift leash, and grinned. "She run off on you too?"

"Yes! She did it to you too?" Jessica couldn't help laughing.

Trent nodded. "She doesn't listen for shit when Mark's not around."

"No, she doesn't. Well, I'm going to buy her a leash. Thanks for the key." She waved at Trent and then continued up the stairs to Mark's third-floor condo. Her right knee was protesting by the time she'd reached the top, which sucked. She'd hoped her symptoms would all go away by the time she finished her antibiotics, even though the doctor had warned her they might not.

She pushed the key into the lock and let herself and Bear inside Mark's condo. Once the door was closed behind her, she knelt and slipped the rope off her head. "All right, girl. You're on your own until Mark gets home."

Bear walked over to the dog bed in the corner, pawing at something lodged beneath it.

"Did you lose a ball under there?" Jessica walked over and lifted the edge of the bed.

Bear grabbed a chewed-up wad of paper from underneath, heading toward the kitchen with it in her mouth.

"And here I thought you always behaved. Now you're chewing up Mark's stuff too?" Jessica followed Bear and pulled the paper out of her mouth. It was crumpled into a tight ball, slobbery and covered with chew marks. Jessica laid it on the kitchen counter, smoothing it out beneath her fingers. It was a note, addressed to Mark, smudged and tattered now thanks to Bear. And Jessica really didn't mean to snoop through his mail, but she didn't look away fast enough, and then she couldn't look away if she'd tried.

Mark,

I'm so sorry. I made a terrible mistake coming here. I thought I could fix things, but it was too late. I'm moving on. If there's ever anything I can do for you, please call.

                                              Mom

A phone number was written below. Jessica drew back, a sick feeling roiling in her stomach. *Mom.* But that wasn't possible...

Mark's parents died in a car crash when he was six. He'd shown her that photo in his wallet, the one of him with his mom and dad. He'd told her...

Oh God.

Was it a lie? No. No way. There had to be some other explanation.

Her head was spinning. Clutching the tattered note in her hand, she slid down to the floor and reached for her cell phone. She started to call Mark, but instead her fingers tapped in the number written on the paper.

It rang twice, and then a woman answered, sounding groggy. "Hello?"

"Hi, um, sorry to bother you. Who am I speaking to?"

"I'm Sharlene Willis. Who are you?" she said, her tone abrupt.

Jessica stiffened. "This is Jessica Flynn. I'm Mark Dalton's girlfriend. I found your note." She sucked in a breath, her heart pounding so hard she could feel it rattling her bones. *Deny it, Sharlene... tell me it isn't true...*

There was a pause. "I...I didn't know he had a girl-friend. Is everything okay?"

"He's fine," Jessica croaked. She swallowed over the pain in her throat. "I, um...you're his mother?"

Sharlene laughed, but it sounded tired and sad. "He didn't tell you, did he? Guess I can't blame him. I fucked up big time where he's concerned."

Jessica couldn't speak. Everything was spinning out of control. She was on the phone with Mark's mother. His *mother*. It wasn't possible. How could he have kept this from her? She choked back a sob as two tears splashed over her cheeks.

After a lengthy pause, Sharlene cleared her throat. "Well, I guess you two have some things to talk about. Sorry for my part in it. Hope you can work it out."

There was a click, and she was gone.

Jessica stared at the phone in her hands. Mark had been lying to her since they'd first met back in high school. How? Why? Sharlene had been here in Haven, re-cently enough for Bear to chew up her note.

Had his mother been here in Haven after he and Jessica were already back together?

A sob broke free. She thought he had finally opened himself up to her, that he'd finally trusted her with all his secrets. That night in the hot tub...he'd *promised*.

But as it turned out, he'd been keeping secrets all along.

CHAPTER TWENTY-THREE

Jessica fumbled through her work day in a daze. Why had Mark lied to her? What had really happened to his parents? Was his dad alive too? Her heart still broke for him because, whatever had happened, his mom was alive but not part of his life. He'd grown up in foster care, for all intents and purposes an orphan. She'd known him long enough to know that much was true.

She desperately needed to talk to him, needed to hear his side of the story. Because he'd told everyone in his life that his parents died in a car crash, not just Jessica, and he must have had a good reason for it. But she was having an awfully hard time with the fact that his mom had been here in Haven this fall because, despite all the intimate conversations he and Jessica had shared, he'd never mentioned a word about his mother to her.

And that felt an awful lot like the way he'd treated her in high school, holding her at arm's length and keeping secrets. Maybe he couldn't help it, growing up the way he did, but she couldn't plan a future with him if he couldn't trust her with his past. They needed to talk after she got off work. It would probably be the most important conversation they'd ever had. And right now, she could hardly breathe past the lump in her throat.

By eight o'clock, she was the last person left at the spa. She sat in her office and stared at the three missed calls from Mark on her phone. They couldn't do this over the phone. His condo was on her way home from work so she'd go straight there and hope to catch him. And God, she hoped he had a good explanation for this. Her heart was so heavy she could barely stand. Sucking in a shaky breath, she headed for the front door. She was so tired, so numb, so *hurt*. And desperate to get to Mark's condo to see him.

Instead, she found him waiting at the front door of the spa, a smile on his face. "Good news," he said as she pulled the door open. "The fire damage was minimal. Water damage from all the fire hoses is worse. Our computers are toast, but we should be able to have a makeshift reception desk in place by next week."

"That is good news." She tried to smile, but her face just wouldn't cooperate.

Mark's smile faded. "What's wrong?" He stepped forward, arms extended, but she backed away.

"I, um... I found the note from your mother." She held her breath, hoping against hope that he'd have some kind of rational explanation for the whole thing.

He dropped his hands to his sides, his expression gone totally blank.

"I called her," she whispered.

"What?" He'd gone into military mode, his eyes dark and unreadable.

"I talked to her on the phone." She hugged herself to keep from falling apart. "Mark, why did you tell me your parents died in a car crash?"

"Easier that way," he said.

"How? Talk to me. Please."

Mark shrugged, but there was nothing casual about the gesture. The tension rolling off him was so thick it enveloped her too, sending a shiver across her skin. Why had it been easier for him to tell the world his parents died? What could be worse than that? Heart in her throat, she flung her arms around him.

He didn't hug her back.

"Dammit, Mark, I'm so sorry. Whatever happened, it's awful and you didn't deserve it."

He stepped out of her embrace. "Doesn't matter. It's ancient history."

"Of course it matters," she said. "You grew up in foster care. That shaped your whole life."

"And there's no changing it now."

"But your mom was here in Haven this fall. You saw her. You talked to her. That matters. That's huge. Why didn't you tell me?"

A muscle ticked in his cheek.

"Say something," she whispered.

But he didn't. He just stood there, still and silent as a statue.

"Help me understand. Please talk to me." *Please let me in this time.* She swiped a tear from her cheek.

Mark looked away.

"Don't shut me out, Mark. When you're in a relationship, you share things, all the things you're going through...even the hard ones. Even the painful ones. I shared all of mine with you." Her breath hitched. "And

I totally understand if this thing with your mom is too painful to talk about yet, but at least say something. Tell me we'll work through this together."

He sucked in a breath, and her heart stopped. She held her breath, waiting to hear what he'd finally say. But in the end, he said nothing.

Goddammit.

He turned away and started walking toward his SUV.

She blinked at him for a moment in shock and then ran after him. She grabbed on to his arm, spinning him to face her. "Don't you dare walk away! You don't get to do that to me again, Mark. Not this time."

He turned to look at her with those dark, empty eyes. "I'm sorry, Jess."

"We can work through this together," she said as tears swam in her eyes and her stomach twisted with fear.

He kept walking. Each thump of his boots against the pavement felt like someone had taken a hammer to her heart, beating it into a million broken pieces. How could he walk out on her now, after everything they'd been through together?

No, no, no...

"If you walk away now, we're through," she whispered, her voice breaking.

Mark gave no indication he'd even heard her, still striding across the parking lot toward his SUV.

"Did you hear me?" she yelled as tears splashed over her cheeks. "If you walk away now, that's it, Mark. We're finished. For good this time."

He paused, nodded slightly, and then climbed into his SUV and drove away.

* * *

Mark thought he knew pain. He'd gone through boot camp, spent a night buried under sand in the desert, and gotten himself blown half to pieces by a suicide bomber, but none of it hurt as bad as losing Jess.

His chest felt like someone had ripped his heart right out through his rib cage.

And the worst part was that it was his fault. He'd gone and fucked it up, just when he'd finally started to think he and Jess might have a future together. He hadn't meant to keep secrets or shut her out. Maybe he just wasn't wired for relationships, for the level of intimacy that involved baring every dark, scarred corner of your soul. When Jess had confronted him with the truth, he'd pushed her away. He didn't even know why he'd done it. All he'd known was that he couldn't breathe, couldn't think...he'd been consumed by the need to escape, to be alone.

And now he'd lost her.

He spent the next day at Off-the-Grid, ripping out carpet, drywall, and everything else that had been damaged by the fire. The entire rear section of the house was smoke-stained and waterlogged. Fortunately, he and the guys would be able to do most of the labor themselves.

In fact, Mark planned to bury himself in work at Off-the-Grid until the pain in his heart had dulled. He might not be wired for relationships, but he was good at this. Between refinishing the inside of the house and building the mountain bike course, he ought to be busy for a good, long time. Long enough to keep him from dwelling on what might have been with Jess. Not nearly long enough to get over her.

He'd never get over her. She'd been the only woman for him since he was seventeen years old, and nothing was going to change it now. He'd already had plenty of experience living without her, but after the things they'd shared these last few months, the memories and the fantasies would never be enough. Not now.

By the time he left Off-the-Grid, it was almost nine o'clock, and he was about to go out of his mind. He had to see Jess. He needed to explain. He could do better than he'd done yesterday. Desperation roared through his veins as he drove toward her house.

He pulled into the driveway and was knocking on her front door almost before he'd realized what he was doing. His heart pounded in his throat.

She opened it, staring up at him with dull eyes, her lips set in a frown.

"Jess..." He had no idea what to say. "I'm sorry."

"I am too," she said.

"I shouldn't have walked out on you yesterday."

"No, you shouldn't have." She blew out a breath, staring at him for several long, painful seconds. "But I meant what I said. I can't do this with you anymore. It just hurts too much." Two tears slid silently down her cheeks.

He stepped back, her words landing like a harsh slap of reality. It was too late. He knew as well as anyone that some things couldn't be fixed. As he walked back to his SUV, he felt like he'd left a vital part of himself behind on her doorstep.

* * *

Jessica stood inside the unfinished walls of her first spa cabin. The bedroom, bath, and lounge area all circled around an open-air courtyard in the center of the space. Here, guests could recline in a hammock or soak in the hot tub and stargaze right in the middle of their cabin.

They could even receive spa treatments right here from the privacy of their courtyard. Retractable screens would soon be installed that could be pulled out over the whole courtyard, allowing it to be used in any weather.

Right now, she was only looking at a skeleton of the finished product, but still...it was amazing. It was exactly what she'd been dreaming about for so many years.

"I love it," she said aloud, clasping her hands in front of her as she spun in a full circle, taking it all in.

"I'm so glad," Melissa Gormier said with a smile. "It's a unique concept. I'm not sure I've seen a spa with resort cabins like this before. I think people are going to go crazy over them."

"I sure hope so." Jessica walked to the back patio and looked out over the woods beyond. All of her cabins featured uninterrupted views of the forest. In the distance, she could hear the stream gurgling. Except...what was that? Off to the left, a raised wooden platform of some sort was visible through the trees.

The mountain bike course.

She let out a growl of frustration, her hands fisting at her sides. Of course. What else could it be? She and Mark had mapped out their prospective territories months ago, when the leaves had still been on the trees. Now her clients would have to watch mountain bikers racing by, interrupting their relaxation with whatever racket the thrill-seekers from Off-the-Grid might make. She should never have agreed to share the land.

She should never have fallen in love with Mark.

Ugh.

Last year at this time, she'd been lonely and frustrated in her search for love, but now...now everything was an even bigger mess. And who knew how long it would take her to bounce back from her broken heart and get back in the dating game? She might as well toss in the towel and accept her fate as an old maid.

Scoffing at her own ridiculous pity party, she turned and stomped back inside to talk to Melissa. Plumbing had already been run for all eight cabins, but if they acted now, they might be able to adjust the angles on some of the decks to protect their view.

They walked through each of the building sites together, and Jessica was relieved to see that the mountain bike course was visible from only three of her spa cabins. Still, that was three too many.

After she'd finished up with Melissa, Jessica went home to shower and get ready for a girls' night out. Thank God she'd finished her antibiotics yesterday because she needed a drink tonight. Actually, she needed several drinks tonight.

"Thank you so much for picking me up again," she told Emma when she got there.

"Any time. You sounded like you needed to drown your sorrows in a tall glass of something highly alcoholic tonight." Emma pulled her in for a quick hug. "You okay?"

"I've been better, but tonight's girls' night out was perfectly timed."

"Well, thank goodness for that." Emma led the way out the front door.

They had chosen The Drunken Bear for their gathering tonight. Mandy, Gabby, and Carly were already there when they arrived. They all greeted Jessica with hugs and words of support.

"I just can't believe it," Emma said after Jessica had filled them in on everything that had happened, or almost everything anyway. She didn't tell them about the note from Mark's mom. He obviously hadn't wanted any of them to know that his mom was still alive, let alone that she'd come to town recently, and Jessica had to respect that.

"I can't believe he just walked away like that." Mandy frowned into her beer. "Why were you guys arguing in the first place?"

"I found out about something he hadn't told me, someone from his past who'd come back into his life." She sipped from her margarita.

Gabby gasped. "Oh, Jess, he didn't... not another woman?"

"God, no. Nothing like that. It's just, it's something personal, and it isn't my business to share it with you guys since you all know him." Jessica took another drink. "In fact, I feel terrible for everything that's happened to him. But this was going on after he and I were back together, and he never told me. When I asked him about it, he just shut down and walked away."

"Oh, Jess." Emma leaned over to give her a hug. "I'm so sorry."

"Men," Mandy muttered. "They all suck, if you ask me."

"I have to agree." Jessica sighed and then polished off the last of her margarita.

Emma, Gabby, and Carly all grinned sheepishly.

"Well, they don't *all* suck," Emma said.

"Fine, but you ladies might have gotten the last three guys with any husband potential." Jessica swirled her empty glass, hoping the waitress came by soon to bring her another.

"I don't even care if they're husband material," Mandy

said. "I'd settle for a steady boyfriend, but I'm telling you, the pickings are slim."

"They're out there," Carly said. "But yeah, they're hard to find sometimes."

"And Mark *is* a great guy," Gabby added. "I hate that he turned out to be such an idiot in the boyfriend category. He's just so closed off."

"That's why I stayed angry at him for so many years," Jessica said, relieved when the waitress brought her another margarita. "I knew that if I ever let my guard down around him, I'd fall for him all over again, and let's face it, I also knew he'd probably never change. But then, for a little while, he really did seem to change. He opened up, and we made promises..." She blinked back tears. "But that whole time, he was keeping secrets. I love him, but I can't keep doing this to myself. I told him that if he walked away this time, we were finished for good. He kept on walking."

"I don't blame you," Gabby said, giving Jessica's hand a squeeze.

"This is so sad." Emma stared glumly into her lemonade. "We all love you, and we all love Mark, and I just hate that it didn't work out for you guys."

"I do too." Jessica gulped from her new margarita. "But enough about me and Mark. Someone change the subject to something cheerful."

"We went for our wedding tasting last weekend," Carly said. "I can't wait for you guys to see this place. It's like a for-real castle up on a mountaintop, and rumor has it, the owner is some kind of reclusive billionaire hottie."

Mandy perked up. "Ooh, is he single?"

Carly laughed. "No clue, but I'll be sure to find out if I meet him."

They laughed, ate, and drank for over three hours, and Jessica faked her way through the whole thing. The truth was that she just felt broken inside. She still had no energy and no appetite, whether it was thanks to the Lyme disease, the antibiotics, or her broken heart, she wasn't sure. The only thing she knew for sure was that it was going to take a long time to recover from losing Mark, maybe even longer than it had taken her the first time.

CHAPTER TWENTY-FOUR

Mark was so miserable that even Bear didn't want to be around him. She pouted in her dog bed in the corner, throwing him baleful looks from time to time, those ridiculously fluffy ears pinned back against her head.

He wasn't enjoying his own company either.

The urge to cut ties in Haven and roam off somewhere new was strong. He'd never stayed in one place this long. Never planned to put down roots. When he'd first come back to Haven, it had been perfect. He, Ethan, and Ryan were living it up just like the good old days, only better this time because they were older and wiser now.

But Ethan and Ryan had settled down, fallen in love, and gotten married. And now Mark was getting itchy again. Maybe, in the not-so-distant future, he'd ask them to buy him out of Off-the-Grid and hit the road.

But that didn't sound good either. Haven felt like home. *Jess* felt like home.

He lurched out of his chair and went to the fridge for a beer.

Someone knocked on his door, and he heard the murmur of a female voice outside. His heart gave a ridiculous leap in his chest. He crossed the living room in about three strides and yanked the door open.

Gabby and Emma stood on the other side, smiling cautiously at him.

He just stared, absorbing the disappointment. Of course Jess wasn't here. She wasn't coming back.

"Mind if we come in?" Emma asked.

"Uh, sure." He stepped back, watching as they walked inside.

They stopped in the living room to pet Bear, who'd come trotting over to greet them. Why were they here? Mark couldn't remember either Gabby or Emma ever visiting his condo before.

Gabby turned and looked at him with a smile. "We couldn't help but notice that you and Jessica both look miserable these days."

"So we're here to meddle a little bit on your behalf," Emma added.

"No thanks." He turned toward the door to show them out. He wasn't interested in anyone meddling in his life, let alone Jess's friends.

"Hear us out," Gabby said, sitting on the couch so that he couldn't kick her out. Emma walked over and sat beside her.

Dammit all.

"Jess has no idea we're here, first of all," Emma said with a guilty grin. "She didn't send us, and she'd be super pissed if she knew we were here."

That made two of them.

"She's also super pissed at *you*." Gabby narrowed her eyes at him.

Well, this was going to be fun. He stood facing them, arms crossed over his chest.

"The thing is, you messed up by not telling her about this thing from your past," Emma said. "But Mark, I've known you since we were kids. I know you had a tough childhood, and I'm guessing you had a good reason for keeping this to yourself so you get a pass on that as far as I'm concerned. But why didn't you fight for her, Mark? Why did you walk away?"

"I don't know." And that was the truth. His skin prickled uncomfortably. He needed this conversation to be over, needed to be alone.

"Look, we realize you don't have much experience with relationships," Gabby said, leaning forward to wrap her hands around her knees. "So we're here to try to help. Because when you get serious with a woman, she expects you to share all these important life things with her. She wants to be a part of your life, every part of your life. Keep her in the dark, even unintentionally, and she's going to get her feelings hurt. She's going to feel like you don't trust her, or you're shutting her out."

"And we know you, Mark," Emma said. "We know you wouldn't hurt Jess on purpose. You're used to keeping all this stuff to yourself because you never had anyone to share it with before. So, here's another hint: Women are really emotional creatures, especially when it comes to love."

Love? He'd never said...Jess had never said...

"The look on your face!" Emma giggled. "You may think you're hard to read, but I've got your number, Mark Dalton. So, here's the thing. If you were to, say, go to her and beg for forgiveness, she might be willing to listen."

He shook his head. "I already went to her and apologized."

"I know." Emma's smile was sad. "But you've got to do more than apologize. You have to tell her everything. Explain the whole story about this person from your past and why you didn't tell her about it before. No detail is too small. Tell her what was going through your head when you walked away and how much you regret it now. Pour your heart out to her. Tell her that you love her. Beg her for another chance."

By the time she'd finished with her little speech, Emma's hands were clasped in front of her as if pleading with him. Gabby sat beside her, nodding in agreement.

Fucking hell. He turned away.

"I don't know if she'll be able to forgive you," Gabby said from behind him. "But you'll never know if you don't try."

"And not for nothing, but you guys all fucked it up before you got it right," Emma said in a laughing tone. "Ryan messed up big time, but he got over himself and came and groveled for forgiveness."

"So did Ethan," Gabby said.

"But we were afraid you'd need an extra nudge, Mark. So here it is. Nudge, nudge. Go after her before it's too late. Beg. Grovel. Do what you have to do."

He felt a hand on his shoulder, and when he turned, Emma pulled him in for a hug.

"We love you too, Mark," she said softly, pulling back. "We want you to be happy. And we want Jess to be happy."

"And we're really hoping you guys can be happy together. We're rooting for you." Gabby pulled him in for a hug too.

His chest felt uncomfortably tight. He didn't have much experience with hugs from anyone but Jess, and it left him feeling somewhat off-balance.

Gabby and Emma walked toward the front door.

"Good luck!" Emma called over her shoulder, and then they were gone.

After they'd left, he took Bear for a long walk while he tried to make sense of their visit. He'd fucked things up with Jess. There was no undoing that. Was there? He walked until a couple of important truths rose to the surface of his mind. He loved Jess, loved her more than anything in the world. And if he wanted a second chance, he needed to offer one first.

When he got back to his apartment, he picked up the note Jess had painstakingly smoothed out and left on his kitchen counter. He typed in Sharlene's number and brought the phone to his ear.

"Hello?"

"It's Mark," he said, his fingers clenched around the phone.

"Mark?" Her voice hitched. "I hoped, but I never thought... I'm so glad you called."

He hadn't thought he'd ever call either. Funny how things changed. "Maybe it's time for us to talk."

* * *

Jessica walked through the woods, a backpack on her shoulders and a blanket clutched in her arms. Today was her day off, and it was unseasonably warm for December so she'd decided to hike to the back of her new property and spend the afternoon by herself. She'd brought a book to read, and she might do a little meditation while she was out here too.

She was tired of moping around, tired of feeling sorry for herself, tired of missing Mark. She was a capable, independent woman, dammit, and it was time to find herself again. She needed to make peace with her illness and losing Mark and move on.

The worst—on both fronts—was hopefully behind her.

She found a leaf-strewn spot on top of a hill with a view of the stream below and spread out her blanket. She sat, pulled out her phone and earbuds, and started up her meditation playlist. A sense of calm flowed through her as she closed her eyes.

This was what she'd been missing.

No more chaos. Just peace.

She sat like that for a long time, eyes closed, as she focused on relaxing her body and letting go of all the negative energy clinging around her. A gentle breeze rustled through her hair, and she inhaled the damp, earthy smell of the forest.

Peace.

How lucky was she that she owned this beautiful spot? She could come out here every day if she wanted to. Yep, she was pretty damn lucky. It was lucky that she'd received a diagnosis, and she'd keep fighting the Lyme disease until she'd beaten it. She'd spent a lot of time in the last few weeks researching holistic treatments to augment what the antibiotics had done for her.

Drawing in another deep, cleansing breath, she opened her eyes.

And tumbled over sideways on her blanket with a shriek.

Mark stood a few feet away, silent as the forest around him, hands shoved into the pockets of his jeans.

"If I've told you once, I've told you a hundred times,"

she gasped, clutching her heart. "You've got to stop sneaking up on me like that."

"Sorry."

She narrowed her eyes at him. "What are you doing out here?"

"Looking for you." The expression on his face was intense, but beyond that, she couldn't read him.

"You found me. How?"

The corner of his mouth quirked. "You left an easy trail to follow."

She glanced over her shoulder, seeing no such trail. "Right. So why did you stalk me out here in the woods?"

"Got a few things to say if you're willing to listen."

She stared at him for a moment, considering. She wasn't angry any longer. Hurt, definitely. Disappointed, yes. Heartbroken, *oh yeah*. But she and Mark were part of the same circle of friends so if he wanted to clear the air between them to make things less awkward when they inevitably bumped into each other around town, then she was willing to give him that chance. She nodded, patting the blanket beside her.

He sat next to her, staring out over the stream as she'd done earlier. "Not sure where to start," he said finally.

Something in his tone caught in her chest. He sounded uncertain, almost vulnerable. Totally out of character for Mark.

So she just sat next to him, taking in the view and waiting for him to sort himself out. For once, she'd be the listener and let him do the talking.

"My parents were only sixteen when my mom got pregnant with me," he said finally, still watching the stream sparkling in the sunshine so far below them.

Her breath caught in her throat. Whatever she'd been expecting him to say, it definitely wasn't this.

"I don't know that much about them. I don't know what it was like for them trying to raise me when they were just kids themselves, and being an interracial couple too. Can't have been easy. I guess both of their families disowned them, but I don't know for sure. I only know that I didn't have any other family around, no grandparents or anyone else. When I was six, my dad died in a car accident."

She reached out and rested a hand on his shoulder.

"After that, my mom had to raise me on her own, and she struggled with it. I went to school a lot without a lunch or missing my coat, things like that. Someone—probably my teacher—filed a report with social services. When my mom found out she was being investigated for neglect, she just... left. Dropped me at school and never came back. She left me a note. In my backpack."

"A note?" Jessica could hardly draw breath. What would that be like for a six-year-old boy, being dropped off at school and never picked up?

"She said I'd be better off without her. She likes to leave notes when she's ready to bail, I guess. Saves her from the tough conversations."

She could hear the pain in his voice, raw and harsh, and it cracked her heart wide open. "Mark, I'm so sorry."

"I waited for her," he said quietly. "Took years for me to realize she wasn't coming back. And somewhere along the way, I just turned into a bitter, angry kid who'd rather tell the world that both his parents died than deal with what really happened."

"I don't blame you."

"She was dead to me. That's the truth." He turned to look at her then, and she saw all the hurt and anger of that abandoned little boy reflected in his eyes.

She wanted to fling her arms around him and hold him and try to make it okay. But she couldn't. Those days were past. And besides, nothing could ever make this okay for him. "I hate that you had to go through that, Mark."

"I know what it's like to wait for someone, Jess, not knowing when or if they're coming back. That's why I had to make a clean break with you when I enlisted. I couldn't do that to you. I couldn't leave you here waiting for me."

"What?" She drew back, reeling from all the information he was throwing at her.

"I should have told you then, but I didn't know how. I was a stupid, messed-up kid, and all I knew was that I needed the Army to straighten me out before it was too late. Actually..." He paused, and a slight smile curved his lips. "I didn't even know that much. Your dad gave me a rather strong nudge in the right direction."

"My dad?" She pressed a hand to her forehead in confusion.

Mark nodded. "He wrote down the address for the recruiting center and told me to get my ass down there and let the Army make me a man."

"He...he sent you away?" Jessica stiffened. Her dad had sabotaged her relationship with Mark all those years ago?

"No." Mark settled his gaze on the stream below them again. "He didn't tell me to break up with you when I enlisted. That was all me. In fact, he was really pissed at me for hurting you like I did. He was...well, I guess he was being a father figure to me, Jess. He saw me headed down a bad path, and he showed me a way to straighten myself out. I owe him a lot for that."

"Oh." Her anger faded into gratitude for her dad, even

if his actions had ultimately resulted in her very first broken heart.

Mark was quiet for a few minutes, and they just sat there, side by side. The enormity of it…of what he'd been through…it made her heart ache. For him, living it? She couldn't imagine.

"When Sharlene came to town this fall, it shook me up," he said, his voice low and gruff. "I didn't know how to handle it so I just shut down, shut her out, tried to pretend it wasn't happening. And I guess I shut you out too. I never meant to lie to you."

She swallowed hard. "Okay."

"All I can say is that I never made a conscious decision not to tell you. I was just so determined not to let Sharlene back into my life, not to even think about her. It was easier for me, I guess, just to not talk about it. To anyone."

"I understand." And she appreciated his honesty, even if it still ripped her to pieces that he hadn't shared the truth with her back when it happened.

"And when she left again, when she left me another fucking note, I just…" He shrugged, his body gone stiff with tension.

"She hurt you all over again," she whispered. *Oh Mark…*

"Stupid, right?" He sounded so tough, but she heard his pain.

"Not stupid at all. You're human. Of course it hurt when she left again."

"So I just blocked it all out and tried to forget."

"Mark, when was this?" *Please tell me it was before we started sleeping together…*

"It was after the meteor shower." He said it in a monotone. "I know I should have told you. I'm sorry. I truly am."

Tears welled in her eyes. "How many times did you see her before that?"

"Two. Three maybe. It wasn't like we were hanging out. She came by a couple of times, asking for another chance. I shut her out, told her to leave me alone. That's all it was."

"Mark, why didn't you tell me any of this when I asked you about it last week?" That was what she still couldn't understand. Why had he walked away when she'd asked him for the truth? Because she would have forgiven him, dammit, and now...

"I don't know." His eyes had taken on that faraway look again, like they had that night at the spa right before he walked away.

"Okay," she whispered.

"I called her last night," he said.

"Called who?"

"Sharlene. We're going to set up a time to meet...talk."

"Wow, that's...that's huge, Mark." She reached out and squeezed his hand. "What made you decide to call her?"

A hint of a smile touched his lips. "I had a little help. And I realized I couldn't ask you for another chance if I wasn't willing to do the same for Sharlene."

Was he asking for another chance? Her heart lurched into her throat. But if she gave him another chance, he'd just shut her out again. He'd walk away when things got tough. "I hope it goes well."

He shrugged.

"I really appreciate your honesty," she told him. "And I'm so, so sorry for everything you've been through."

"But some things can't be forgiven. I know that better than anyone." He kept his eyes straight ahead.

Dammit. "I do forgive you, Mark. You never meant to hurt me. I know that."

"But I hurt you anyway." He turned to look at her, and the raw emotion, the pain, in his eyes knocked the breath from her lungs.

She dabbed at the tears that streaked her cheeks. "We keep repeating the same cycle, Mark, and it's just too painful for me...for *both* of us, to go through it again."

He nodded. He swiped at his eyes and then got to his feet. He started walking away, and the pain that rose up inside her was so strong that she pressed a hand to her chest. *Don't go*, she wanted to scream. But he had to. There was no other way. She watched as he walked through the trees toward Off-the-Grid, his steps heavy as if walking away hurt him every bit as much as it was hurting her.

Gah. Life just sucked sometimes.

And then he stopped. He stood there for a few seconds with his back to her, and her breath caught in her throat. What was happening?

Then he was walking back toward her, each stride swallowing the distance between them. She stood, her heart thumping in her throat, her knees weak and shaky.

Thank God. Oh, thank God...

Nothing had ever felt more right than the sight of him coming back to her. He stopped in front of her, his face so full of emotion—of pain, and fear, and love—that she almost didn't recognize him. "I can't do it. I can't walk away from you this time, Jess."

And it was her turn to stare, speechless.

"I—" His voice broke. He cleared his throat and then reached out to take her hands in his. "I panicked last week when you asked me about my mother. I realized how badly I'd fucked up, and I was afraid you wouldn't be able to forgive me so I acted like an ass and walked away. Biggest mistake of my life."

Holy shit. Her heart tripped all over itself, thumping painfully against her ribs.

"I wish I could promise that I'll never hurt you again, but I can't. But I can promise you this ... my eyes are open now, Jess. I get it. I see what I did wrong, and I promise you I'll do my very damn best not to make the same mistakes again. If you'll give me another chance, I think I can be a better man."

"Mark—" More tears splashed over her cheeks. The truth was that he couldn't possibly be a better man. He'd come here today and opened himself up, laid himself bare. *He'd come back this time.* And in doing so, he'd told her everything she'd needed to know.

"There's never been anyone else for me, Jess, and there never will be. I think ... I think I've been in love with you since I was seventeen."

She gasped. "Did you just say..."

He smiled, and she could swear his eyes were damp too. "Yeah, I did. I love you, Jess. I've been all over the world, but I can't forget you. You're it for me, whether you give me another chance or not."

She just stared at him for a moment in shock, and then she flung her arms around him, tears streaming down her cheeks. "I love you too. God, I love you so much."

He kissed her, sliding one hand around to cup her head, so gentle, yet so fierce and protective. "Please say it again."

There was something fragile in his tone. He hadn't heard those words nearly enough in his life, but she could make up for it now. "I love you. I've always loved you, and I always will. And I promise I'll help you work out this stuff with your mom. Whatever you decide to do, I'll be here with you. And you have a new family here in Haven. Me, Ethan, Gabby, Ryan, Emma... we're family now."

"I like the sound of that."

And this time she wasn't imagining it. An honest-to-God tear ran down his cheek. She kissed it away, and then she kissed the scar beneath it. *She loved this man so much, every perfectly imperfect inch of him...*

"I love you." He tugged her in for another kiss. "I'm not sure I've ever said those words out loud before today."

"I'll make sure you get lots of practice."

"Good." His arms tightened around her. "Because I don't want to waste another minute."

And neither did she.

$\mathscr{E}$PILOGUE

$\mathscr{M}$ark walked down a flagstone path into the woods behind the spa. His heart pounded in his chest, and adrenaline flooded his body, leaving him jittery. He'd faced down armed mercenaries in some of the most dangerous places in the world without breaking a sweat, but right now, he was so nervous he was about to jump out of his own skin.

A cabin came into view ahead, wood-paneled with lots of windows. Brightly colored flowers bloomed along the walkway. Jess's new spa cabins didn't officially open until next week, but he was staying here with her tonight, a reward for all their hard work over the last six months as they got her spa resort and Off-the-Grid's mountain bike course completed and ready to open for business.

And Jess was inside that cabin right now, waiting for him. He quickened his pace. Last month, they'd driven to South Carolina together to visit Sharlene. The three of them had sat and talked. It had been awkward and painful, but good too somehow. He didn't know what the future held, but if it brought Sharlene back into his life, he was okay with that now.

Life was short. Family was precious. And love was something never to be wasted.

When he reached the cabin's front door, he paused, drew a deep breath, and then knocked. Jess pulled it open, wearing a purple sundress. Her cheeks were flushed, and her brown eyes sparkled with health. She still had bad days when the Lyme disease flared up, but for the most part, she was as good as new. Better, because now she was his.

"I'm spending the night at the spa. You know what this means, right?" He pulled her into his arms.

"What?" she asked with a smile.

"It means I'm totally whipped."

She laughed, pressing her lips to his. "It means you're a smart man who realizes he gets to do all kinds of naughty things to christen this place tonight with the woman he loves."

His dick stirred in his pants. "Well, in that case..."

"Come on in. Dinner's being delivered in a little while, and I've got champagne for later." She stepped back, tugging him inside with her.

"That so?" He closed the door behind them and looked around. He'd seen the place a few times during construction but not since it was finished. There was a bedroom to the left and a lounge area to the right, but he followed Jess through a doorway into the open-air atrium at its center. A hammock was strung between two trees, and behind it the private hot tub beckoned. He'd had all kinds of plans for tonight, rehearsed how to do this right, but he blanked on all of it as he stood in the courtyard with Jess.

The sun shone down on them, warm and bright. A robin landed in the tree beside them, hopping from branch to branch and twittering happily.

"It's amazing, isn't it?" she said.

"It really is. Jess?" His stomach tightened, and his palms grew damp.

Her smile faded. "Are you okay? You look…"

Like he was about to hurl? Because that's how he felt. "Yeah, I just…" He paused and drew a deep breath. "I have something to say, and I'm afraid I'm going to mess it up."

She took his hands, giving him an encouraging smile. "What is it?"

Here goes nothing. "For a long time, I thought I wasn't cut out for anything but a life in the military. The Special Forces gave me a purpose, a reason to keep getting up every day. And I was damn good at my job. After the explosion, I thought I'd lost the only worthwhile thing in my life, but I was wrong."

Jess's eyes widened.

"I'm happier now than I've ever been before, and it's all thanks to you. I never really knew what love was until I met you, Jess. And then I fucked it up…several times." He grimaced, and she laughed softly. "Thank God you kept giving me second chances."

"There's a learning curve for everything," she said, reaching out to touch his cheek. "Even love."

"Well, I hope I've mastered it this time because, Jess, I need to ask you something really important."

"Okay," she whispered, her eyes locked on his.

"I've always known I wanted to spend the rest of my life with you, but… well, what I'm trying to say is…Jess, will you marry me?" The words just tumbled out of him, and his heart was beating so fast he could hardly breathe.

Jess was already nodding as tears spilled over her cheeks. "Yes."

A funny lightness spread through his chest. *She said yes!* He must be the luckiest sonofabitch in the whole world because the most amazing, gorgeous woman had just agreed to marry him. But...*fuck.* "Wait. I forgot..."

"No, you didn't. It was perfect." She flung her arms around him, kissing him through her tears. "I'm so happy."

Hooah! "Me too, baby. Me too. But I forgot the most important part."

"I'm pretty sure the most important part was asking me to marry you." She kissed him again, and he was so happy he felt like his chest might explode trying to contain it.

He stepped out of her arms and reached into his back pocket, pulling out the little black box he'd been carrying around with him all day. He dropped to one knee and held it up. "Amethyst is supposed to be good for peace and meditation...and health. So—" He opened the box, revealing the ring he'd had made for her. A diamond glittered in the center, flanked on either side with amethysts and set in white gold.

When he looked up, Jess was sobbing. "It's so perfect. Oh, Mark..."

"Really?" Because it was an unusual ring, but he'd thought it suited her. An ordinary ring would never do for his extraordinary Jess.

"I love amethysts for all the reasons you just said, and purple is my favorite color too. Mark, it's the most beautiful ring I've ever seen. I love it. I love *you*. So, so much."

His hand shook as he slid it onto her finger. "I love you too, Jess, more than I ever knew it was possible to love someone."

She touched her ring finger, smiling, then flung herself into his arms. "I could have never picked out a ring I'd love more or envision a more perfect way for you to ask me to marry you. I will never forget a single moment of tonight."

He kissed her, holding her tight while his pulse slowed and peace descended over him. He felt calm, centered in a way he never had before, like for the first time in his whole life he was where he was supposed to be. His heart swelled with warmth when he saw his ring sparkling on her finger. So this was what it felt like to be happy, to be loved, to be part of a family.

It was the best goddamn feeling in the world.

Gabby Winters pretends she's dating red-hot troublemaker Ethan Hunter to avoid breaking his matchmaking grandmother's heart. But there's serious sizzling attraction between them—and this charade may lead to the real thing…

An excerpt from *Run to You* follows.

CHAPTER ONE

*E*than Hunter braced his feet against the edge of the wooden platform, glanced down at the ground some forty feet below, and pushed off. With a yank from the harness, he was flying. The wind whistling in his ears, combined with the scream of the hand trolley over steel cable, silenced his thoughts for the first time all morning.

He let out a whoop, an adrenaline-fueled war cry, as he soared between trees and over a small ravine. The zip-line carried him about eight hundred feet, ending on a wooden platform similar to the one he'd kicked off from minutes earlier.

Here he unclipped from the line, unfastened his harness, and took off his helmet to check the Go-Pro camera he'd attached. He thumbed through its menu, searching for the video he'd just recorded. It wasn't there.

He swore under his breath. Somehow he hadn't recorded a single moment of his trip down the zip-line.

And he had to get this video sent off tonight to the college student he'd hired to design the website. He'd have to hike back and take the whole course again. His empty stomach grumbled in protest.

Ignoring it, Ethan climbed down the ladder and headed for the trail that would take him back to the top. This was the end of the line, the fifth and last leg of the series of zip-lines he'd built, taking him from the main building deep into the forest behind. For now, the zip-lines were his, a place for him and his buddies to get their thrills without putting anyone's lives at risk.

But soon, when Off-the-Grid Adventures opened, this would be the start of a business venture that could set him, as well as his friends Mark Dalton and Ryan Blake, on the way to fulfilling a dream. A way to put their dare-deviling ways to good use, cementing themselves as upstanding citizens and making some money while they were at it.

And as of last night, bringing this dream to fruition had taken on a new urgency. His grandmother's words haunted him like an unwelcome ghost, flitting in and out of his vision and making his chest feel too tight.

"An aneurysm," she'd told him over supper. "I saw it myself on the scan. Because of the location, it's inoperable. The doctor said it could stay like that indefinitely, but he thinks chances are high that it will rupture sometime in the next few weeks or months."

Weeks. Months.

Dixie Hunter was the strongest woman he knew. She'd endured more in her lifetime than anyone ought to, had raised him since he was twelve with a firm hand and a smile on her face, and at seventy years old, she still walked a mile into town each morning to have breakfast at The Sunny Side Up Café because, as she said, she had two perfectly good legs and needed the exercise.

And now he was to believe that a bulging blood vessel in her brain was going to take her life sometime in the next few months?

She'd taken his hand across the table, tears shimmering in her eyes. "I need to see you settled before I go, Ethan. I need to know you've got something or someone to keep you out of trouble when I'm not here to nudge you back into line."

A hawk called overhead, drawing his gaze toward the blue sky peeking through the swaying treetops above. Settled for him would never include a family, but this place would keep him out of trouble. He just needed to make sure Off-the-Grid Adventures opened in time for Gram to see it.

He picked his way across the stream, taking a shortcut back to the start of the course. One more ride on the zipline, and this time the damned camera had better work. He absolutely could not afford a delay.

Up ahead, a woman sat on a large, flat rock by the stream, her back to him, arms crossed over her knees. Ethan stopped in his tracks. He owned this property, but it bordered the public forest so it wasn't unheard of to find a hiker wandering through his neck of the woods.

What was unusual was that he didn't recognize her. The population of Haven, North Carolina, numbered somewhere in the vicinity of seven hundred, and he could say with some confidence that he was acquainted with all the female residents in his age range.

The woman before him had light brown hair hanging almost to her waist in long, loose waves. She wore a white tank top that hugged her slender frame, accentuating the curves at her waist, and a billowy blue skirt that swirled around her ankles. Intriguing. Different. And without seeing her face, he knew he had never seen her before.

"Hi there," he called out.

She scrambled off her perch with a startled squeak, almost pitching face-first into the creek. With one hand on the rock for balance, she turned to face him.

And *hot damn*, she was gorgeous. Her eyes were a shade darker than her hair, as wide as they were wary. She looked a little out of place here in the woods dressed like that—he didn't know any local women who went hiking in a skirt—but most interesting were the black leather boots peeking out from under its folds. Not girly dress-up boots. These looked more like combat boots, and for some reason, paired with the blue skirt they were smokin' hot.

"Sorry." He held his hands out in front of him. "Didn't mean to startle you."

"I—well—oh!" She swatted at something near her face. "Ouch!"

He stepped closer. "Something sting you?"

"Yes, it's okay. I'm not allergic. Ack!" She let out a little shriek, ducking and swatting around her head.

Ethan lunged forward, spotting several yellow jackets buzzing around her head. "You must have disturbed a nest." He put a hand on her arm and tugged her away from the rock where she'd been sitting.

With another shriek, she jumped, landing flush against him, her face pressed into his shirt. Just as quickly, she pushed past him, leaving behind the faint scent of honeysuckle and the warm impression of her body on his.

Something he'd like to explore...later. He glanced back and spotted the nest she'd accidentally trampled, now easily visible thanks to the swarm of angry wasps flying in and out. "We've got to get away from that nest."

He nudged her ahead of him, swatting at yellow jackets. One of the little fuckers stung his arm, and it hurt like a son of a bitch. He smashed it beneath his palm. "You doing okay?" he asked the woman ahead of him. His arm was on fire from one sting, and she'd received several.

"There's one in my hair. Oh God—" She clawed at her head.

"Let me." He disentangled her fingers then combed through her hair until he found a yellow jacket busily stinging her scalp. He squashed it. "Got it."

He inhaled the scent of honeysuckle from her hair, then winced at the angry welt already forming on her scalp.

"My skirt—" She grabbed it in her fists, shaking madly.

They'd gone up her skirt? *Oh hell.* Ethan wasn't touching this one with a ten-foot pole. "Ah—"

She stomped and twirled until thankfully a yellow jacket escaped from the folds of her skirt. Ethan ground it into the dirt before it could strike again.

"Please tell me that was the last one." Her hands flitted anxiously by her face, which had flushed a dark pink. Two red welts had risen on her left cheek, and another was visible on her forehead.

Damn. "I don't see any more. You said you're not allergic, right?"

"Yes. I mean, no, I'm not." She dabbed at one of the welts on her cheek and winced.

"Either you really pissed them off or they like the smell of your shampoo. Let's keep going to put a little more distance between us and their nest." He led her along the path by the stream, walking briskly.

"I came from that way." She pointed in the direction of one of the town's hiking trails.

"I figured, but you wandered onto my property, so I'll drive you back to wherever you're parked."

"Your property?" She pulled back. "I'm sorry. I—"

He shook his head. "Don't even worry about it. I think we lost the yellow jackets. Let me have another look at you."

She stopped short, her pretty face now alarmingly red and splotchy. "Thank you for your help, but I should really go back the way I came."

"No way I'm letting you out of my sight right now. Hang on. I have an ice pack." He reached into the pack he wore slung over his right shoulder. "I'm Ethan Hunter, by the way."

"Gabrielle Winters—Gabby. An ice pack does sound great. You're awfully well prepared." She blew out a breath and waved her hands in front of her cheeks.

"I like living on the edge, but I always keep a basic first aid kit on hand. Then I can at least patch myself up...well, most of the time." He winked at her.

Her lips curved in the faintest of smiles.

Ethan found her 100 percent captivating, even in her current wasp-stung condition. He cracked the ice pack to activate it, then handed it to her.

She pressed it against her forehead with a sigh of relief.

"You got a lot of stings. Sure you're okay?"

She grimaced. The hand holding the cold pack, he noticed, was shaking. "Actually—" And then she stepped backward, tripped, and landed with a splash in the stream.

* * *

Gabby let out a startled squeak as she landed flat on her butt in the stream. But then…oh, the cold water felt so good. Her skin was on fire, like a million stingers were never-endingly piercing every inch of her body. She lay back in the stream, splashing more water over herself.

"You okay?" Ethan leaned over her, offering a hand to pull her up.

She shook her head. The cold water felt too good. Her skin might burst into flames if she got out now. She pressed a cold, wet hand to her forehead and squeezed her eyes shut. Why did she hurt all the way to her toes when she'd only been stung on her face? Somewhere in the back of her pain-wracked brain, she was aware she was making a total fool of herself in front of Ethan Hunter.

Of course, if she had to get stung by yellow jackets after wandering onto some guy's private property and then fall on her butt in a stream, of course said man would have to look like he belonged on the cover of *GQ* magazine.

With his tousled blond hair and tanned, muscular arms, Ethan Hunter looked more like a movie star than a Boy Scout. He might be the hottest guy she'd ever met. And *oh God…*

She moaned, watching as his cold pack floated away. Her heart was racing, and her skin…her skin felt like it was being devoured by ants.

"Gabby, you're scaring me."

"I'm okay," she answered, this time letting him pull her to her feet. The pain increased tenfold as she left the cold caress of the water. She was torn between the desire to claw at herself until she bled or cover her eyes and scream.

Speaking of eyes, Ethan's had darkened considerably.

Following his gaze, she looked down to see her breasts outlined beneath her now soaking-wet white tank top, her nipples visible through the thin shell of her bra. Her skirt was also plastered to her skin, probably highlighting her panties in similar fashion. Crossing her arms over her chest, she turned away.

What a nightmare. She needed to send him on his way, pronto. This little encounter was headed from bad to worse, and if she didn't get into a cold shower in the next ten minutes, she might spontaneously combust.

He pulled out a cell phone and held it to his ear. "Hi, Max. I'm so glad I caught you. Got a minute?" He paused. "Great. I'm with a hiker who got stung by yellow jackets, at least half a dozen stings, and most them are on her face and scalp. She says she's not allergic, but—"

"I'm not," she repeated, "but my skin is on fire."

Ethan repeated this to whoever he was talking to, then looked at her. "Are you having any difficulty breathing? Any itching or swelling in your throat?"

She shook her head. "Just my skin. And my heart is really racing."

He spoke into the phone again. Gabby knelt by the stream and scooped a fresh handful of water to splash over her face. Who cared what kind of impression she made on Ethan at this point?

"Hey." He came up behind her. "My friend Maxine is an ER nurse. She says you're probably just reacting to the amount of venom in your system, but we should get you checked out to be safe. I'll drive you to the clinic. I wish I had some Benadryl to give you in the meantime."

"Oh." She stood, backing away. "I guess it's probably a good idea to get checked out, but I can drive myself."

He gave her a look that said *hell no*. "I have a change

of clothes in my Jeep. I doubt the shorts would do any-thing for you, but I can at least offer you a dry T-shirt."

"That's really not necessary. I'll drive myself straight to the doctor, I promise." She yanked at a chunk of her hair, desperate to relieve the burning, crawling sensation on her scalp. She had to get away from Ethan. He was too charming, too smooth...too *everything* she no longer trusted. She'd come to Haven to take care of herself for a change, and that's exactly what she intended to do.

He shook his head. "You can call someone to meet us at the road if you want, but there's no way I'm leaving you out here by yourself."

She shivered, biting her bottom lip to keep from screaming in pain and frustration. There was no one for her to call, and the longer they stood here talking, the more likely she was to strip naked right in front of him and jump back in the stream to sooth her wasp-bitten skin.

Ethan's blue eyes narrowed, and he shoved his hands into the pockets of his cargo shorts. "You're not from around here, right? I'm a strange guy you met in the woods. How can I put your mind at ease?"

She shook her head. "Forget it."

He cocked his head with a smile that might have made her swoon if she wasn't so miserable. "I could get my grandmother on the phone for you. She'll vouch for me, and she knows everyone in town."

"It's okay, really. I trust you." She shouldn't, but she did—enough to let him drive her to the clinic anyway. And maybe he was right. Maybe she shouldn't be alone right now in case it turned out she was allergic after all. "Thank you for caring."

He shrugged. "Of course. I imagine you'd do the same for me if I'd been the one who stepped in a wasps' nest."

This was true. With a resigned sigh, she clenched her fists against the urge to claw at her flaming skin and started walking beside him, presumably in the direction of his car. Her misery was compounded by the wet clothes that clung to her with each step.

Ugh.

"You new in town or just visiting?" Ethan asked.

"Both." She wiped a strand of wet hair from her face, grimacing when her fingers brushed against one of the wasp stings. "I've been here since April."

Two months, spent mostly holed up inside the little cabin she'd rented or wandering the woods behind it. A habit she'd modify now to make sure she stayed far the hell away from Ethan Hunter's property. She couldn't wait to forget today ever happened.

"But you're not staying?" he asked.

She shrugged. "I'm not sure how long I'll be here."

"You have family in town?"

She shook her head. After she'd left Brad, she'd stayed with her parents for a while, but it hadn't taken her long to realize she'd merely left one suffocating situation for another. So she'd packed up her SUV and hit the road, leaving her hometown of Charlotte behind. A quiet mountain town called Haven sounded perfect. And it had been, more or less. She'd needed a place to curl up and lick her wounds before she was ready to go back out and face the world, and she'd found it.

"Been to the spa yet?" Ethan asked.

She shook her head again, rubbing her hands up and down her arms, which only seemed to intensify the burning sensation in her skin.

"Definitely check it out. You've heard of the natural hot springs here, right?"

"Yes." Not only did they sound fantastic, but they were rumored to have medicinal properties that calmed the soul. And hers could certainly use calming.

"How're you holding up?"

She paused and pressed a hand against her heart. It raced like a runaway train, making her light-headed. "You ask a lot of questions."

"You seem kind of quiet, and I need to keep you talking to make sure you're okay." He gave her an easy smile, but his eyes were sharp, watchful.

"I could use a cold shower and some Benadryl, but I'll be okay." She bit her lip. "In fact, I'd really rather go straight home."

"No way. I'd never forgive myself if I sent you home and you went into anaphylactic shock or something. There's a clinic on Weaver Street that'll get you right in. I've been there more times than I care to admit. The nurse practitioner who works there is an old friend of my grandmother's. You'll be in good hands."

They came out into a large grass yard behind a little white house. A red Jeep Wrangler was parked in the driveway. She'd seen this house before, driven by it many times. In fact, the cabin she was renting was just up the street. "You live here?"

"Nah. I used to, but I bought a condo downtown last year. My friends and I are turning this place into an extreme outdoor sporting facility—Off-the-Grid Adventures."

"Extreme outdoor sports?"

"Yeah. Zip-lining, rock climbing, that kind of thing." His eyes gleamed with pride.

"Wow, that sounds, um ... exciting."

His lips quirked. "You look horrified."

"Sorry. I guess I'm not adventurous."

He looked like he was about to say something, but then he shook his head. "I'll drive you to the clinic and then take you home. Where are you parked? I can get someone to drop your car off at your place later."

"I walked."

"Really? Where do you live?"

"Just up the road actually."

His brows lifted. "Oh, you must be renting the Merry-weather place."

"Yes."

He opened the back of the Jeep and pulled out a light blue T-shirt that said, I'D RATHER BE GETTING HIGH, with a graphic showing someone hang gliding. "Sorry. This is all I've got."

"It's okay. I'd rather be getting high than stung by wasps." She laughed in spite of herself. "Thanks for the shirt."

"My pleasure." His gaze flicked briefly to her breasts, still outlined in embarrassing detail beneath her wet tank top.

Her cheeks burned even hotter as she turned her back and pulled the shirt over her head.

* * *

Lord have mercy. Ethan scrubbed a hand over his eyes and tried to wipe the dirty thoughts from his mind. Gabby Winters was turning him on big time, even red and blotchy from the wasp attack, still slightly bedraggled from her tumble into the stream, and wearing his ridiculously oversized T-shirt.

Nurse Meyers had examined her, dosed her with Benadryl, and given her a tube of anti-itch cream to take home. Her symptoms seemed to be a reaction to the amount of yellow jacket venom in her system, not an allergy.

Gabby settled on the front seat of the Jeep, looking slightly more relaxed, probably thanks to the Benadryl. She leaned back and closed her eyes.

"I'll be right back." He left her in the Jeep and walked into the pharmacy next door. He grabbed a couple of jumbo-sized candy bars, a bottle of water, and a package of Benadryl tablets. After paying for his purchases, he snagged one of the candy bars for himself and walked out to the Jeep. He handed the bag to her. "For later."

She peered inside, her eyes widening. "Thanks, but you didn't have to—"

He waved her off. "The least I could do. Now let's get you home."

Neither of them spoke on the short drive to her house. It was a classic-looking mountain cabin, with wood-paneled walls and a real wood-burning fireplace. He knew because he'd done some work on the deck a while back. The Merryweathers had moved to nearby Boone a few years ago and now rented the place out to vacationers.

In the driveway, Gabby climbed out of the Jeep and gave him a small smile. "Thanks again for all your help today."

"Any time. See you around." He watched until she was safely inside, then turned back toward the center of town and his condo. He ripped open the wrapper on the candy bar and took a big bite. His stomach had been growling since before he'd found Gabby in the woods. It was too late now to go back and make a video of the zip-line. He'd have to shoot it tomorrow morning and hope it didn't delay production on the new website for Off-the-Grid Adventures.

He chewed through the candy bar in the time it took to drive home, but it didn't come close to filling him. The leftover pizza in his fridge ought to do the trick. The roar of a Harley behind him on Main Street could mean only one thing: His good buddy Ryan Blake had arrived in town. A grin worked its way across Ethan's face. Tonight was looking up after all.

He swung into the space behind his building and watched as Ryan parked beside him. Shit was getting real now. Ryan was here, and Mark planned to arrive by the end of next week. They'd requested to have the property on Mountain Breeze Road rezoned from residential to commercial to allow Off-the-Grid Adventures to operate there, and it was taking longer than expected, but with any luck, they'd be accepting customers by the end of the month.

He stepped out of the Jeep. "Well, look what the cat dragged in."

Ryan grinned at him from behind mirrored shades. "Good to be home."

Ethan pulled him in for a hug and a clap on the back. "Good to see you, man. You check out your new digs yet?"

Ryan nodded. "Got here this afternoon. The place looks nice."

The old brick building in front of them had once housed the town's newspaper offices. It had sat empty for over a decade, but last year, Garrett Waltham, a local businessman, had bought it, renovated it, and converted it into three spacious condos. Ethan, Mark, and Ryan bought them, ready to turn this old building into their newfangled bachelor pad.

Ethan's stomach growled again. "You want to head over to Rowdy's for a beer and some wings?"

"Definitely."

They walked down the block to Main Street. Rowdy's was just around the corner, ambitiously named for this laid-back town, but occasionally, if enough alcohol was consumed, it lived up to its name.

Ethan and Ryan took a table near the front where they could see the game on the TV behind the bar.

"Hi, Ethan," their waitress, a pretty blonde named Tina, said as she approached their table.

"Hey, Tina."

She adjusted the neckline of her top, giving him a better view of her cleavage, then turned to his friend, her eyes widening. "Ryan Blake?"

"Yo." Ryan gave her a friendly look, his gaze sliding from her face to her breasts.

Dog. Ethan shook his head with a grin.

"I'm Tina Hawthorne. I was in class with your brother."

Ryan's eyes narrowed. "Excuse me?"

"Bro, she means Mark," Ethan said.

"Right. Good to see you, Tina." Ryan's posture relaxed. He and Mark had been foster brothers for a few years in high school after they'd both been taken in by Howard MacDonald in Silver Springs, the next town over from Haven.

After being bounced around the foster care system, Old Man MacDonald had been a welcome respite, a stable home where they were treated fairly and with respect. Ethan had gotten even luckier. After only a year in the system, Dixie had shown up and taken him in. Luckiest day in his damn life.

Tina had her hand on Ryan's biceps, admiring his tats. He showed her an eagle he'd had inked on his right arm, and next thing Ethan knew, she had lifted her shirt to show Ryan a little blue bird tattooed on her hip.

It was cute. So was she. Ethan sometimes flirted with Tina when he came here, which was often. She'd never shown him her tattoo. But tonight he didn't care because his thoughts were still occupied with Gabby, her honeysuckle-scented hair and those gorgeous caramel eyes. There was an air of mystery around her that intrigued him.

He wanted to see her again. Soon.

He and Ryan ordered a pitcher of beer and a platter of wings from Tina, then settled back to watch some baseball.

"You heard from Mark?" Ryan asked.

Ethan shook his head. "He said he'll be in next week, so he'll be here."

His phone pinged with a text message. He swiped it from his back pocket and grinned.

What's this I hear about you escorting our lovely friend Gabby Winters to the clinic?

It was from Gram, the tech-savviest seventy-year-old he'd ever known.

She stomped on a yellow jacket nest. She's pretty sore, but she'll be okay, he wrote back. How do you know her?

Silly question. Gram knew everyone in town.

We met at the garden store. She's a sweetheart.

Entirely too sweet for the likes of him, and they both knew it.

"Who are you texting?" Ryan asked. "You better not be planning to ditch me for a chick on my first night back in town."

Ethan held his phone up so that Ryan could see the screen.

His friend chuckled. "Tell Gram I said hi."

He did, and Gram replied that she'd like to have them all over for dinner soon. Ethan's gut twisted uncomfortably. He'd scheduled her to see a specialist in Charlotte on Monday for a second opinion. This guy was supposed to be the best. Surely he could find a way to save her life.

Because Ethan had no fucking clue what he would do without her.

About the Author

Rachel Lacey is a contemporary romance author and semi-reformed travel junkie. She's been climbed by a monkey on a mountain in Japan, gone scuba diving on the Great Barrier Reef, and camped out overnight in New York City for a chance to be an extra in a movie. These days, the majority of her adventures take place on the pages of the books she writes. She lives in warm and sunny North Carolina with her husband, son, and a variety of rescue pets.

Rachel loves to keep in touch with her readers! You can find her at:
   RachelLacey.com
   Twitter @rachelslacey
   Facebook.com/RachelLaceyAuthor

Fall in Love with Forever Romance

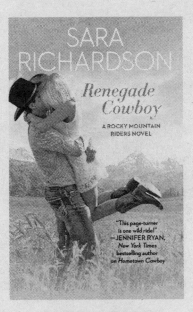

RENEGADE COWBOY
By Sara Richardson

In the *New York Times* bestselling tradition of Jennifer Ryan and Maisey Yates comes the latest in Sara Richardson's Rocky Mountain Riders series. Cassidy Greer and Levi Cortez have a history together—and a sizzling attraction that's too hot to ignore. When Levi rides back into town, he knows Cass doesn't want to get roped into a relationship with a cowboy. So he's offered her a no-strings fling. But can he convince himself that one night is enough?

Fall in Love with Forever Romance

THE HIGHLAND GUARDIAN
By Amy Jarecki

Captain Reid MacKenzie has vowed to watch over his dying friend's daughter. But Reid's new ward is no wee lass. She's a ravishing, fully grown woman, and it's all he can do to remember his duty and not seduce her...Miss Audrey Kennet is stunned by the news of her father's death, and then outraged when the kilted brute who delivers the news insists she must now marry. But Audrey soon realizes the brave, brawny Scot is the only man she wants—though loving him means risking her lands, her freedom, and even her life.

Fall in Love with Forever Romance

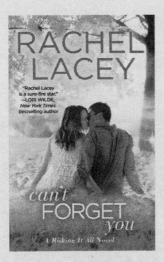

CAN'T FORGET YOU
By Rachel Lacey

Jessica Flynn is proud of the spa she's built on her own. Now that the land next door is for sale, she can expand her business... Until Mark Dalton, the man who once stole her heart, places a higher bid on the property. Mark doesn't want to compete with Jess. But as he tries to repair the past, he realizes that Jess may never forgive him if she learns why he left all those years ago.

BACK HOME AT FIREFLY LAKE
By Jen Gilroy

Fans of RaeAnne Thayne, Debbie Mason, and Susan Wiggs will love the latest from Jen Gilroy. Firefly Lake is just a pit stop for single mom Cat McGuire. That is, until sparks fly with her longtime crush—who also happens to be her daughter's hockey coach—Luc Simard. When Luc starts to fall hard, can he convince Cat to stay?

Fall in Love with Forever Romance

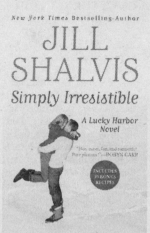

SIMPLY IRRESISTIBLE
By Jill Shalvis

Now featuring ten bonus recipes never available before in print! Don't miss this new edition of *Simply Irresistible*, the first book in *New York Times* bestselling author Jill Shalvis's beloved Lucky Harbor series!

NOTORIOUS PLEASURES
By Elizabeth Hoyt

Rediscover the Maiden Lane Series by *New York Times* bestselling author Elizabeth Hoyt in this beautiful reissue with an all-new cover! Lady Hero Batten wants for nothing, until she meets her fiancé's notorious brother. Griffin Remmington is a mysterious rogue, whose interests belong to the worst sorts of debauchery. Hero and Griffin are constantly at odds, so when sparks fly, can these two imperfect people find a perfect true love?

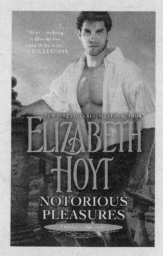